MORNING MORNING TRUE

A Novel of Intrigue in New Guinea

MORNING
MORNING
TRUE

A Novel of Intrigue in New Guinea

ERNEST HERNDON

Zondervan Books
Zondervan Publishing House
Grand Rapids, Michigan

Morning Morning True:
A Novel of Intrigue in New Guinea
Copyright © 1988 by Ernest Herndon

Zondervan Books are published by
Zondervan Publishing House
1415 Lake Drive SE
Grand Rapids, Michigan.

ISBN 0-310-27270-X

Printed in the United States of America

88 89 90 91 92 93 / EE / 10 9 8 7 6 5 4 3 2 1

New Guinea, the world's second
largest island, is located northeast of
Australia, just south of the equator. It
contains some of the most rugged landscape
and primitive people on earth.

It was so bizarre to hear Johnny Cash singing "Ring of Fire" out there in the sprawling tropical night that Roy Williams strained to listen. Laced with the thud of drums from an all-night native singsing, the grind of diesel engines, a man's shout, and a dog's howl of pain, the distant American song triggered a moment of distorted perception in Roy's mind. In fact, the country singer was so out of place in the New Guinea night that a strange, lost sensation swept over Roy, and it seemed that he looked down on the cozy scene from the top of the room where the ceiling fan whirred.

Dark-haired Jeri, heavy-fleshed in the mid-trimester of her pregnancy, stooped over Powers's shoulder as he sat at the coffee table with the big yellow map spread before him. At his left sat Pamela, her hair a long, dark dimension to her seemingly taciturn being. Clad in crisp khakis and oversized boots, the type of clothing travelers new to the tropics frequently wore, she concentrated on the energetic ramblings of Powers's hand and voice.

Almost as an afterthought, Roy saw himself, the journalist, observing the scene. Tall, lanky, a little slouchy, he stood off to the side where he could see the map and follow the discussion

9

without taking part. Like Pamela's clothes, his pale skin betrayed his recent arrival from a temperate climate.

Only Powers and Jeri Stivell seemed at home, which indeed they were. Jeri wore a large sleeveless print dress; her arms glistened with perspiration. Powers was dressed in ragged jean cutoffs, tennis shoes, and a faded T-shirt bearing the logo "Lae Racquet Club."

Roy descended back to floor level when the distant country and western song subsided into a garble of static indiscernible from the clamor of insects and the whoosh of fruit bats' wings outside among the trees. When he thought of the bats, their wingspread sometimes reaching six feet, the thrill of newness and adventure came over him again, and he looked at the map with interest.

"It's going to be tough, but I wish I was going with you," Jeri was saying to Pamela.

Powers laughed. He had an easy laugh; his teeth glimmered and his eyes radiated both warmth and cunning. Powers was a hotdog missionary, and no expedition was too ambitious for him.

"You'll get a taste of bush life, if that's what you want," he said.

Pamela Carpenter was a Canadian, fresh out of a Christian college in Arkansas. She'd been in New Guinea a week and was about to embark on this rugged patrol into a little-known area of mountainous jungle with Roy and Powers. The inhabitants there were the sort the missionaries referred to as "very bushy."

"They've had very little contact with civilization," one had explained to Roy.

"You'll find out what being a missionary is all about," Powers went on, obviously relishing whatever effect he imagined he was having on his audience. He enjoyed playing the seasoned veteran, which indeed he was, though he was only twenty-six. These visiting "short-term zealots" from the States wanted a taste of exotica for a month or so, and he was happy to oblige — in triplicate.

"Oh, Powers," Jeri said, resting her hand on his shoulder. "Don't mind him," she said to Pam. "There's more to being a missionary than going on patrols. There's a lot to be done in the towns without ever going out into the bush."

Roy spoke up. "What she's saying is that even if you don't like the bush you can still be a missionary."

The three looked at him as though he had just dropped from the ceiling. Perhaps they suspected him of irony, since he professed no interest in anything religious. He smiled, as though to say he hadn't meant it that way, and studied their reactions.

Jeri returned his smile, which didn't surprise him. Though only twenty-two, she struck him as amazingly mature, kind, and straightforward. He would never expect deception from her. She had married Powers on his stateside tour a year ago and was now a missionary wife in New Guinea, ready to start a family.

Powers was more complex, but Roy had liked him instinctively — liked his easygoing bravado, his offhand arrogance, his strange brew of laziness and determination. Powers glanced at him now with that sleepy-eyed smile, as though Roy had just tried to one-up him in a match of wits.

Then there was Pamela. So far, she was an enigma; one moment warm, the next cold. She looked at him from an expressionless face, then looked away, as though rejecting any terms of intimacy or even friendship. Probably she was just homesick, Roy figured. Her most striking feature was her hair. When unbraided it hung in a straight, dark brown mass to her hips. When braided it formed a single rope that looked thick as

11

a hangman's noose. Her eyes were as brown as her hair, and their dark luster seemed secretive; she gave nothing away. Roy wasn't sure he liked her.

But it didn't matter. He was not here to like anyone. In a month or so he'd be on his way again along his journalist's tour of these sultry parts of the earth: Manila, Cairns, Jakarta. The pay for his random feature stories and photos would not make him rich, but the experience was fantastic. For a twenty-five-year-old journalist he had it pretty good.

When you do New Guinea, of course, you do the bush. He'd known that from the start. So with the help of his contacts, he'd hooked up with these missionaries in Lae and now, thanks to their hospitality, was about to embark on a patrol that promised to exceed even his expectations. The prospect set his heart thumping. For Roy had to admit to himself that, while he wanted a good taste of the bush, he was not sure he wanted as big a gulp as Powers was promising. But then Powers might be exaggerating. No matter. Roy knew how to play the greenhorn.

In fact, he was pretty much of a greenhorn. He had no illusions on that score. He'd been in Honduras, only to be yanked out by his syndicate as soon as trouble started. They did not do war correspondence, his boss said. Leave that for the big boys, the Associated Press and UPI.

What the syndicate wanted from Roy were features: colorful, exotic, titillating perhaps, and always with the sort of vicarious thrill that makes readers tingle with adventurous excitement. A cynical description of Bangkok here, a laconic float down a Borneo waterway there. It was not his job to serve up the horror of war, and that suited him fine.

In a way. Still, part of him dreamed of setting out on some expedition in the grand explorer style. Crossing a continent, wrangling through mountain passes, walking between the teeth of death, and sitting by the campfire with a daring grin. But his more practical side had given serious thought to applying for a position as staff writer at one of the travel mags, the sort whose writers spent their time at hotels, cafés, and poolsides, and whose closest experience with the jungle came on a guided tour up an estuary by a token native: "The silence of the jungle was unsettling and seemed to carry me back to a time before man's tread first broke the stillness of the primeval vegetation." He knew the sort.

"Up here is a place called Noa," Powers was saying. His finger touched a twining line of blue that closer inspection showed to be the Markham River. Pamela leaned forward to look for the word Noa on the map. There wasn't even a dot. "We'll just have to hunt for it," Powers said. "They tell me that's where we can catch a boat and head upriver."

"Boat?" said Pamela. Her voice, even with that one word, conveyed a sense of displacement.

"Dugout canoe." Powers smiled. "Outboard motor. I don't know what it'll cost, but probably not more than ten kina apiece — huh, Jeri?" She shrugged.

"We go up here," he said, moving his finger slowly, following the river's course, "then branch off up the Watut and on up here to Maralinan."

Aha, a dot, Roy thought. A name. Must be a place.

"And then?" Roy said.

Powers shrugged. "We'll have to get carriers. Let's see." He made mental calculations. "I figure at least six."

"Six?" said Roy. He thought in terms of American-style backpacking, carrying it all yourself.

"Well, there'll be our own personal gear. That's three."

"You don't plan to carry a pack?"

Powers laughed. "Not me, brother. You can carry one if you like, although I advise against it. I don't carry anything. I've

13

trekked over those mountains enough to know what they're like."

Roy said nothing, but his opinion of Powers faltered. Roy had carried packs, and heavy ones, in the Ozark Mountains as well as the Great Smokies back in the States. Still, he tried to give the missionary the benefit of the doubt.

"Then I plan to carry a big bag of rice to leave with the boys. And I figure another couple for pots and pans, extra food and gear." He turned to Jeri. "I don't know. You think we'll need seven?"

"It depends on what you can get, Pow, and what they'll cost."

"I figure, what, three kina each day per man? That's pretty good money for these fellows."

"How many days?" asked Roy, calculating.

Powers turned back to the map. "From Maralinan we go this way — southwest — up over these mountains, then follow this river up a ways, then more mountains and we get to Engati."

Engati. No dot. No name. Nothing except a big blank area and a word spanning it — Menyamya.

"We'll have to have a guide," Powers said. "It's so far back it's a wonder the devil himself found his way in there."

"The devil lives there," Jeri murmured. She sounded as though she knew it for a fact.

"I only know of one white person who's gone in this way before," Powers said. "Phil Sparks. You two haven't met him. He was sent back to the States."

"Why?" It was Pamela who asked. Her soft, husky voice sounded very large in the night.

"Health problems," Powers said lightly.

"Blackwater fever," said Jeri. "Very serious. He's in the hospital now."

"Is it likely we'll get it?" Roy said.

Powers leaned back in his chair. "It's no picnic."

Suddenly they were all conscious of the sounds around them — sounds always there but seldom heard. Inside, the ceiling fan hummed comfortingly. From outside, through the screen walls, came natural sounds — fruit bats, and insects — and the far-off drums. The drums beat like a pulse — bum-BUM, bumBUM — and had been beating like that ever since they finished supper. Chances were, Powers had said, they'd continue to beat until shortly before dawn.

Roy tried to imagine what was going on at the place where the drums were beating. Somewhere in the bush outside the town there must be a fire with bodies moving around it, mostly bare, black, glistening with sweat and pig grease, adorned with feathers. Or was that pure imagination? Was it just some lonely drunkard sitting in his backyard, locked into a hypnotic thud?

"You've never been to Engati, right?" Pam said to Powers and Jeri.

"Right," Jeri said. "But we've been to Aiwomba. We came in from the opposite side of where you'll be coming from."

"How did you get there?"

Jeri and Powers looked at each other and grinned. "We drove," Jeri said. "But I'd rather walk any day."

"A group of us in four-wheel-drives tried to follow what they call a road," Powers said. "It was hairy. In some places the road was wide enough for one vehicle, straight up on one side, with a sheer dropoff on the other — hundreds of feet straight down."

"He's not exaggerating," Jeri said.

"We went as far as we could on the roads, and then we got out and walked," said Powers. "From where we parked it took about a day to walk to Aiwomba. Engati is another two days'

15

walk over the mountains — or so they tell me. So that's why we're coming in from this other way. We hope it'll be easier."

"What do we do at Engati?" asked Roy.

"Stay a few days, preach, visit. These are hospitable people, friend. In Aiwomba they feasted us the whole time. When I first went in, before I met Jeri, they offered me a wife, begged me to settle there with them. It was very tempting." He laughed.

"They're the friendliest people you'll ever meet," Jeri said. "I made some real friends in Aiwomba, and the people in Aiwomba and Engati are kinsmen. That's why I wish I was going with you. It's rough getting there, but it's worth it."

"Fresh pawpaws, sweet bananas, sweet mulis — oranges. They may even kill a pig in our honor. It's great. You may want to stay there, Pam — which can be arranged," Powers laughed again. Pam smiled at him in her shy, secretive way.

"Or you," he said to Roy. "Who knows? You may find the girl of your dreams."

Roy felt drawn to the bearded, easygoing fellow who at twenty-six was already a five-year veteran of New Guinea bush patrols.

"Have you decided who you're taking?" Jeri asked.

"Peerson and Ramel," Powers said. "Don't you think?" Jeri nodded her agreement.

"They're native teenagers from the mission school," he added for Roy's and Pam's benefit. "They're both Chimbus, who are pretty much fearless. That's what we'll need."

"Why do you need them?" asked Roy.

"They're going to stay there for a month and preach," Jeri answered.

"Well, how do we plan to get back?" Pam said. She sat forward and propped her elbows on the table. The overhead light picked up the deep auburn sheen of her long hair. Roy

16

wondered if she wore it long for religious reasons, even as he admired its rich color.

Powers was laughing again, warmed and relaxed. "That's up to us." He put his finger on the blank yellow space that was Engati. "We can walk on to Aiwomba and visit awhile and then go on to Menyamya Station, two more days' walk from Aiwomba. From there we can catch a bush plane back to Lae."

"In other words, Menyamya Station is four days past Engati?" Roy said.

"Based on what the natives tell me. Like I said, I've never been to Engati. And the only person I know who has wasn't in much of a position to talk about it." His tone changed abruptly. "Phil didn't have any sense! He'd walk himself to death trying to keep up with the natives — and you just can't do it. He said it took two days to walk from Maralinan to Engati. I'd add at least a day to that. I'm not one for setting records. Anyway, I don't know about the walk from Engati to Aiwomba. The natives say it takes one day; that's why I say two. You can usually double whatever they say."

"So there's an airport at Menyamya Station?" Pam asked.

Jeri and Powers exchanged smiles. "If you call a strip of grass and a single-engine plane an airport," Powers said.

"What about going back the way we go in?" Roy said. "Back to Maralinan and then float back down to Lae?"

Powers nodded. "That's another possibility, though I always hate to retrace my steps. The third way — " He searched with his finger on the map. It grubbed like a mole in the dirt and found nothing. "There's a river between Aiwomba and Menyamya Station. I don't see it here. If you two like, we could maybe buy a canoe from some natives there and float down to the sea."

"Where does it come out?" Roy asked.

Powers grinned and shrugged. "To tell you the truth, I don't even know what side of the island it comes out on — the Port Moresby side or the Lae side. Or even if it's navigable. But it might be fun to find out."

Roy looked at Pam to see her reaction, but her face was expressionless.

"Sounds good," he said perfunctorily. "Doesn't matter to me. I'm just along for the ride."

"How will the boys get out later?" said Pam.

"Oh, they'll go on to Menyamya Station and Hugh will go get them. No problems."

"No worries, man," Jeri laughed.

"That's what the New Zealanders say," Powers explained. "'No worries, mate.'"

Jeri clamped her hands on Powers's shoulders. "Let's play Scrabble. Or do the men have a prayer session tonight?"

Powers glanced at the heavy black watch on his wrist. "I forgot all about it. It's in five minutes."

"Maybe we can play afterward," said Jeri. "Pam, I've got some good books on New Guinea you might like to look at while the men are praying."

"You want to come, Roy?" Powers asked.

Prayer session? Men only? Roy felt both revulsion and curiosity. Jeri and Pam were talking, closing him out. It was only eight o'clock. He could go to his room and read. He only had a few books — *Alone* by Richard Byrd, Captain William Bligh's account of the mutiny on the Bounty and his subsequent escapades, and Thor Heyerdahl's *Kon-Tiki.* He wanted to ration his reading material carefully. He planned to save the Heyerdahl for when he got back from this patrol, which was expected to last about two weeks. He would take *Alone* on the trek. Reading about Antarctica could take him away from the tropics when he got fed up with the jungle. And he'd take Bligh in case he finished *Alone.*

18

He supposed it wouldn't bite into his reading ration too much if he started in on *Alone* now, but he decided to go to the prayer session. It might be an interesting cultural experience — good preparation for sitting around with jungle natives and observing their religious rituals.

Most of the men were already gathered in the big mission meeting room. Like all the rooms in the mission center this one had ceiling fans and screen exterior walls to get maximum air circulation in the tropical heat. There was also a communal kitchen and a large table.

In addition to Powers and Roy there were six other men present. Roy had met them all the day before when he arrived, and he liked Powers the best. He seemed the most energetic and down-to-earth. Powers was the patrol man for the missionaries. It was Powers who ventured into places where no one else went, to villages on the back side of mountain ranges or the edges of swamps.

The men arranged the folding chairs into a circle, and as the chatting subsided they assumed postures of prayer. For most of them this meant leaning forward, heads bent over knees, eyes tightly shut. Roy slouched in his chair and shut his eyes.

Hugh Larsen was the first to pray. When he finished, the man on his right began, and so it went around the circle. Each man prayed at great length, and Roy realized with some dismay that this was going to be a long ordeal. He opened his eyes and gazed at the floor. The words of the prayers wandered in and out of his consciousness.

"I have had harsh words with Tim," one man was saying. "I said things in anger that I shouldn't have said, Lord. We have not always acted toward one another in a Christian manner. Open our hearts, Father, and let your love guide our thoughts, our words, our feelings. Heal the rift that has grown between us" — Roy realized that the man being talked about, Tim, was sitting just across the circle — "And forgive me for any wrong I might have done him. And help me to be more understanding, not only toward Tim, but toward Ruth" — Ruth was one of the native women who worked in the dispensary — "and toward everyone, God. Let your love guide my heart and keep it open and free from anger and from childishness and wrongheadedness. Please heal the rift, any rift, which springs up among us, God. Weld us into perfect union so that we may effect your will and spread your word in these regions. . . ."

After every few phrases, almost in a rhythmic pattern, there were scattered "amens." To Roy's cynical and impatient ears they sounded like frogs croaking along a pond. Galled by the endless redundancy of the prayers, his mind drifted idly. He thought of frogs and ponds and frog-gigging as a boy in Louisiana, chewing rich black Bloodhound tobacco that made him slightly sick and a little giddy. He thought of the light swinging soundlessly across the swamp, picking up myriad eyes — mostly the red eyes of spiders. Once, a nice-sized bass, attracted by the light, jumped right into the boat and lay there flopping. Roy's cousin, who was sitting in the front of the boat, had turned with a grin and spat a hefty stream of Bloodhound juice into the weeds along the boat. "Nice catch."

"That's my method," Roy had said. "I usually don't bother with hook and line and all that nonsense. Just get them to jump in the boat."

Then he had flashed his light upward and a pair of bright green eyes did a double loop-the-loop in the air. The two young men were startled. When the eyes settled above a tree limb, they saw it was an owl. The beauty of the swamp, its silent mystery, its absurd humor, its croaking bullfrogs, and the thrilling knowledge that somewhere out there were alligators made the night resonate.

The words of the prayers mingled with the swamp sounds of

20

Roy's memory and with the night sounds outside. Fruit bats flapped close to the screen walls around the mission compound. They must be large, judging by the sound of their wings. Natives hunted them, blinding them with lights and shooting them, just as he had gigged frogs by catching the light in their eyes. Roy had seen the fruit bats, dead, smoked, disemboweled, for sale as meat at a market in Lae.

Powers was praying now. "Please go with us on this patrol into the wilderness, Lord," he said earnestly. His voice had a slightly higher pitch, seeming to blend sincerity with a hint of the theatrical. "Let our footsteps not falter as we try to bring your word to people who are lost in darkness."

More amens. Croaking frogs, flapping wings. Roy thought again of Johnny Cash pining out in the Lae night on radio or cassette player: "I fell into a burning ring of fire." He heard no radio out there now, just an occasional motor vehicle.

"Be with Pam as she faces the hardships of being in a strange land," Powers continued. "Help her find the best way to serve you in her life and to do your will."

Roy wondered if Pam could hear him from whatever room she was in, through the screens.

"Bless Roy; let him accomplish his goals, and let his goals be in accordance with your will."

Roy's heart began to race with embarrassment, hearing his name mentioned in Powers's prayer.

"Bless Peerson and Ramel as they embark on this mission of learning and teaching. Be with them in those dark regions where we're taking them, O God. Guide their footsteps. . . ."

Roy's heart pounded faster as he realized he was next in line to pray. Did they expect him to? So far no one had questioned him about his religious beliefs, nor had anyone tried to convert him. Did they assume he was one of them? Or had they decided he was a sinner, not worthy of their spiritual clique?

Whatever the answer, Roy was grateful the subject had not arisen. Indeed, he respected the missionaries for leaving him alone.

As Powers's prayer wound down, Roy's heart continued to thump. Maybe he would pray. But what should he say?

Then he heard "Amen" and it was his turn. There was a silence — a crucial silence, for if he did not speak the next man would start.

"O God," he said, his eyes tightly shut, and with a rush became aware of the wonderfully rich texture of night sounds. "Thank you for this world around us." He was unsure whether he was making a speech for the benefit of these human listeners or whether he was really praying. "Thank you for the fruit bats. For the sounds of the night. The insects." Each thing, as he named it, became almost painfully audible, as though God were turning up the volume. "The voices." He had not heard them until that very instant — human voices. A woman, a man, far away. "The trucks." He felt silly. Why thank God for the trucks?

He ended quickly and somewhat pompously to hide his growing discomfort. "Thank you for the world around us with its sights and sounds and smells and feelings and textures, O God." His voice trailed off and he heard every rustle of every insect on each leaf; he heard the fruit bat as it swooped, opening its mouth and gulping. Then the deafening surf of banality drowned these rich sensations, and once again he was sitting with a boring gang of zealots.

He was surprised to hear, toward the end, one of the older missionaries mention his name again. "Thank you for Roy, for letting us hear through him the sounds and the wonders of the night."

Now he was acutely embarrassed. He wished he were in his bed reading about the Antarctic. The intimacy of this situation

22

appalled him, gave him a horrible feeling of nakedness, like a child dressed in his underwear in a room full of adults. He feared what might happen when this interminable praying was over. What would they do? Hug? Shake hands and smile meaningfully?

But when they finished there were no such intimacies. The men drifted apart, speaking of plans for the next day. Some headed to the refrigerator; others went to find their wives or to their empty rooms of God-devoted bachelorhood.

"How about a game of Scrabble?" Powers said, at his shoulder. "You up for it? It's only ten."

In truth he was tired. He had yet to recover fully from jet lag. The thought of his book and bed was seductive. But stronger still was an underlying zest for anything in this new and unusual place, even a game of Scrabble.

"All right," he said.

"I have to warn you, though," Powers said. "I'm the undisputed world champion Scrabble player."

Jeri and Pam had entered the room, Jeri carrying the Scrabble box and a dictionary. "Watch it, Powers. You're talking to a journalist," she said.

"A man of words," Pam added. She seemed to have loosened up in their absence. She was smiling and warm.

"True," Roy said. "It might not be fair to you folks."

Powers snorted smugly under his beard. "Bold words from a rank newcomer. Set it up, Jeri."

"You set it up," she said. "I'll get drinks."

"Any gin?" Roy asked, then realized his error. There was a sudden silence. He glanced around. No one remained except Powers, Jeri, Pam, and one of the missionaries, a young man named Tim, who was headed for the door and seemed not to have heard.

"No gin here," Powers said, and Roy wondered if he had

only imagined the awkward silence. "You can get some in town."

Jeri added softly, "You might not want to bring it here, though."

Still self-conscious, Roy glanced at Pam. She was setting up the Scrabble board and either had not heard his remark or was pretending she hadn't.

"The undisputed champion," Powers said, his mind back on the coming contest. "You're sure you all don't want to back out now while you have a chance?"

"No way," said Pam.

"Many have tried and many have died," Powers said. "I guess it's time for two more to bite the dust."

"And Jeri?"

"She gave up trying to beat me long ago."

"Oh, come on, Pow," Jeri said as she set four glasses of lemonade on the table. "I beat you last week, and you know it."

"One game — one out of a thousand."

"Oh, please."

"We all have our weak moments. But I have a feeling tonight will not be one of mine."

They shuffled the wooden tiles and each drew seven. The glasses of iced lemonade sat neatly on squares of napkin. The tiles were lined in their racks.

"There's crackers and cheese if anybody wants some," said Jeri.

"I don't," Pam murmured.

"Yes, my dear, I believe I do," said Powers in a W. C. Fields voice.

"Here, let me get it," Pam offered, but Jeri had already risen.

"No, I know where everything is. Roy, do you want some?"

24

"I guess."

"Hurry, would you?" Powers said. "The champion is straining to assert his titlehood."

Jeri set a plate of cheese and crackers on the table and said, "How about some music? It won't take a minute."

She left the room and came back with a portable cassette player and a handful of tapes. Roy looked through them. Contemporary religious music, some popular middle-of-the-road performers. Nothing he liked.

"What sort of music do you like, Pam?" Roy asked.

"I like Kenny Rogers," she said, pointing to the tape in Roy's hand. "Let's see. Gordon Lightfoot." He was not surprised; Lightfoot was Canadian and mellow. "Creedence Clearwater Revival."

Roy did a double take. "Oh, yeah?"

"*Requite* is not a word," Jeri said to Powers who had just taken his turn.

"Look it up," he said smugly.

"It is a word," Roy said gently.

Jeri thumbed through the dictionary, looked closely at a page, then slammed it shut.

"Beautiful *Q*," Powers gloated, writing down the score. "What does it mean?"

"Get even," Roy said. "Also return. You know, 'unrequited love.'"

"Yeah, I knew I'd heard it somewhere."

"You see the kind of luck he has," Jeri said. "It makes me sick." Her love for her husband was evident in her eyes and her manner, contradicting her words.

"I remember the best breakfast I ever had in my life," Roy said. "My father and I were going to a college football game in Oklahoma. He's the sort who likes to leave on a trip early. We left at something like two in the morning."

"Horrors," said Pam, gazing intently at her tiles.

"And it was cold. I mean cold. It was still dark when we got to Little Rock, and we stopped at a truck stop to have breakfast." He paused. "*Queer.* Thanks for the use of your *Q*, Pow," he said as he placed his tiles with a triumphant flourish. "I was hungry. Dad said I could order anything I wanted for breakfast. Can you imagine? That was rare for him, for my dad. So I ordered steak and eggs and hash browns and I think grits and toast. Also orange juice and milk and coffee."

"A man after my own heart," said Powers. "I want you to take note of this, Jeri, for in the morning."

"Cold cereal will have to hold you, sweetie." She frowned at Powers's latest experiment. "*Lumbar?*"

"It's a word," Roy nodded, but Jeri reached obstinately for the dictionary.

"He doesn't know these words," she said. "He just guesses and gets lucky sometimes."

"That's why I'm champ."

"Anyway, I ate that breakfast — I was fourteen — and it was perfect," Roy said.

"It's a word."

"Huge, thick steak. First time I'd ever eaten steak and eggs. Scrambled eggs. Ketchup on the hash browns."

"Come on, journalist, this is getting boring," said Powers. "Next you'll tell us the kind of jelly you put on your toast."

"Grape. Or apple. Anyway, when we left the restaurant, it was just getting daylight. And it was cold! The wind cut you in two. We got in the car and set off down the highway, and the sun was coming up behind us, and I lit up a big Roitan cigar and turned on the radio. And guess what they were playing."

"The Bellyache Blues," said Powers, hunching over his tiles intently.

"No. Creedence Clearwater Revival's 'Doo-doo-doo lookin' out my back door.'"

Pam laughed and clapped her hands, but Jeri just frowned. "Your father let you smoke cigars when you were fourteen?"

"Occasionally."

"*Rapell.* Look it up, Jeri." Powers was beaming.

"Good word, wrong spelling," Roy said.

"Look it up, look it up."

In a few moments she said, "*Rappel — r-a-p-p-e-l.* You see?"

He wrinkled his nose in disgust. "That would have been a triple word score too."

"I told you he was a journalist," Jeri said.

"Just wait and let the score do the talking," Powers said.

"I think 'Run Through the Jungle' is one of my favorites. And 'Suzie Q'," said Pam.

"What are we talking about?" asked Jeri.

"Creedence Clearwater Revival," Pam said.

"Run through the jungle, huh?" said Powers. "You'll be getting plenty of that."

"What's the best breakfast you've ever had?" Roy asked Pam.

"What an intelligent conversation," Powers said. "And you said this guy was a journalist? A gourmet columnist, maybe?"

"Pow!" said Jeri.

"I can tell you the worst breakfast, only I didn't eat it," Powers went on. "And it was close to where we're going. Aiwomba. Really, I didn't see it, but an old man told me about it."

"Powers! They don't want to hear that. Besides, we're eating."

"I'm just trying to prepare these two. If they've got weak stomachs, they better not come along on a New Guinea bush patrol. You got weak stomachs?"

27

"Not me," said Roy.

"I worked in a hospital," Pam said.

"All right," Powers said. "The Menyamyas — they used to be called Kukukukus, but don't call them that now, they don't like it — are notorious for their taste in — how shall we say it — the delicacies of the human form. Flesh, that is." He chuckled. "They call it 'long pig.'"

"Powers!" said Jeri, rolling her eyes in disgust.

"Cannibalism. They still practice it, you know."

"I thought cannibalism wasn't practiced anymore," Roy said.

"That's what the government wants people to think. Cannibalism's not good for the tourist trade. But it still goes on in secret. Anyway, these Menyamyas not only eat their enemies, they'll eat their own kinfolks when they die. Say, for example, if Jeri were to get malaria tonight and die. Well, I'd have a real feast for breakfast."

"That's disgusting," said Pam.

Powers laughed. It was obvious he loved to shock greenhorns. "That's only during time of famine, of course," he said.

"Well, I hope there's no famine now," Pam said.

"In normal times they just hang their dead up in trees." He was concentrating on the game board again. "*Factory*. Good word, Roy. This boy's got learning potential."

"For how long?" asked Pam.

"Till they rot off."

Jeri spoke up. "Come on, Pow, that's enough. You're making us sick."

Pam did, indeed, look distressed. "It sounds like a place of the devil," she said.

Powers leaned across the table and looked at her seriously. "It is, sister. That's why I'm going there." He sat back with his hands on his hips. "I don't like these patrols. I hate them. I don't care about adventure. I've had enough adventure to last me a lifetime. It's just work to me. It's just taking the word of Jesus."

Roy felt suddenly alienated. The game had stopped and an uneasy silence hung over the table. Roy glanced at his tiles, then looked into Jeri's face — that frank, honest, and loving face he had come to admire in such a short time. "And what's the best breakfast you've ever had?" he asked.

The group did not exactly dissolve in laughter, but the tension broke. The images of cannibals and rotting human flesh disappeared.

Pam had been frowning over her tiles for a long time. Now she began laying them on the board, asking with mock innocence, "Is *ozone* a word?"

"Triple word score!" Powers clamped his hand to his forehead in despair and slumped in his seat, surveying the evident poverty of his own tiles. "It's not over with yet."

Roy was awakened long before his mind and body had had the rest they needed. He must have been sleeping with his mouth open, for his tongue was dry and his pillowcase was damp with drool. His bed lay next to the screen of the east wall of the room, and he quickly became aware of the intense morning heat. Still struggling with some jumbled dreams, he floundered in the kaleidoscope of sensation that was thrust upon him on his third morning in Lae.

Once in the night he had awakened and had not known where he was — Louisiana, Honolulu, or the brig of the

H.M.S. *Bounty*. He had lain there in the darkness, looking at the shadowy forms of his room, seeing them perfectly but having no idea what they were. In that lost state a claustrophobic panic nudged him, but he was too tired to give in to it, and some part of him remembering where he was, he drifted back into demanding slumber.

The early morning glare outside was filled with the sounds of screeching parrots — oh yes, this was the tropics — and high-voiced children, either imitating the birds or trying to make the birds imitate them, and a woman telling them to "Shut up! Can't you be quiet out there? Please! Some people are trying to rest!" That must be Miss Nellie, the elderly Canadian missionary nurse.

Roy turned over toward the shaded side of his room and tried to sleep again, but the heat was stifling. He sat up and turned on the ceiling fan. It ladled the air like hot syrup. He sat up again and turned it higher, and this time it sprang into a loud, energetic roar. He gave up. Screeching birds, giggling children, and now the sounds of pots clattering and water running in the mission center. Obviously, he was not going to get any more sleep this morning.

He lay still in his undershorts, sheet thrown off, body damp with perspiration, and smelled the smells of the musty guest room. His tired mind thought about the new and strange land just beyond the screen and the thin curtains, where the tropical morning sunshine crouched like a gigantic, slavering tiger.

Later, dressed in white shorts and a lightweight rugby shirt, he headed for the showers. There was nothing but cold water here, and it brought him stunningly awake. Shaving was a scratchy, slow process, and by the time he was slapping aftershave on his face other half-awake men were drifting into the bathroom.

In the cool darkness of the mission center he ate bananas

and papaya — pawpaw, they called it — for breakfast. Then he poured himself a mug of hot tea and walked outside.

The morning was full of fragrances found only in the tropics. In the middle of the mission grounds was a patch of jungle with paths and a creek and a bridge with log handrails. Roy crossed the driveway, walked down to the bridge, and leaned against the railing, completely shaded by the tall trees around him. The sound of water was refreshing, and though it did not cover the noises of traffic and voices coming from the main road a few hundred yards away, it gave him the promise of a peace to come — some sanctuary he hoped to find.

The tea was rosy, stout, and good, especially after the mild fruit breakfast. The cool shower had left him feeling invigorated, despite his lack of sleep. But he dreaded the thought of the two days before they set out on the patrol to Menyamya. There were things to do: buy provisions, hire a guide, write letters. Yet he feared the time would drag by, hot and dull.

"So who do you write for?" Pamela's voice asked from behind his right shoulder. She moved up beside him and leaned against the railing. He didn't know whether to resent her intrusion or welcome her as a fellow-stranger.

He named the syndicate; she had not heard of it.

"I do feature travel articles mainly," he explained.

"And they pay you to travel?"

"You might say it's an experiment. This is my first big trip. Well, second, really. The first one wasn't much though. If this one draws reader interest, maybe I'll get to do more. If not, I guess it's back to city life."

"What city?"

"New Orleans," he said. He thought about whether he wanted to pursue a conversation, then said, "And you are considering being a missionary?"

She didn't answer immediately. She seemed taciturn like she

31

had been yesterday. Not really cold, but not warm. Thoughtful perhaps. Her hair hung straight and damp from the shower. She wore a matching khaki shirt and hiking shorts but had shed her heavy mountain boots for tennis shoes.

"Yes," she said at last. "I'm here on a post graduate program. Sort of our introductory field course. It's a way of making sure you want to be a missionary before the long-term commitment. Or finding out if you're suited for it."

"Then you've more or less already decided you're going to be a missionary."

She made a gesture — part nod, part shrug.

"Why New Guinea?" he asked.

"A lot of people from school have been here. My dad came here on a mission tour too. He told me about it. It seemed like a good place. And there's plenty of need."

"Need for what?"

"Christianity," she said, frowning. "Aren't you a Christian?"

He hated that question. It went with door-to-door salvation peddlers. "Are you saved, brother?" they'd say. "Are you going to heaven?" Implying, "If not, you'd better get that way or the devil will kick your tail."

"I guess that, being part of a Christian culture that embraces Christian values — in that context, yes, I'm a Christian."

"Oh," she said.

He waited for the next question, the one he had been waiting for since he'd arrived: "Yes, but do you believe Jesus Christ to be the son of God?" That, Roy thought, was what the church-goers' questions always boiled down to. And the answer had to be either, "Yes, I'm one of you, brothers," or "No, so leave me alone to my fate." Roy was not comfortable with either answer.

But she did not ask it. She did not even seem to be thinking it. Instead, she was staring up into a tree.

"Are you nervous about this expedition?" Roy asked, his

gaze following hers to the treetops where a large black bird with a big beak was cleaning its feathers.

"It does sound pretty scary, doesn't it?" she said. "Have you ever done anything like this before?"

He was tempted to say yes and compare it to some campout he'd been on or maybe to some of his experiences south of the Rio Grande. Somehow though, he knew Pam would detect any dishonesty. "No," he said. "Sounds interesting, though. I'm excited about it. I can't wait." Adrenalin coursed through him at the mere memory of last night's plans over the map.

"Isn't that a hornbill?" she said after awhile, still watching the bird.

He glanced up again. "I don't know." He was not interested in birds, although this one was beautiful in a harsh, abstract way. Huge, jutting beak. Brilliant orange head, black body. Sort of like a crow decked out for a tribal dance.

"So how do you like it here?" she said.

"Here as in the mission, or New Guinea in general?"

"Take your pick."

"New Guinea I like, so far anyway. Like when I first landed at the airport in Port Moresby. I was standing waiting for my luggage and I looked across the crowd and saw this black man staring at me. Fierce, like a real warrior. He was frowning like he was ready to start chucking spears.

"I wasn't sure how to react. Ignore him? Try to look fierce myself? Well, I decided to smile and wave. And the funny thing is, he broke into the biggest grin I ever saw. Just like a kid."

She nodded. "Yes, I like the people, too. What about the mission?"

A sudden feeling of bitterness unaccountably swept over him. "Oh, I don't know," he said. "I like to drink; I like to smoke cigars. All this praying — "

33

"My father smoked cigars," she said, interrupting him in a quiet, musing voice.

He waited, slightly surprised. He had been prepared to alienate her.

"The doctor told him to quit, and he did. He was afraid of lip cancer." She looked at Roy's mouth.

"Pam!" Jeri's voice called from the mission center.

Pam walked across the patch of open sunlight to where Jeri was standing on the porch, then turned and called, "She wants you too, Roy."

In the mission center Powers was slapping a tennis racket against his leg. "Do you play?" he asked when Roy came in.

"No." He went to the sink and washed out his tea mug.

"Powers wants to play some tennis," Jeri said. "How about if he and Pam go play, and I'll take you around town, Roy? Anything you'd like to see?"

Roy shrugged.

"You want to swim? There's a pool by the tennis courts, and there's a pretty good public beach."

"Better take advantage of the offer," Powers said. "This may be our last day of fun. Tomorrow it's all work. We're supposed to meet a guide at dawn to plan out the details. Then find us somebody with a boat and buy supplies." He shook his head. "Thursday morning we leave, you know."

"The beach sounds good," Roy said.

The four of them crammed into the Stivells' small car and Jeri drove out onto the road into town. Hunched up in the back seat, his elbow jostling against Pam's arm, Roy watched the natives along the roadside: all ages, all postures, all manners of dress. An old woman, bare-breasted, sat in the shade of a palm tree. A group of men wearing ragged T-shirts and shorts talked and spat great gobs of red betel-nut juice onto the pavement — like bloodstains. A slender young man

34

with the light skin of a coastal tribesman, wearing a brilliant blue sarong, stood in the center of traffic for no apparent reason. An old man carrying a bow and arrows, fresh out of the bush by the looks of him, wore a grass loincloth in front and an astanket — a large, single leaf — in back; the leaf bounced up and down as he walked. He was bedecked with shells, and a tusk pierced his nose.

"Tonight we'll eat out," Powers said, turning his head to address Roy and Pam. "It may be our last feast in quite a while. There's a real good restaurant up the coast."

"They have native singers and everything," Jeri said.

She dropped Pam and Powers off at the tennis courts and, after stops at the post office and the bank, drove a short distance up the coast to a public beach.

"You swim all you want," she said. "I'm going to sit in the shade and read. Be careful though. Sometimes sharks come in." She cut off the ignition and got out. Large palm trees leaned toward the sea, shading the car and a long edge of coconut-strewn sand.

Jeri sat down, leaned against the trunk of a palm, and opened her book while Roy stripped down to his swimming trunks and walked across the hot sand. A few other swimmers and sunbathers played along the beach.

He waded out into the water, dazzled by the expanse of sea and sky, sun and heat. In the distance, the palm trees formed an arboreal chorus line along the coast. He waved at Jeri, hunched over in the shade.

He waded out, chest-deep, and stood bracing himself as each foamy mound moved into him, lifting him and pushing him backward a little. He tasted the brine, felt the coolness of the water washing over his sun-warmed skin.

He floated on his back, letting the waves carry him under. Then he backstroked farther out, watching the perfect blue sky

35

puffed with small white clouds. A trio of seagulls wheeled by, squealing. He flipped himself upright and treaded water, over his head now. He thought of sharks, of the saltwater crocodiles he'd been told about, and turned to face the open sea, an instinctual thrill of fear kissing his spine. The crocodiles grew to twenty or thirty feet long, they said, and were extremely aggressive, ranging the coastal waters of New Guinea and southeast Asia, traveling up freshwater rivers as well. They made freshwater crocs seem like Boy Scouts.

Thirty feet long! How many tons would they weigh? What would happen if a thirty-foot croc met a thirty-foot shark?

Driven back to the shallows by his imagination, Roy felt the pure pleasure of the warm wind on his salty, wet body. He walked up the beach to Jeri and spread a towel out in the sun a few yards from her. Rubbing down with suntan lotion, he lay on his back to sunbathe.

"I wouldn't do that long," she said. She was knitting now.

"What are you making?" he asked, one arm thrown up over his eyes.

"Booties."

"You want a boy or girl?"

"We'd like a boy."

"Have you picked a name?"

"Hundreds of them. We can't decide. I like Aaron. Powers likes Mark."

"Mark Aaron sounds good."

"If it's a girl, we've agreed it will be Rebecca Ann."

Roy thought about Jeri having her first baby in this strange land. Did she worry about that? He didn't think so. Somehow, as young as she was, Jeri was at home, even knitting booties among the coconuts.

"You'll stay here then, after the baby?" he asked.

"Oh, yes. Powers and I plan to make our home here."

36

"For good?"

"Let's say indefinitely."

"You like it that much?"

"We like it, and there's so much work to be done. Oh, Roy, if you could see some of these people. The need here is so great."

"And you really feel like you're helping them?"

"Yes."

"What about the money? Things are pretty high here."

She sighed. "It's tough. Our church at home won't send us our money on time."

"You're kidding."

"Well, it goes deeper than that. But we're already behind in our notes on the car. Powers is going to call the elders today and try to find out what the hold-up is."

"It's not cheap calling overseas."

"No, but . . . I don't know. There are just problems."

"Like what?" he asked, sensing that his curiosity would not offend her.

"Doctrinal beliefs. We don't always see eye to eye with the church. They expect you to toe the line all the way. And through our studies and prayer, Powers and I have come to believe differently on some things than what they teach."

"Like what?"

"Like the Holy Spirit. He's alive. Today, now. But they seem to think the Holy Spirit quit working when Christ was crucified."

Roy was out of his depth now. Religious discussions were beyond him. But he did care about the Stivells' plight. He sensed the gap that lay between them, but not an awkward gap.

"I was raised in the Methodist church," Roy said. "But religion was never very important to me."

"When you're out here," Jeri said, "dealing with people in real, genuine, sometimes life-and-death situations — well, the people back home just don't understand what it's like."

"So what will you do?"

"I don't know. They're wanting us to come home, to tell you the truth. I'm afraid we may have to go back and find another supporting congregation."

"Sounds like fun."

"It's a headache. It really is. You can't imagine."

"And you with a baby coming."

"And then there's this patrol."

"Are you worried?"

"Oh, Powers can take care of himself. I mean, he's been on plenty of patrols. He knows the bush and the people."

"It's just a bad time for him to be gone, right?"

"Right."

"Want me to talk to him?"

"What do you mean?"

"Try to get him to cancel it."

She laughed. "You don't know Powers. No, he's going. He's got faith. I wish I had his faith."

Roy turned over on his belly, adjusting himself on the towel and applying more lotion. Then he closed his eyes again. "I haven't known you long, but I'd say you have at least that much faith."

He felt her smile.

At the restaurant that night there were the four of them, along with Tim Harkins, and Hugh and Janice Larsen and their two children. The restaurant, at one of the country's few hotels, was a house-wind, a large open-sided building with a thatched roof. It allowed a view of the sea, and the breeze kept insects away.

The buffet was outrageously sumptuous, with roast pig, tenderloin, shrimp of all sizes, crabs, fish fried and broiled, vegetables both native and European, every sort of tropical fruit, rich highland coffee, and homemade rolls.

"You won't find a feast like this for many a mile," said Powers as they sat down, their plates loaded, at a large table.

"You can count on that," said Hugh, a pudgy, jolly fellow with a full, black beard.

"Madang's got a good restaurant," said Janice, who spent most of her time attending to the two squirming youngsters. Though in her twenties, she looked older. Perhaps dealing with the endless hardships, petty and otherwise, involved in raising a family in a place like Lae caused the dark circles under her eyes. And Roy sensed that jolly Hugh might be something of a bully.

Tim, a bachelor in his late twenties, was a strange sort, too. Roy had seen him consume thirteen pancakes, a piece of chocolate cake, and two bananas for breakfast the previous morning. Though intense and friendly, he seemed a bit slow mentally — or perhaps not so much slow as on a different track altogether. Despite his legendary appetite — a source of pride to him — Tim was gaunt with a scraggly goat's beard and thick, rimless glasses. He made rather an odd figure, and his speech seemed slightly impeded, his words like pieces of a jigsaw puzzle cut not quite to form. But Roy warmed to the rare sincerity radiating from the man — the sincerity of Dostoevsky's Mishkin, whom society called an idiot but whom other, wiser persons might have called a saint.

"Yep," said Hugh knowingly, "eat up, Pam and Roy. Starting Thursday it'll be kaukau and pitpit."

"Sweet potatoes and edible grass," Jeri translated. "Actually, I like pitpit."

"Well, when we went to Aiwomba — remember, Powers? — I got enough kaukau and pitpit to last me a lifetime," Hugh said.

"Pitpit's a little like asparagus tips," Jeri explained.

"You can have your pitpit and your kaukau," Powers said. "I've decided to hire an extra carrier just to carry canned hams."

"Rice and tinned fish is more likely what you'll be eating," Janice said. "That's the usual patrol diet."

"Hey, they can take whatever they want," Powers said. "We'll go to Burns-Philp, the grocery store, tomorrow and stock up. You don't know, Pam might be a caviar eater."

"I'm pretty much an omnivore," she said.

"A who?" said Hugh.

Tim, his thick spectacles glinting, broke in with a voice that was always a shade too loud. "There's plenty to eat in the bush. Pawpaws, sweet bananas, cooking bananas, maritas, tree pineapple, sweet muli — "

"Look," Janice interrupted. "They're setting up."

"What do you call that?" said Pam. A group of native performers dressed in colorful sarongs had brought in a huge bundle of hollow bamboo tubes lashed together. Some of them had guitars, and with no ado, the music began.

"I don't know, but it's nice," whispered Jeri. Janice agreed.

The bamboos were played by a man who sat astraddle them and slapped the open ends with rubber flip-flop sandals. Each tube produced a different note, and all were deep, hollow, calming, like the heartbeat of a big friendly beast. The air was rich and warm with the sound and feel of the South Pacific.

40

The sea stretched out in the blue dusk, framed by thatch. The breeze carried a suggestion of bougainvillea and raintree, brine and brown skin.

Roy excused himself and took his coffee cup into the bar to have it laced with amaretto. Then he returned, wandering easily past the performers, among the ranks of food, through the humming conversation, the candlelight and dim yellow incandescence. The sea breeze and the music flirted with him.

At a small table in a corner sat an extraordinarily attractive couple: a young man and woman, both deeply tanned and dressed in cool tennis whites. Her hair was honey rich in the warm light, and Roy could see her tanned skin under her thin white blouse. At another table sat a white man with a black woman. She was dressed in a dark blue floral print wrap-around dress, and the rich tones of her skin glinted warmly. A group of men sat around another table, drinking beer with their meal and talking too loudly, ignoring the music. A solitary gentleman sat at a small table watching the musicians, his head moving back and forth with the music. The scene filled Roy with a strange sensation, and he half expected to have that ceiling view again. He took a gulp of coffee to steady himself and returned to the table. The coffee, rich but not dark like Colombian — in fact, almost as pale as tea, but quite strong — warmed him and added to his light-headed sensuality. The gentle music sang of easy living in paradise.

"Get some more food," Hugh urged him.

"Eat up, man!" Powers agreed. "You'll be dreaming of all this soon enough."

Roy got another roll and a slice of pork and ate that, then slid his chair back from the table, disengaging himself from the conversation. Occasionally he heard Hugh's loud laugh, the Larsen kids whining for ice cream, an earnest conversation between Jeri and Pam, Powers's energetic description of a

41

tennis match, Tim's awkward attempts to join in, but for the most part he tuned them out.

Soon — much too soon — the musicians quit and another group, utterly different in appearance, brought in a huge hollowed-out log. The men were much darker skinned and wilder looking. They wore loincloths, shell necklaces, and head plumage.

"What's this?" Roy asked Jeri.

"Looks like a Sepik River group," she said. "That's a garamut — a big drum. On the Sepik each village has at least one."

Roy excused himself again and slipped into the bar for another drink. When he came out, he leaned against the wall to watch instead of joining his group at the table.

Some of the Sepik group carried small wooden drums with tops of reptile skin, and they began the same pulse-beat — bumBUM bumBUM — Roy had heard last night. Women had joined the group, and they stood in place, swaying with the music. The loud, deep garamut sounded and the group danced out into the circle.

Roy's eyes were drawn to the women, their bare skin glistening with oil and sweat. All of them were young and shapely, but one in particular caught his eye. Her face was fierce-looking but arrestingly attractive. Haughty. Around her neck and ankles she wore circles of fur, and there were feathers in her hair. Her only clothing was a dark loin cloth. The dance was not especially erotic — it was mostly a jog-trot movement, each dancer holding the waist of the one in front — but Roy felt a stirring of desire. He glanced at the table of missionaries across the room. No outrage, no curiosity. To them this was just another group of native performers.

Half-ashamed, Roy devoured the dancer with his eyes, now and then looking away idly so that no one would notice his fascination. He sipped the strong mixture of coffee and alcohol. The drums added another dimension to his passion: it was a pulse-beat, all right, the pulse of dark jungle passion that lived in his heart and brain and blood and muscle like a caged, drugged tiger.

And yet, how foolish he felt — like a kid sneaking his first copy of *National Geographic*. Foaming at the mouth like a teenaged boy. His own desire bewildered him. Yet the drum-pulse had settled in his throat, in his chest, spreading down like raw heat.

He gulped the last bit of coffee and returned to the table. "Those are some dancers!" Powers was saying.

Everyone had finished eating, and they got ready to leave. On the way out Powers stopped beside a black man in a suit who stood watching the dancers proprietorially. "Who are they?" Powers asked, nodding toward the entertainers.

"The Sepik Group," the man said, and the pure unimaginativeness of the name almost made Roy laugh.

"What do they charge?" Powers said. "I might like to hire them sometime." He turned to Roy. "Don't you think some visiting church members would get a kick out of being met at the airport by a group like that? It'd be great, man!"

Roy turned and followed the others to the cashier's desk.

Roy was being dragged deeper and deeper into fatigue. He was not sleeping well at night. Each morning he woke with raw, burning eyes, cotton mouth, and skin slick with perspiration. He braced himself with a cold shower and strong tea, but his brain was clogged with aching tiredness.

Wednesday morning at dawn found him sitting in the church minibus on a deserted jungle road. He blinked at his surroundings, half-awake. Powers was outside somewhere. In the seat behind him sat Peerson and Ramel, who would be their native companions on the patrol. This morning was the first time Roy had met them. They were about sixteen years old and were training to be preachers. Now they sprawled in the back of the bus, half-asleep, as tired and uncommunicative as he was.

All around was jungle — towering trees slung with vines — except off to the right, where there was a clearing of sorts. It was not a natural clearing. Someone had made it by cutting down trees, burning them until they were reduced to gigantic black carcasses, and planting sweet potatoes, pumpkins, bananas, and pawpaws among the rubble. The potato and pumpkin vines had spread out rapidly to form a jungle of another sort. Two or three huts stood in the middle of this jumble.

A heavy mist lay in the clearing and among the trees. The sun was not up yet. *It lurked behind the huge jungle of trees, waiting to spring on the world and seize it by the throat.* Roy tried to think of other metaphors. After all, he would eventually have to produce an article. He really needed to get one off today before they left, so he toyed with ideas.

The mist lay coiled among the trees like a huge serpent. Trite, overused. Everything was serpentine, especially rivers.

The mist lay entwined with the jungle like a lover. Leave out the entwined. *The mist lay with the jungle like a lover.* That was good. It reminded him of last night's dance. He looked at the mist and the jungle and the clearing and the huts. In fact, the mist did not lie with the jungle like a lover. They were just words.

44

The scene itself was just jungle and fog. But everything has to be like something else — the writer's trade. You don't have white hills; you have hills like white elephants. Only by thinking of something else could you imagine the actual thing. Just tell the actual thing like it is and what do you have?

The article should begin: *There was jungle and fog.* Nothing especially exotic about that. *The mist lay with the jungle like a lover.* Exotic? Maybe. But it didn't describe the scene before him now. He'd probably use the line in his article anyway. They'd like it back at the office.

Powers emerged from the thicket of the clearing followed by a small brown man. Roy clambered down from the bus into the clammy dawn heat.

"This is Yalu," said Powers. "He's a Menyamya, and he'll be our guide."

Yalu was the shortest native Roy had seen; he could almost be classed as a pygmy. His skin was the color of dirty copper, his hair slightly darker. His eyes glittered like the flat black ivory pieces of a Chinese Go game. Wild, blank, animal eyes.

He appeared to be young, perhaps twenty or so, and had evidently never known soap. He wore ragged khaki shorts and a T-shirt so faded and filthy that whatever logo it had once sported was now an indiscernible smudge. His legs were scaly, his feet broad and tough.

"Yalu, this is Roy." The small man grinned and nodded.

"Yalu is a new Christian," Powers said. "He's been coming to our church about a month now. Engati is his place. True, Yalu?" Again Yalu grinned and nodded. "Engati place belong you?" Powers said.

"Ah, yes, Engati place belong me — true!" Yalu said in a high, emphatic voice.

"And you savvy the road to Engati?"

"You think what?" Yalu said disparagingly.

Powers turned to Roy and smiled. "I explained to him that we'd leave with the boys and Hugh would pick him up in a month at Menyamya Station."

He turned back to Yalu. "True, Yalu? You stop in Engati one moon something with two-fellow boys. All right? Then you fellows walk-about to Menyamya Station and whiteskin missionary Hugh get you then, and you fellows come back to Lae. Savvy?" Yalu grinned and nodded.

"You sure you know the road to Engati?"

"You think what?" Yalu repeated with mock contempt.

"All right. Morning morning true we will come and get you here. You be ready. Have all something you like carry to Engati for one moon. All right? Morning morning true, same as now." He motioned to the sun just clearing the treetops. "You be here; we get you." Yalu grinned and nodded.

"All right," said Powers, offering his hand. Yalu took it heartily and they shook. "See you."

Roy shook Yalu's hand. It felt crusty. "See you," he said.

"Now we've got to make arrangements for a boat," said Powers as they got into the bus.

When Roy looked back, he saw that Yalu stood by the road watching them.

As a boy, Yalu remembered, he had been so frightened he wanted to vomit. He had to fight down the sensation. He and the other boys his age — they were still young, just about to enter young manhood — sat for interminable periods in the hut listening to the old men hammering at them with their words.

Then, weary from listening, they were led down a path through the thick jungle. The path led to a low tunnel of brush, and one by one they were forced to squat down and crawl into the tunnel. Once inside they heard monstrous noises, the sounds of masalai, spirits of the dead, spirits of the mountain and jungle. At the end of the tunnel — hurrying, hurrying — hard hands clamped over their eyes and they heard horrible bird shrieks from the other world, the world of the dead that lives in the jungle. The air roared like thunder.

They were halted in a line before a log and the hands were removed. Angry men surrounded them, men who looked like their elders but were full of rage and madness. He remembered the feel of cold water rubbed against the septum of his nose. He wanted to flinch, but strong arms held him. Fingers pinched his nose and held it out and a sharp bone pierced the septum. Blood ran in a trickle over his upper lip; he felt the slide of a tiny bone into his nose. For the first time he knew a sensation of strength amid the howl of his fear.

The boys were led to an altar and shown the three sacred foods — foods they could not touch until they passed the rites of manhood many years later: red maritas for blood; black sugar cane for skin; a dead tree opossum for flesh. His bowels had trembled with fear and power as they were warned not to eat the sacred foods until the right time.

Then they were forced to run, run, while the men shouted and whipped them with barbed canes. But the running was happy now, and free. Even as the blood ran down their backs and shouts filled the air, they glimpsed the road to manhood before them, a destination they would someday reach with power, treachery, and fearlessness.

By mid-afternoon they were back at the mission center where the floor was a mountain of gear and food. Powers sorted through it while Jeri checked off a list of items.

Powers looked exhausted from the day's scrambling. After several wrong turns that morning they had found Noa, a little clearing on the Markham River, where they made arrangements with a man who owned a motorized dugout canoe to meet them in the morning and carry them upriver to Maralinan. At Burns-Philp they had purchased a twenty-kilo sack of rice plus a dozen one-kilo sacks, a carton of tinned mackerel, a carton of hard biscuit — plain unleavened crackers — a canned ham, and odds and ends such as canned grape juice (for communion services in Engati), chocolate powder, tea bags, peanut butter, honey, cheese, salt and pepper, dried soups, and drink mix.

Back at the center, Jeri had already dragged out Powers's patrol gear: duffel bags, backpacks, socks, boots, tennis shoes, cutlery, cookware, primus stove, fuel, sleeping bags — all the thousand and one things required to make life bearable for the civilized person in the jungle.

Roy had his own camping gear, and Jeri was loaning her gear to Pam. Miss Nellie had assembled a well-stocked first-aid kit inside a small, water-tight metal chest. She had included aspirin, chloroquine, bandages, gentian violet ("blue paint"), sulfa powder, sunburn cream, swabs, disinfectant, and ointments for ear, eye, and skin infections. Pam would be expected to administer medical treatment to the natives at Engati. With her limited knowledge and experience, this would essentially amount to first aid.

As the four of them sat around organizing the various items, Roy sensed a dual air of excitement and fatigue. Why did they need so much gear for a mere two weeks? he wondered. The bush natives could go anywhere with a string bag full of sweet potatoes and a machete or bow and arrows.

"What about a tent?" he asked Powers. "Do you have one?"

"I usually just stay in the huts. The villagers always provide you with a house."

"What about on the trail?"

Powers shrugged, preoccupied. His lack of attention irked Roy, who prided himself on his camping skills. "I've got a little two-man tent," Roy said.

"Take it if you want," Powers said, not looking up.

It was after dark by the time they had assembled the mass of bulging packs and duffel bags into a stack against the wall. Jeri had gone out for fish and chips, and they ate hurriedly. The other missionaries had already left for the Wednesday night church service.

"Are we going to try to go to services?" Jeri asked when they had finished eating and sat slumped around the table. They could hear the group singing the first hymn.

"I'd like to," said Pam.

"Might as well," Powers agreed. "Coming, Roy?"

He nodded and looked at the others as they stood up. What a ragtag crew, he thought. They would not have been ready for church services in the United States. Powers in his ragged jean

49

shorts and a sweat-soaked T-shirt, Jeri in a sleeveless maternity dress, and Pam in jeans and a "Lae" T-shirt. Roy wore a pair of old khaki trousers and a rugby shirt.

But this was not the United States, where Sunday-best clothed church-goers and a clean, temperature-controlled building housed the family of God. It was Papua New Guinea, where no amount of grooming could survive the withering heat, where church doors stayed open to admit the slightest breeze, and where dogs or pigs sometimes took advantage of those open doors and wandered in to check out the commotion.

The four left the mission center and headed across the grounds to the church, which glowed cozily in the early tropical night.

Nine o'clock. Roy sat in his room with his portable typewriter and stared at the blank sheet he'd just inserted. The hymn-singing of the native congregation hung resonant in his memory. They'd sung in pidgin English with full-hearted feeling, and the service had been entirely in pidgin, so he was able to follow only some of it. But it was one of the nicest services he'd ever attended. The broad, beaming smiles of the people made him feel welcome, and many of the hymn tunes were familiar. He had hummed along, sometimes even singing the English equivalent.

Now, staring at the white sheet, he had no idea what the topic of his article should be. He did not feel like writing at all. He should turn in; the next day promised to be long and hard, the beginning of the Menyamya patrol. Yet he felt obligated to send something to his editor before taking off for two weeks. If he could get something on paper, Jeri could mail it for him in the morning. He had a couple rolls of film he had shot, just general photos. They would do.

He rehearsed the experiences he'd had since leaving New Orleans. The flight over? Tiresome, uneventful. The Honolulu layover? Ditto. Guam? He had only been there a few hours, and that at night. Port Moresby? Just one night there, and on to Lae.

And Lae? Visits to the market, around town, the beach, the mission, the restaurant, the dancers. Nothing that would make an article. He'd have to write a general, local-color, feel-for-the-tropics piece. He sighed with boredom and typed, "The mist lay with the jungle like a lover."

Then he stopped, reviewing his impressions of Lae. Certainly he'd been struck by the colorful clothes, the anything-goes attire. He liked his own new shirt, purchased in Lae the day before. T-shirts with logos abounded in New Guinea, and his was the most cryptic and arresting he'd seen. On the front, in blue letters, it said "The One to Eat" with no punctuation. Just under that was the word "Man" in red letters followed by an exclamation point. He had seen a native wearing one of the shirts in town and had thought the slogan was a tongue-in-cheek reference to the nation's history of cannibalism: "The One to Eat Man!" When he saw the back of the shirt, which read "Morobean Biscuits," he realized it was merely an advertisement for a biscuit company. He preferred his original, more macabre interpretation.

Scratching the line about the mist — he'd save that for another time — he started an article entitled "Tropical Attire: Anything Goes" and did not emerge until eleven o'clock, when he slid into the inviting embrace of the sheeted mattress.

51

. . .

By the time they had loaded the church bus with gear, picked up Yalu, and soared up the straight, flat Markham highway, then turned off onto the twin dirt ruts that carried them, jouncing and bouncing, through head-high kunai grass to the edge of the wide muddy Markham River and a view of the green grassy mountains beyond, it was no longer "morning morning true." No, nor anywhere near it. It was after nine o'clock on a hot and brassy tropical morning. Blackskins sat around the smoking embers of cooking fires in sparse shade; they turned and looked at the minibus and the people and gear pouring out of it.

While Ramel, Peerson, Roy, Pamela, and Jeri unloaded the bus, Powers found his boatman and began the usual harangue over details. When the gear was at last heaped beneath a solitary tree on the short bluff overlooking the mud flats leading to the river two hundred yards out, Powers returned with the news that all was ready except that the boatman had no fuel for his motor.

To Pam and Roy with their American view of schedules, of making plans and following through on them, this was a disappointing setback. To Jeri and Powers, well acquainted with the way things worked in the tropics — the way gears don't mesh, cogs don't fit, and plans are made to go awry and be reformulated — it was "something-nothing," as the pidgin expression so appropriately put it.

"We'll have to go back to town for fuel," Powers told Jeri. The boatman, a lank black ostrich of a man wearing a weathered and crumpled black golf hat, stood behind him sheepishly. "Why don't you and Ramel go and we'll stay here with the gear?"

Jeri frowned, a hand over her brow to block the sun. It was a frown that could easily become a habit to her pretty, young face. Observing it, Roy remembered Janice Larsen's young-old face and wondered if this was what happened to white women in the tropics.

"Take him with you," Powers said, pointing to the boatman. "Have you got plenty of money?"

Roy turned away from the discussion to the broad river vista. The water was not particularly wide, but the riverbed was. Obviously there were floodtimes when this river became angry. Right now it would be a long, hot, muddy trek to haul their bags of gear out to the beached canoes. Across the slow-swirling brown water the mountains rose abruptly like emeralds. The kunai grass that covered them looked close-cropped from this distance, showing their soft, numerous spines. Farther back were dark jungles, slung like capes over the shoulders of the mountains.

Around him, soft voices mingled with gentle acrid smoke. An old woman poked sweet potatoes in the embers. Naked fat-bellied babies with caterpillars of snot molded under their noses stared with the frowning curiosity of infants.

"All right," Jeri was saying. "We should be back in an hour."

As she backed out and drove off with Ramel, Yalu, and the boatman, Powers turned to Pamela and Roy and said, "It looks like we wait."

"How long do you think it will take us to get to Maralinan?" Roy asked.

Powers shrugged. "We ought to get there today." He stood with his hands on his hips, surveying the surrounding natives

53

with a friendly gaze. Their returned glances were equally mild. "Might as well get comfortable," he said and went to the foot of the single big tree. After checking its base for ants and clearing away the twigs, he sat down, leaned back, and tilted the wide brim of his leather hat down over his eyes.

"Well," Roy said to Pam, feeling awkward, uncertain what to do next. Pam shrugged slightly, and together they walked over and joined Peerson who was sitting with his back against a duffel bag. Peerson smiled broadly at them as they leaned comfortably against the gear.

"All right, man," Roy said, feeling the strange discomfiture of eagerness deferred. He'd been ready to embark into the wilderness and here they sat on a riverbank. "Are you ready?"

"Oh, yes, I'm ready," Peerson said.

"Are you excited? Scared?"

"Yes."

Roy laughed. For breakfast he'd eaten only a few bananas, but he'd stowed away a sack of cold fish and chips from the night before. He rummaged through his pack and pulled out the paper sack.

"Pam, you want some?" he asked.

She shook her head. He suspected she felt more out of place than he did. A straw mesh safari hat threw a tight grid of shade across her face. Beneath it her hair was braided into a thick rope, pulled tightly behind her head. The tip of the braid peeked around her waistline like the head of a python. She wore what Roy assumed was her safari outfit: the khaki shirt and hiking shorts and huge, red-laced mountaineer boots with thick white socks pulled halfway up her smooth brown calves. A yellow bandana was tied scout-fashion around her neck. The entire outfit looked crisp and new and, although ostensibly designed for a tropical safari, seemed incongruous here. As his article last night had indicated, natives wore catch-as-catch-can outfits. Peerson's oversized hand-me-down trousers were rolled up around his calves. He was barefoot, of course, and wore a T-shirt of indiscernible parentage. The natives around the clearing wore similar motley outfits.

Missionaries dressed only slightly better. Powers's blue jeans were stuffed into laced green canvas jungle boots. He wore a long-sleeved red plaid shirt with the sleeves rolled up, a big hunting knife on his belt, and his crowning glory, a wide-brimmed leather hat that appeared to be the veteran of numerous bush patrols.

Roy wore lightweight canvas pants and Vietnam jungle boots he'd picked up at an army surplus store back home, along with his new light blue "One to Eat Man" T-shirt. For headgear he had a baseball cap with an extra-long bill and the emblem of a leaping bass on the front.

After a while, Roy fished out his Olympus and snapped pictures. The others dozed.

It was nearly one in the afternoon when the minibus bumped back down the road to the clearing. The clutch had malfunctioned and they'd spent two hours in a repair shop. In the interim Peerson and Roy had devoured the fish and chips, exchanging details of their lives with growing friendliness. Pam had joined in occasionally but mostly dozed. Powers had slept, waking only once to tell some of the natives a fabulous story about the time a crocodile had bitten his leg off and he'd had to replace it with a steel one. For a moment they had believed him, then broke into laughter.

Now, in the blazing heat of the day, assisted by the boatman and his partner, they toted the gear across the mud flats, arranging it in the long dugout canoe. Roy and Pam found seats in the boat while Powers and Jeri said good-bye. Powers held her by the waist and kissed her lightly. Roy heard their low voices and soft laughter.

"Rebecca Ann will be waiting for you," Jeri said, apparently referring to their unborn child. Powers gave her a final kiss and stepped into the canoe.

The motor caught after several false starts, and suddenly they were in motion, motoring up the Markham River.

Roy sat near the front directly behind the boatman's assistant, who used a pole when necessary to push away from shallows. The boat was narrow and cramped, and there was half an inch of water in the bottom in which he sat. The duffel bag immediately behind Roy was uneven and poked him uncomfortably in the back. He was too hot to be hungry, and the water in the canteens was warm. His bare arms were cooked in no time, and the area of his chin not shielded by his cap brim began to burn among the stubble of his new beard.

He glanced around behind him. Peerson's open face was a blend of boyish excitement and anxiety, while Ramel's Chimbu features were set into a sullen mask; Powers flashed an adventurer's grin; Pamela surveyed the scenery impassively from behind the shade of her cool straw hat; and Yalu watched his surroundings with the glitter-eyed gaze of a forest animal. At the rear the boatman, his hand on the tiller of the outboard, smiled placidly, constantly watching the river.

Roy turned back to the view of his own boots and the assistant boatman's bare black back. The man was smoking tobacco rolled in newspaper; it smelled like wild perfume.

This is great! Roy thought, looking up into the blinding tropical blue with its islands of white cloud. The brilliance was unbearable. He watched the land — the mountains on his left, thick grass on the right. Here and there he spotted a native with bow and arrows. Despite the sun's searing heat, the movement of the boat created a pleasant breeze. It felt good to be moving at last, upriver where the roads ended and there were no newspapers or phones or electricity — just wild country and mystery and things that were going to happen to him which he could not imagine no matter how hard he tried. The pit of his stomach tingled.

They stopped once, a few hours later, to stretch their legs, beaching at a spot where a small clear stream ran into the Watut; they had left the Markham behind at a big fork and turned up into the Watut, which, like the Markham, was the color of gravy. If Pamela had not been there, Roy would have stripped and plunged into the cool water. As it was, he and the rest waded out into the shallow stream. The water soaked his trousers and cooled his legs.

There was a clear line of demarcation where the stream joined the muddy Watut, from jewel dark to opaque gray. Roy waded out thigh-deep and stood in the muddy part. He turned back to Peerson and Ramel, who crouched in the shallow, pebbly water of the stream.

"Come on out here and swim!" he called to them.

They just shook their heads and grinned. The assistant boatman muttered something in his tribal language; it went the rounds of translation, and Powers said to Roy, "They won't swim out there. They're afraid a crocodile might come up and they won't see it."

Roy felt foolish but not fearful. Pamela was grinning at him.

Soon they were under way again. When the sun went down, the air cooled noticeably. Roy's exposed skin had gone through several shades of redness, and the cool dusk air felt good against his blistered, burning arms and face.

57

They were far up the Watut now, which had become shallow and rocky, making navigation difficult. The assistant boatman used his pole frequently and signaled the boatman with his hands. Towering jungle lined the banks, and mountains ranged away in all directions.

As darkness fell the man in front took out a weak, battery-operated flashlight; its yellow beam limped ahead into the blackness. He shouted directions back to the boatman. It seemed to Roy that they were zigzagging back and forth across the river.

At last up ahead there was a dim light. The assistant boatman shouted; voices answered. The canoe puttered over to the light, and the voyagers clambered out stiff-jointed into mud. A little boy held a kerosene lantern to guide them up the slick bank. Villagers grabbed gear and trotted with them along a damp grassy path overhung with the shadows of great trees and into an open village where fires twinkled like amber.

"This Maralinan?" Roy asked Powers, who walked beside him.

"I think it's the boatman's place." Powers called to the boatman, who answered back in pidgin that Roy could not follow. "We'll come up to Maralinan tomorrow," Powers said.

Roy's main sensation was thirst. They had long ago finished the tepid water in their canteens and hadn't dared drink the water of the Watut. The gear was heaped around a small house-wind, and Pam and Roy stood beside it in exhaustion and confusion while villagers babbled, Powers conversed with the boatman, dogs barked, and hogs snorted.

"Hey," Roy said, interrupting Powers. "Tell him we're dying of thirst."

"Yes, please," Pam said weakly. Roy looked over at her sympathetically. She'd hardly spoken all day. How was she feeling, this Canadian girl ten thousand miles from home?

Powers and the boatman talked some more. "The only water is the river," he said after awhile.

"We can't drink that," Roy said, figuring he'd opt for perishing thirst over a case of dysentery.

Pamela slumped down against one of the corner posts of the house-wind. Ramel, Peerson, and Yalu had hauled out the primus and were firing it up to cook a pot of rice with river water. Suddenly a little child padded up to Pam and held out a fat green coconut with the top lopped off. Pam looked at it wonderingly.

"Drink," said the boatman.

She tilted it to her mouth and, once drinking, could scarcely bring herself to stop. Then she passed it to Roy, who guzzled his share of the sweet, cool coconut water, then passed it on to Powers.

"More, please," Roy begged. The boatman spoke to the child, who soon returned with two more coconuts.

Soon the scene was orderly again. The three boys sat around a big pot of simmering rice. Pam, Roy, and Powers shared biscuits and cheese, none of them being especially hungry. The villagers, not far enough from civilization to be fascinated by whiteskins, had retired to their own huts, leaving the travelers in peace under the house-wind, which was just a thatched roof set on poles with neither walls nor floor.

"I don't know about you people," Powers said, wiping his knife on his jeans, "but I'm about ready to turn in. I'm beat, and we've got a long day tomorrow."

"Me too," Roy said.

"Do you know how much more river we've got ahead of us?" Pam asked.

"I'd guess not much," Powers said. "Probably a couple hours. We want to get started early, before the sun comes up."

"Morning morning true, huh?" said Roy.

59

"Yeah."

"I'm so tired," Pam said.

"Probably never got over your jet lag," Roy said sympathetically.

"Well, kiddies," said Powers, standing up, "you ain't seen nothing yet."

They spread their sleeping bags on the ground and burrowed in. Sleep did not come easily in the tropical night, however. One of the villagers had a battery-powered cassette player. The fact that the batteries were nearly dead did not keep this household from playing a recording of a Lae radio show late into the night. The program was a motley blend of island music, drum-throbbing singsings, and American country and rock.

Tired and overheated from the long day in the sun, Roy's brain swirled around like taffy — pulled in outlandish and sickening shapes, stretched thin as thread, then massed into fat, sticky lumps. Woven throughout was the ridiculous cacophony of music, voices, laughter, hogs grunting around the crumbs they had left, the fitful breathing of his companions, and the hungry refrain of mosquitoes defying the acrid scent of the repellent they had so ardently applied before retiring.

On the first day of their final initiation into manhood their foreheads were pricked with sharp quills while they were told of their inadequacy as boys and their mandate to become men and warriors.

On the second day they were painted with maritas juice, which dried sticky and crisp along their flanks and chests. They were then given sips of the blood-red juice, and in the night they heard their elders dance and beat the drums and sing the deeds of old battles, prowess, treachery, and victory. The old men, becoming excited, grabbed some of the boys by their cane-pierced noses and dragged them to the ground, shouting, stomping, until the boys thought they were about to be killed and their red nose-blood spilled into the dirt.

On the third day they arose as men.

Groggy and stupefied, they at last were allowed to partake of the sacred feast at the altar in the clearing which they had witnessed years before in their first ordeal. This time the three sacred foods were imbued with the richness of their imminent manhood. He would always remember their flavors: the maritas juice, thick and pasty like hardening blood; the sugar cane, sweet as a man's toasted skin; and the opossum, rich and meaty as a man's thigh.

The ceremonial supper over, it was time for celebration.

Wakefulness arrived as spitefully as sleep had been kept at bay. Roy heard what he fancied to be a dysenteric splatter, followed by the raw gurgling bugle of a rooster. He realized the screeching roosters had been chasing him in and out of slumber for some time now. A newly wakened baby screamed with displeasure at its surroundings. The hogs, returning from their dark grovels, mulled around the house-wind, and Roy felt one nuzzling the mound that his feet made in the sleeping bag.

He sat up angrily. "Get back!" The hog trotted off.

His eyes were grainy and sore, but his heart throbbed with novelty and anticipation. Pam and Powers were still lumps in their respective sleeping bags, but Roy's exclamation must have sifted through to Powers. He sat up groggily, rubbing the back of his head with one hand.

"Morning," said Peerson. Roy looked around and saw the boys hunkered around the stove again, heating water. Hot tea!

"No time for rice," Powers said, clambering out of his sleeping bag.

"But let's have tea," Roy hurried to say.

The sun was not up. The air was gray and thick with cool mist.

Pamela rolled over. "Already?" she said with a sour face.

"Rise and shine," Powers said cheerfully. "You two aren't big breakfast eaters, are you?"

They had biscuits and honey and hot tea, eating and drinking with little talk. Roy was wide awake with adrenalin. The tea was ambrosia. A coffee-drinker back home, he felt a novel pleasure in drinking hot tea here. No sugar — just rosy, clear, and strong. Bitter and biting to the stomach.

The village, which last night had been hidden in the darkness, was alive with sounds and smells. The houses were simple huts surrounded by bare dirt; smoke sifted through their thatched roofs. Coconut palms rose here and there.

Pamela stood looking around her, apparently lost in thought. "Just anywhere you can find," Powers told her with the wisdom of one who had been on many patrols.

Within an hour they were headed upriver in the canoe. The air felt cool as they motored through it; its briskness was invigorating. The hot tea had charged Roy, and the coolness renewed that energy. Life was clean and new and exciting. Pure mystery lay before him like a deep-sea dive or a space voyage. The waiting was over; he was moving into a story that had not yet been written.

"Surely this is not why they put the dot on the map," Pam said, standing with her hands on her hips in a clear, sandy spot in the shade of some big trees on the river bank. The boatmen were pushing off, drifting downstream without a word of good-bye.

"This is it," said Powers. "Actually, there's probably a village back off the river. It's nearly one. What say we have some lunch?"

"I'm famished," Pam agreed, and she and Peerson began to rummage through the packs. Two young native boys had appeared and stood watching.

"Hey, you two-fella," Powers said in his friendly, laconic way — the result of years of dealing with natives and knowing how to put them at ease. "Drinking water close-to?" The boys looked at each other; then one nodded.

"What about sweet muli? You got sweet muli?"

They shook their heads.

"There's got to be some oranges around here somewhere," Powers said. "I saw some floating in the river."

"I would love an orange right now," said Pam, who was setting up the stove.

"Yalu, you and Ramel go fill up the water bottles," Powers said. "When you get back we'll make rice." Yalu and Ramel gathered up canteens and cooking pots, and the two young boys led them down a path into the woods.

"There's only one thing to do at a time like this," said Powers. "Sleep." He arranged himself a resting place among the duffel.

"Well, I'm not sleepy," said Pam.

"I hope you two aren't gung-ho hikers," said Powers, tilting his hat brim over his face in his tough cowboy manner. Roy and Pam looked at each other. "I'm not out to break any records," Powers went on, talking to his unseen audience. "Tony Hill tried that. You haven't met him; he lives in Goroka. He was a Marine, figured he was tough. He was going to out-hike his carriers. Carried his own pack." He laughed. "Had to fly him out on a stretcher."

"Why?" asked Pam.

"Malaria. Exhaustion. Who knows what else? Like the time I got shipped home. Before I was married." Powers was obviously relishing any effect he might produce with his jungle tales. "They sent me to a hospital in Houston, connected to a medical school; those med students clustered around me like flies. Said I was a living textbook of tropical diseases." He chuckled.

"I wonder how long it'll take them to get water," Pam said, sitting down beside Roy, who had found a comfortable spot under a tree.

"Malaria, dysentery, liver disease, worms . . ." Powers was lost in his recital. Then, realizing what Pam had asked, he said, "Why?"

"I wonder if I'll have time to brush my hair out."

Powers raised his hat brim, fixed her with a skeptical stare, then pulled the brim back down. "You've got time."

She looked at the unkempt braid as though wondering if it was worth the trouble. "Do you think we'll find a place to wash soon?"

"There's a place," Powers said, raising his arm in the general direction of the river.

She eyed it doubtfully. "Think there're any crocodiles?"

Roy could not see Powers's face, but he could tell the missionary was smiling. "Not this high up." He paused. "I doubt."

"I'll just brush it dry."

"Isn't that long hair a problem?" Roy asked, then felt tactless. "It's beautiful hair, really — but like on this patrol. Do you have it that way for religious reasons?"

She laughed. "I'm not Pentecostal."

"What's wrong with Pentecostals?" asked Powers, and Pam looked at him in surprise.

"I don't remember anything in the Bible about women having long hair," Roy put in.

"Yeah, but when's the last time you read your Bible?" said Powers.

"So you think women can't cut their hair?" Pam said. "What about Jeri?"

"She has to look out for her own soul. I can't look out for mine and hers too."

Roy smiled slightly, but he could see that Powers's brand of humor — half-serious, laced with arrogance — did not succeed with Pamela. She had unbraided her hair and spread out the thick ropes. With a brush retrieved from her pack she began struggling with the immense, tangled mass, frowning and at times biting her lip.

"So you don't carry a pack," said Roy.

"That's right," Powers agreed.

"I'll carry mine," Pam said. Again Roy felt Powers grin. Maybe he could tell by the slight movement of the hat as it responded to the facial muscles, or maybe he was developing some sort of harmony with the missionary.

"It's tough out there, sister."

Roy could imagine her retorting, "Don't call me sister!" but she said nothing.

"Those mountains aren't like the mountains back in Canada," Powers said.

"I'm from Toronto. No mountains there."

"See what I mean?"

"Where did you go to college?" Roy asked her.

"Searcy, Arkansas."

"Good school," said Powers.

"Searcy," said Peerson, who had been sitting cross-legged trying to take in the strange repartee. "I hear of that plenty.

Plenty missionary go to Searcy school." Pam favored him with a winning smile.

Roy was enjoying the cool shade, the sultry air, the mild river breeze. He dug into his pack until he found the hard wooden box containing his cigars. "I hope you people don't mind," he said as he lit one.

Powers lifted his hat, then lowered it. "I don't mind. I've had plenty of experiences with outhouses."

Peerson's face showed profound puzzlement. "That is tobacco?" he asked.

Roy nodded, savoring the long cigar, fresh and, to him, pleasantly fragrant.

"But isn't it a sin to smoke?" Peerson said doubtfully.

Roy suddenly became aware of the web of religious complexity into which he had blundered. He was a guest of the missionaries; it would not do to undermine their teachings.

"I didn't tell him that," Powers muttered.

"Brother Larsen told me," said Peerson.

"Hugh's father," Powers explained, with a note of deprecation.

Roy breathed a great cloud of smoke, feeling like an Indian chief about to bluff his way through a powwow. Pam, brushing her hair, watched him with curiosity and amusement.

"Oh, yes, smoking can be a sin," Roy said. "That is, much smoking, plenty smoking. You savvy? Suppose a man gets up in the morning and smokes. And then he does not stop until night. Yes, you're right, Peerson. That is a sin."

Peerson nodded. "It buggers up the body, temple of Holy Spirit."

Roy agreed, nodding his head sagely. "Yes, of course, a little smoke — oh, one cigar, you know, or two — that does not bugger up the body. Yes, I think one or two is okay."

Peerson brightened. "Then I smoke?"

Roy thought fast. "Peerson, you got how many years?"

The youth thought a moment, calculating. "Sixteen," he declared.

Roy shook his head sympathetically. "Ah, sorry. You're too young yet. You must be a man to smoke. Say, twenty."

Peerson grinned. He was no dummy; he was just young. "And buai?" he asked.

Chewing buai, or betel nut, was a native habit like tobacco was for Americans: Many abused it horribly, while others used it in moderation. Missionaries did not agree on whether to condemn it or ignore it, since the habit was so deeply ingrained in the culture.

"I think the same," Roy said. "But I don't know. I never tried buai. I think a little buai, maybe okay. Plenty buai, no good." Peerson nodded, satisfied.

"Tell him what buai's like," Powers said.

"Oh, I think you no like it," said Peerson, unaware or uncaring that in answering he was admitting familiarity with the vice. "Make you dizzy, you know?"

"But tell him how it affects you," Powers said.

"Oh. All right. Suppose you no sleep; it help you sleep. Suppose you tired; it make you feel good. Suppose you hungry; you no need food. Suppose you old; it takes pain away."

"Sounds pretty good, eh?" Powers chuckled. "Maybe we should market it in the States."

"I like the smell of a cigar," said Pamela. She had brushed her hair into a smooth fall and was now braiding it again.

"You're one of the few," Powers said.

"Well, there's a difference between a good cigar and a cheap one," said Roy. "I can't stand the smell of a cheap cigar myself. But this is a good one."

"They all smell the same to me," Powers grunted.

"Reminds me of home," Pam said, wrapping the end of her braid in a rubber band and leaning back against a duffel bag. "My dad always smoked them." She stared at the high, clear sky and the slightly shifting tree fronds above her. "I don't know if they were cheap ones or not, but they smelled good. Like that."

They were quiet awhile, drowsy.

"So what do we do next?" said Roy.

"After we eat, we'll go in to Maralinan and try to find carriers," said Powers. "I don't know if we should get started today." He glanced at his watch. "It's 1:30. I don't know. We might want to stay in the village tonight. Start in the morning."

"Do patrols always have these delays?" asked Pam.

"This is New Guinea, darlin'."

He wasn't joking. They did not arrive in Maralinan until an hour before sunset. A small settlement near the river was able to provide them with only two carriers, and they would only agree to carry to Maralinan, which turned out to be a two hours' walk from the river across blazing kunai fields and through muddy patches of jungle.

Since they had only two carriers, everyone was overloaded, except Powers, who did however agree to carry his camera bag and two canteens. Pam carried her pack, and Roy carried his pack plus his camera bag. The natives toted impossible loads with little apparent effort, tossing heavy duffels over their heads and setting off down the trail almost at a trot, until Powers yelled at them to slow down.

Walking across the wide flats of kunai, they headed straight into the blinding sun snarling over the humps of the mountains they would later have to enter. These mountains, covered with grass, looked massive and imposing. They were mere foothills, Powers told them, compared to the ranges further back in Manyamya country.

* * *

Powers and Roy sat in the cold water of a creek. The village headman had brought them here after showing them to a house. Although the air was slightly cooler with approaching dusk, the cold water felt exquisite to their hot, dirty bodies.

"I think we can get two," Powers said. "It doesn't look encouraging."

"That about the baptisms is a lot of bull in my opinion," Roy said.

"They're just afraid of the Menyamyas."

They'd canvassed the village, seeking young men to hire as carriers. The elders had told them all the young men were gone to be baptized somewhere. In the end only two men had agreed to carry, and then only for one day — by no means all the way to Engati.

"I think once we get out there we can convince them to carry all the way to Engati," said Powers.

Roy agreed. "Just offer them more money."

"But we need more carriers, man. And according to what Phil Sparks said, this is it. There ain't no more villages between here and Engati. Nothing but bush true."

"What kind of bush?"

"Mountains. Big ones," Powers said, shaking his head.

"You think Pam can make it?"

Powers laughed. "I'm not sure I can make it. I tell you one thing: I'm not going to carry a pack, even if we have to signal a helicopter to take us out of here."

"What's with you and packs?" Roy said testily. "I don't mind carrying a pack."

"You haven't been in those mountains, brother. That's all I can say. You'll see. Who knows? Maybe you're man enough to hump a pack over those mountains. I sure don't want to. I've done it. Never again."

"Well, if we can't find enough carriers, I'm willing to haul my pack."

"Good on ya, mate."

"And I guess Pam will carry hers."

"She's a stubborn one."

"You two don't exactly hit it off," Roy said.

"My fault," Powers said. "I should take it easy on her. Actually, I feel sorry for her. She's had a tragic past."

"Yeah?"

"Yeah. Jeri told me. She was going with this guy — a biker. I think it might have been before she was a Christian. It was a few years ago. Anyway, he got killed in a motorcycle accident. Really tore her up."

"That must have been rough. So then she becomes a Christian?"

"I don't know. I'm just telling you what Jeri told me. I'm a louse to hurt her feelings, I guess. But, I don't know, everybody's got a tragic past."

"Yeah, but that doesn't make it hurt any less."

"Right-oh, mate. We may all have a tragic past pretty soon if we don't get enough carriers."

"Maski carriers."

"Learning pidgin, eh? Yep, maski's one of the best expressions they've got."

"Maski — as in 'the hell with.'"

"That's one way of putting it. I'll go with 'never mind'."

"Look, I'm determined to get to Engati. I came around the

world for a story, and I don't want to go back just because all these Watut gents are scared of the — what? — Kukukukus?"

"Menyamyas. They've got reason to be scared. Wasn't too long ago the Menyamyas made raids down here. Cannibals, man. Look, when I was in Aiwomba this old tribal elder told me they still do it. That was just two years ago. He said he'd take me to one of the feasts if I wanted to see it. I wish now I'd gone."

"I thought the last act of cannibalism was 1968 or something."

"The last official act of cannibalism. There's a difference. You look at Engati. Takes two days to get there, any way you go. No constables, no nothing. Who's to say what they do when they catch one of their enemies? There's a dozen clans, and each one is feuding with the others. If you're from one clan and out walking and a group from another clan gets you, your number's up. Tribal warfare is common all over this country — all the time. Who's to say whether they eat a man after they kill him? If they don't report it to the local authorities — assuming there were any to report to — who's to complain?"

"What about us? What's to keep us from getting eaten?"

"Oh, no. This is strictly an intertribal thing. Hey, they'll take you out to watch the battles at Goroka. They don't bother whiteskins. It's like the Hatfields and McCoys. If you're a Smith, no problem."

"I hope you're right."

Powers grinned. "Why? You worry about these little details?"

"Yeah."

"I'm about to freeze. That's what I'm worried about."

They climbed out and dried off. "We need to tell Pam about this spot," said Roy. "She'd probably appreciate a good bath."

Walking back through the village, they passed women

cooking over outdoor fires, men sitting around smoking. One old man, toothless and gaunt, offered them a bunch of sweet bananas. Powers took it with a great display of gratitude. He offered money, but the old man refused it.

As Powers had promised, the village had a hut for visitors. It lay at the outer edge of the village, not far from the dusk-blue mountains which rose abruptly from the flat savannah. A group of villagers, mostly youngsters, clustered around the open-sided hut where the boys were cooking rice over the stove. A fire had been built nearby for warmth and light.

While Powers joined the throng, Roy walked off on a little path into the grass and stood alone looking at the closest mountain. Covered in soft grass, it stood silent and blue-gray in the dusk that was rich with the smells of tropical vegetation mingled with smoke from the fire and native tobacco.

"Sizing it up, huh?" Pam had come up from behind him. She was towelling her hair.

"Looks like you found a place to wash, too."

"Some women took me to a spot. Beautiful. Water gushes out of this bamboo pipe, ice cold. Like a shower."

"We found a creek."

"They got supper cooking?"

He nodded.

"Great. I'm hungry. See you in a little while." She walked on, leaving him alone again. He savored the aloneness. Tomorrow, when he had to climb that mountain and the ones beyond it, he would probably have different feelings. But just now he relished its extraordinary, dream-soft quality. The grass overlaying each ridge of the mountain looked as smoothly sculpted as a golf course. Runnels of dark jungle probed down along apparent ravines.

The sky was a deep glowing blue, with one brilliant star. Was it the evening star? He didn't know, being in an alien hemisphere. The air was clear and cool. Yet somehow the scene was closed to him. His heart wanted to capture its ecstasy but could not. It was just a view; the essence remained a mystery — like a screen he could not see through. He sensed the vastness behind it.

He returned to the hut, which was now a smoking, buzzing hive of smells and voices. The cooking food smelled good. After a meal of rice mixed with tinned mackerel and dried soup for flavor, and a cup of hot chocolate, he had a jovial chat with the villagers, some night-time talk with his companions, and then sleep.

This Jesus was an interesting character, one worth emulating. He was a wise and crafty warrior, possessed of great powers. He deceived his enemies by letting them hang him on a tree and throw spears into him, even though his magic powers protected him from harm. He played dead and let them carry him to a cave. Then he sneaked away and would soon take terrible vengeance. Indeed, it was so. The preacher men said he would come back and burn the houses and bodies of all his enemies. It was a crafty thing to be his friend and follower.

To partake of his power was also wise. The preacher men said the white biscuit was the flesh of this Jesus. In eating a man's flesh one acquired a portion of his spirit power. The dark red juice, sweeter than maritas juice, was his blood. It was good to join the clan of Jesus and eat his flesh and drink his blood. From these actions surely a man could become a great warrior, restoring to himself the powers his forefathers had — powers to fling arrows and deceive the enemy, making them run with fear and killing the stragglers.

He was a lucky man to be among these people of power. Christian spirits, he was told, were more powerful than the masalai of the jungle. The biscuit and juice were more potent even than the three sacred foods of his clan. These Christians, as time went on, would divulge to him the secrets of their magic and the means of putting it into practical use. He would return to his village a man of power and authority.

Roy drifted in and out of sleep. During one of his conscious spells, he turned on his side to gaze out into the moon-drenched kunai. It was a silver-blue world out there; at times he did not know what it was or where he was.

Fragments of his late-night conversation with Peerson resonated in his sleep. Peerson, whose sleeping bag lay next to his, had tossed fitfully for a while, prompting Roy to ask in a low voice, "Thinking about tomorrow?"

"Yes," Peerson whispered. "I'm afraid."

Roy was truly amazed at the boy's admission. Of all the emotions vying within him, fear was not among them. A streak of nervousness, yes; even some agitation and anxiety. But not actual fear.

"Afraid of what?" he had asked.

"Menyamya men." Roy became aware that Peerson did not see the world, or the bush, through the same eyes as a white American tourist. "Also fear big mountains," Peerson went on. "Not enough carriers. I think road will be hard too-much."

Roy could not deny the reality behind Peerson's worries, but for him they seemed minor. He lay for a while before replying. "No good to worry," he said at last, then added, "God will look after you," thinking that might help the boy.

Peerson did not reply. His steady breathing indicated he had fallen asleep.

As Roy himself drifted off, scenes of the day passed through his mind. He remembered swimming in the Watut with the boys after lunch and chatting with a group of villagers who were down at the river working on their canoes. He recalled the little river village, where old men sat on hand-carved log stools smoking long droopy cigarettes rolled in leaves or dirty paper. Flies buzzed around their bristly gray hair and beards; the pungent smell of tobacco surrounded them. It was the heat of the day, and no one stirred.

Then they had set out for Maralinan, walking down a narrow trail through patches of garden where women weeded sweet potatoes with their bare hands; through belts of muddy forest and into big areas where the jungle was being felled, where gigantic trees lay charred on the ground and the air was spiced with smoke, axe-blows, and distant shouts. Vines lay around the tree trunks like parasites feeding on corpses.

Roy remembered finding Ramel, who usually walked ahead with Yalu, sitting hunched by the trailside. "What's the matter?" he had asked the youth, for Ramel's face was creased with worry.

"I've got to pekpek," he said.

"So?" Roy said. "Go ahead." He had motioned to the dense jungle next to them.

"I'm afraid some man will court me."

Then Roy had remembered reading or hearing of some of the curious customs centering around defecation, one of which was that a person could be hauled before tribal court if caught defecating on another person's property. His first urge was to laugh, but realizing how serious the matter was to the boy, he said, "Go ahead. I will watch for you." Ramel had scampered instantly into the woods.

They'd crossed a huge plain of searing kunai, into and out of stretches of jungle, occasionally meeting villagers headed to the river. Always before them in the distance were the grass-covered mountains.

A conversation Powers had had with the Maralinan headman revolved through Roy's sleepy mind.

"We come to talk the good news of Jesus," Powers had said.

The headman nodded sagely. "You come from what place?"

"From Lae."

"No, you come from what first-place?"

"My home place is America. United States."

"Ah." The old man's eyes widened. "America. Yes. Place belong to Jesus."

"No, Jesus belong all place. Jesus belong here too."

The old man shook his head. "First-place belong Jesus is America."

"You talk what?"

The man's eyes glowed with enlightenment. "I hear of star of David. Big-fella star. Star belong Jesus. All right. Now one time I looked at airplane belong America. Airplane he got star, all-same star belong David, belong Jesus. Yes, true, first-place belong Jesus is America."

Powers had looked at Roy; it was the look of a man facing a portentous task, a task with no end of complexity or incongruity.

The memory of Powers's eyes was replaced by stars as Roy gazed out through the open side of the hut to the dark line of mountain and the starlit sky above it. Sometime later, the sky became brighter, gilded. Despite the warm comfort of his sleeping bag and the enticements of slumber, he roused himself.

"Powers. It's getting light," he said and received a grunt in reply.

• • •

Two hours later they were hoisting their loads. Roy's pack was an old Boy Scout canvas backpack, a veteran of many treks. Pam's was a yellow nylon pack on a streamlined aluminum frame. She had it loaded neatly, with a pair of lightweight tennis shoes tied to the back. Today she wore stylish, well-fitted khaki trousers that would have looked good on any college campus. They seemed to be made of tough drill, however, and would probably be good in the bush. Her lightweight navy blue shirt had long sleeves — a good choice, for her arms had been badly burned on the river trip. With her safari hat, mountaineer boots, and clean hair in a braid, she looked trim and attractive, though it struck Roy that she would look more appropriate in a safari fashion store in the States than here in the ragtag bush.

Maybe he was just jealous of her neat appearance. Today he was wearing shorts, hoping to get some sun on his legs; they were baggy old denim things that, had they not been cinched tightly with a belt, would have drooped around his hips. Chastened, like Pam, by the river sun, he wore a long-sleeved shirt as well. Rubber flip-flops and a drinking cup dangled from his swollen pack, and he had carelessly stuffed his raincoat in at the top.

Powers, in cutoff jean shorts and a T-shirt with "Good News Bilong Jesus" printed across the front, hoisted his concessions to the carrier shortage — his camera bag and a canteen — grabbed his walking staff, which had been cut on the walk from the river, and announced that he was ready.

Ramel, Peerson, Yalu, and the two carriers hoisted loads that would have been too heavy for a single man in ideal circumstances. Yet they seemed eager to go, shuffling their feet restlessly.

"Let's move," Powers said. Before the words were out of his mouth, Yalu and the two Maralinan carriers were zooming down the path, followed by Ramel, Powers, Pamela, Roy, and Peerson, who evidently liked to assume the role of herd dog for any laggers.

Roy saw immediately that the road to Engati would be unlike anything he had ever traversed. The trail in from the river had been rough, but it was a highway compared to what they were embarking on now. Walking fast to keep up with the breakneck pace set by Yalu and the carriers, he slithered precariously down a narrow mud-slick trail, over slippery logs spanning ditches, and up sudden rises that left him panting and eyeing the big mountain fearfully. And yet they were within close proximity of a major village — one which merited a dot on the map. What would the trail be like deep in those mountains where there were no dots, no villages?

The pace allowed him little time to worry. Struggling to keep his balance, he resolved to have one of the boys cut him a staff with one of their machetes at the first opportunity. Up ahead Pamela was having the same trouble. Her heavy boots had clogged with mud and offered her little traction, despite their tractor-tread lugs.

The trail rose through waist-deep, dew-soaked kunai grass, and they were soon drenched from the waist down. The heat of the rising sun soaked the rest of their bodies in sweat.

Halfway up the mountain — one of those Watut River foothills — Roy was gasping for breath. Fit! he thought contemptuously. You thought you were fit. Fit for a lazy, television-bred American flatlander, maybe!

He had bragged to his colleagues at home that he was "training" for the trip. By that he meant he took a two-mile stroll around his neighborhood each evening for two weeks prior to leaving and did some calisthenics and some kenpo exercises at night before bed. The calisthenics consisted of pushups, sit-ups, deep knee-bends, and the like. The kenpo exercises were basic self-defense techniques he had learned during a semester course in college. He had forgotten most of them, not being interested enough to pursue the art but proud enough of his achievement — orange belt — not to have abandoned the exercises entirely. So every night for two weeks he had practiced the stances, the straight punch, the eye-gouge strike, the low front kick, then retired to the shower, winded and sweaty.

Two weeks of that, and he had "trained" for New Guinea. Panting and sweating, hardly a half-hour into the hike, he reviled himself thoroughly. Still, Powers had claimed to be a take-it-easy man, so maybe he could toughen up gradually. But those mountains!

Roy stopped to catch his breath and look up at the grassy trail ahead where the others walked. They were still on the first mountain, the one he had eyed wistfully last evening. He took a deep breath and sensed Peerson — ten years younger, barefoot, and carrying twice the load — waiting patiently behind him.

Later that morning they reached the top of the mountain. There on the peak, leaning against some boulders, the carriers were waiting for them. Roy heaved off his pack and took a mighty chug from his canteen.

"Look," said Pam, pointing to the view behind him. He turned and looked out at the Watut River valley. The village of Maralinan was a soft Chinese painting in the mist below, the sun carving wands of texture across the expanse; the mountains lay with serrated flanks covered in soft blond grass. He now understood the meaning of each of those soft ridges — understood that every outlined rise meant aching toil and that the soft sculpted grass meant sharp blades that lacerated his legs.

The trail forked here at the top of the mountain and Yalu had already started down the left fork. The carriers smoked their homemade cigarettes and chatted softly while Powers, Pam, and Roy sprawled on the ground for a brief rest. Roy mustered the energy to take some photos, as he had done periodically since they left Lae.

"Well," Powers said after a few minutes, "I guess we ought to hit it."

Roy followed him down the long sloping trail that Yalu had taken. In places the grass was head high, the trail a narrow parting through it. At the bottom was a grove of trees, a beautiful creek, and Yalu. He squatted there with his broad calloused feet, his scrawny, dirt-caked legs, his pot belly, his strangely glittering eyes, and an expression that seemed about to be something but never turned into anything — about to be a smile, a laugh, a frown.

"Look at this!" Powers said, gesturing toward the idyllic tropical scene. The creek was pure and clear, babbling over pebbles, with a deep hole that looked perfect for bathing. The belt of jungle was not wide, and they could see the open, sunny slopes through the tall, vine-draped trees.

"Feel like a dip?" asked Powers.

"Why not?" Roy said.

They shed their packs and shirts and waded in. Roy had learned already the uselessness of undressing to cool off in a creek while on the trail. Clothing dried out in no time, only to get soaked again at the next creek crossing. The cold water made them catch their breath as they went under and came up spluttering.

"This is great!" exulted Powers.

"Man!" said Roy. "I just hope some nine-foot python doesn't come slithering out."

They both looked around quickly, then relaxed again in the water.

"I wonder where the rest are," Roy said.

"I don't know. I imagine Pam's going pretty slow. What do you think? How do you like it?"

"It's great. Wouldn't it be neat to have a house here? Like up there, maybe at the edge of the trees." Roy tried to envision the scene: a solitary writer, living here far removed from everything and everybody; a simple thatched hut set up to catch the breeze; a daily swim down here in the creek.

They heard voices somewhere in the distance.

"Down here!" Powers shouted. "Come on!"

They splashed around, washing off grime and sweat.

"Might get boring out here," Powers said.

"Yeah," Roy said. "You'd have to have a woman."

"Even that would get old after awhile."

"Yeah? Oh, yeah, you're a married man."

"That's got nothing to do with it. I'm just thinking long-range."

"You're probably right," Roy acknowledged. Despite the idyllic nature of the scene, after awhile it would have to get dull.

"Down here!" Powers shouted again, responding to the approaching voices. "What's taking them so long?"

"Pam ought to like this."

"You think she'd come in?"

"Why not?"

"Church girls are funny."

83

"Well, you're a church boy."

"But I haven't always been."

"From what you say, neither has she. But I have to admit, you're the most unusual missionary I've ever met."

Just then Ramel appeared on the bank. "They say this is wrong road," he yelled.

"What?" Powers and Roy stared at him.

"The Maralinan men say this is road to Wau."

"What do you mean?" Powers shouted. "Yalu! Come here! This is the right road, Ramel. What do they know? You tell them to get down here!"

Ramel walked away. They could hear him shouting to the others.

Yalu appeared. "Yalu," said Powers. "What do they mean — this is the road to Wau?"

Yalu did not answer. Just then Ramel came back. "They say they won't come here; this is the road to Wau. Road to Engati the other way."

The peacefulness of their swimming hole shattered, Powers and Roy climbed out.

"Yalu, is this the road to Wau?" Powers demanded angrily, pulling on his shirt.

Yalu shrugged sheepishly.

Powers turned to Roy. "I don't believe it. All this time wasted! Come on!"

They started back up the hill with Yalu following.

"This is the most ridiculous thing I've ever heard of," Powers ranted.

Roy too was furious. How stupid to have to make this wretched climb for nothing. It took a long time to reach the top again, and when they did they were exhausted. Peerson and Pam were still there with the two Maralinan carriers, who both wore expressions of contempt.

84

"We shouted after you," said Pam, "but you didn't hear us. They say this is the road here." She motioned to the right fork.

"Yeah, yeah," said Powers. Yalu trudged up.

"Yalu, talk up. Which road goes to Engati?"

All eyes were on the impish Menyamya gnome, his expression about to be sheepish, about to be belligerent. At last he pointed almost angrily to the right fork. Powers snorted in fury. The Maralinan men laughed contemptuously at the ignorant little Menyamya — the Kukukuku, the bush kanaka true who did not even know his own way home.

Powers shook his head disgustedly. "We've wasted enough time as it is. Let's get going. You two fellows lead. I don't think Yalu knows the road."

As the two Maralinan men led off toward the southwest, Roy wondered if Yalu felt shamed. But he was from a different culture. Who could estimate the emotions of such a man? Besides, Roy was furious at Yalu. He could not have cared less, just then, about the guide's humiliation.

Roy reached into the breast pocket of his shirt and retrieved his survival compass, one of those devices sold in camping catalogs. He always carried it on camping trips. It fit easily into his pocket and featured a loud whistle, a waterproof match case, and a simplified compass that showed directions but not degrees. From now on, he decided, he would keep tabs on their direction. From this height he could sight Maralinan, which lay northeast of where they stood. The trail went southwest. From time to time he would take a general compass bearing — just in case. After all, if the guide got lost, who knew what to expect?

For the rest of the morning the trail was more of the same: deep kunai, belts of jungle, steep slopes. The unshielded sun blistered every inch of unprotected skin, so despite the heat, Pam and Roy kept their long sleeves rolled down, and Roy wrapped a handkerchief around the back of his neck. The deep grass protected his bare legs from sunburn, but irritated them with scratches. Peerson had cut him a walking stick, and Pam carried one also. The staff came in handy on uphill climbs, like an extra leg pulling and hauling him up the steep muddy path.

The sky stayed pure blue with handfuls of drifting white clouds, while the mountains wore every shade of grassy beauty — golden, emerald, blue in some shadows, jade in others. Roy's jungle boots were excellent for crossing shallow creeks; the vent holes in the sides allowed the water to flow in and right back out, so the boots did not waterlog. Crossing logs spanned the deeper creeks. Frequently slippery, these were sometimes so precarious that the whiteskins had to sit and straddle them, inching across ignominiously. Peerson always waited patiently behind them, then darted across; his bare feet seemed incapable of misstep.

Yalu was in front again. Some tricky forks in the trail had left even the Maralinan men wondering, and Yalu seemed to be in control once more.

Shortly before noon they came to a good resting place: a wide, clear creek with broad sandy banks and a clear view across a grassy rise. Powers instructed Peerson and Ramel to set up the cooking pot for a midday meal. The hasty breakfast of crackers, jelly, bananas, and tea had long since lost its staying power.

"Pam, you missed a good swim back there when we took that wrong turn," Powers said. "Feel like a dip?"

She eyed the creek with an uncertain frown. Roy sympathized with her. She must feel rather awkward being the only woman, besides not knowing either himself or Powers well. Along with that, she was in a land which could be savage and frightening, and she had no one to share her impressions with. But what could he, a man and a virtual stranger, say or do to help her?

"It'll feel good," he said to her now in a soft voice. "Don't bother changing into your bathing suit. Your clothes'll dry out again in no time. Come on." His encouragement sounded stilted to his own ears.

"You two go ahead," she said. "I may come in later. I think I'll help the boys." Indeed, she seemed more at ease with Peerson and Ramel. They were friendly boys and responded to her mothering gestures.

"Do we want to go to the trouble to make rice?" Roy asked. The boys looked at him almost fearfully.

"I think the boys are hungry," Pam said solicitously.

"We've got plenty of rice, that's for sure," Powers said. He had removed his boots and shirt and was wading gingerly out into the cold water. Roy began unlacing his boots.

"Hoooo! It's cold," Powers said. "What would we do without creeks, man?"

Roy wondered the same. The tropical heat raised such fearful temperatures under his skin that he felt he would perish without the cold dips. He eased down into the water, sitting on the pebbly bottom so the cold water lapped at his belly.

"Aiiieeeee!" he shouted in a surge of pure exultation. Pam looked at him and smiled. The Maralinan men, puffing their cigarettes, permitted themselves half-amused smiles. "It feels good, ladies and gents!" Roy said.

"Don't it now, me lad?" Powers responded in a mock Irish accent.

"If it's that good I'd better try it," Pam said. "Can you boys take care of the cooking?"

"Oh, yes," Peerson said.

She took off her gigantic boots; without them, her feet appeared slender and frail. "Wow! How can it be so cold?" she said as she waded in beside the men.

"One of the mysteries of nature," Powers retorted, easing

backward to float in the water and gazing straight up at the sky. Roy suddenly longed for a cigar. He clambered out, retrieved one, and lighted up.

"Now this is the life," he said when he returned to his place in the creek.

"Well, you two boys certainly seem to be having a good time," Pam said, smiling at their enthusiasm.

"What about you one girl?" Powers asked. "Aren't you?"

Roy wished Powers knew how to remove the arrogance from his voice when he spoke playfully, but it seemed beyond him.

"Well, I must admit it's like nothing I've ever experienced," she said, sitting down in the shallow water and exclaiming at its coldness.

"Not like Toronto, eh?" Powers said.

"New Orleans either," Roy interjected, blowing a trail of cigar smoke and watching it linger uncertainly over the water before being caught up in a current of air and twirled away.

"New Orleans," Powers mused. "Well, I'm from Texas, and it ain't like Texas either."

"Texas," said Pam. "Is that why you wear that hat?"

Powers grinned. His hat lay atop his pack on the bank. "If you're implying that I'm a rootin' tootin' cowboy, ma'am, I guess you're right."

"Gee," she said sarcastically, "I've never met a real cowboy before."

"Now boys and girls," Roy said. They all laughed. Underneath the slight current of tension was a growing layer of camaraderie.

"Listen," Powers said suddenly. "Is that a chopper?"

"What if it is?" Roy said.

Powers stood up, water dripping from his hairy chest. "Maybe we should signal."

"Whatever for?" Pam asked.

He stared at them seriously. "We've got carriers for one day — today. After that, zilch. Who knows how far Engati is? Yalu! Engati how far from here?"

Yalu shook his head. "Ah, Engati long way true."

"You see? What'll we do with all this gear? If we signal a helicopter, we can go back to Lae, regroup, get some carriers, and come back."

"No!" Pam and Roy chorused.

"Look," said Roy. "I've got less than a month before I have to leave. This is my only chance. If we go back now —"

"Same here," said Pam.

"How about if I go back and you two go on to Engati?" Powers said. Was he serious or joking? With Powers it was hard to tell. "All right," he said, shaking his head and sitting back down. They could hear the helicopter clearly now. "You don't know what you're letting yourselves in for though."

"We can handle it," Roy said.

"Yeah. Brave words."

"Well, I'm determined," Pam said. "I'm here to see what the bush is like. If the bush means sometimes you don't get carriers, all right, then we'll experience it that way. God will look after us."

"Yeah, God will look after us all right," Powers said. "But he expects us to look after ourselves too."

"I know that," she said peevishly. "But is this normally what you do on patrol? Turn back at the first setback?" It was a low blow, and Powers did not respond.

"I don't think signaling a helicopter is a bad idea," Roy said, wanting to make peace. "Pam, you and I are looking at it like tourists, which is really what we are. Powers lives here. What's the difference to him whether he makes this patrol now or two months from now? He'll be here. We'll be gone."

She nodded. "You're right. I apologize, Powers."

He looked at her with a strange, intense expression. Was it hurt, anger, forgiveness, or a combination of the three? He wasn't saying.

"Anyway, it's going to be tough," Roy said. "I don't doubt that. Not after this morning."

"Yes," Pam said. "I'm sure this is just a taste of what's to come." They were both trying to placate Powers now, conscious that it was through his hospitality and generosity that they were even on this patrol.

Roy puffed his cigar thoughtfully. Why is it, he wondered, that in the midst of this vast silent solitude, this immensity of wilderness, all it takes is a handful of humans to stir up a ruckus? And two of them are missionaries!

The others, meanwhile, had remained silent. Peerson was overseeing the rice, with Yalu beside him. The two Maralinan men were dozing. Ramel was reading in his New Testament.

"Now that boy is setting a good example," Roy said, nodding to Ramel.

"Ain't he, though," Powers acknowledged.

Pam looked over at Ramel, who was wholly absorbed in his reading, a puzzled frown on his face. She laughed.

"Well, I'll say this for you, Miss Carpenter," Powers said. "You're not the mousy type I thought you were when I first met you."

"Mousy?" She seemed astonished.

"You know — quiet, shy."

"Not mousy-looking," Roy put in. To the contrary, he thought.

"I can see you have a mind of your own," Powers said. "And that's good. That's the type we need to spread the gospel."

Ah, thought Roy. They're back to being fellow missionaries now.

"We get some over here that're well-intentioned and everything, but good intentions just don't cut it," Powers went on. "This is a hard country."

"Rice is ready," Peerson said.

"Good," said Roy, standing and taking a final deep drag on his cigar, billowing the smoke up into the sun-dappled shade. "This discussion's getting too deep for me."

An hour later they were on the trail. Pam lagged behind close to Roy. "Is he always such a — excuse the expression — such a horse's butt?" she asked. Her attempt at vulgarity made him laugh.

"You've known him longer than I have," he said.

"Not much. But anyway, you've been around him more."

"Well, I admit he's kind of a smart aleck, but I like him," Roy said.

It was Pam's turn to laugh. "You know, maybe part of it is that you two are southern and I'm not," she said. "I thought I'd gotten completely used to you southerners, living in Arkansas, but I guess not."

"Do you have trouble talking to me?"

"No. Just him."

Warmed by her remark, Roy thought maybe he could establish some kind of friendship with her. "Well, I know it must be hard on a girl out here alone," he said.

She shot a look over her shoulder that clearly expressed what she thought of his condescending tone. Then she walked on ahead, leaving him feeling slightly confused and foolish. But the sudden uphill climb made petty emotions fade.

The trail grew harder to discern. Although Roy checked his compass faithfully — due southwest — there were so many minor forks that he could not keep track of them. The climbing pumped his lungs like bellows, overtaxed his legs and hips, back and shoulders. The canvas pack was a coarse, sweat-soaked load blistering his lower back. He envied Pam her streamlined backpack, resting trimly on her hips. And he marveled at the ability of the boys to trot up these mountains balancing a forty-pound duffel on their heads or carrying a heavy load slung from a single shoulder strap without showing the slightest discomfort.

In the midst of the brutal exertion, however, there were scenes of inestimable beauty. The sun burnished the kunai ridges like melting candlewax. Mountains fell away like discarded centuries. It was geology gone berserk.

In mid-afternoon they came to a way station in a patch of jungle, a house-wind erected by natives for sleeping on the trail. This, the Maralinan men announced, was where they got off. This was the place for the travelers to sleep for the night. As for them, well, they would take their pay and set off for home immediately.

Roy tossed his gear down under the thatched roof, but one of the Maralinan men warned him against lice: better to sleep outside the hut, unless it rained. So they heaped the gear in the cleared space outside the hut. All around was jungle, but a creek ran nearby and through the treetops Roy glimpsed sunlit kunai ridges rising above them.

"Everybody gather round," Powers said. "We must talk."

Relieved of their gear, everyone sat. Yalu moved off to himself, leaning sullenly against a tree. Ramel and Peerson looked troubled and depressed.

"I know it's a hard road to Engati," Powers began, addressing the Maralinan men. "We pay you what, three kina a day?" They nodded.

"I tell you what," Powers said. "Suppose you carry for us to Engati, I will give you five kina a day."

There was no hesitation as one of the men, the spokesman

92

for the two, shook his head. "No," he said. "We said we carry one day. That's all. Now we go back."

"Oh, brother," Powers said, a theatrical note of woe in his voice. "We have a big heavy. We have all this cargo and no one to carry it. What will we do?"

"This is something belong you. We must go back now."

"Ah, brother, brother, hear me. I will give you ten kina a day to carry to Engati."

The man shook his head.

"Fifteen."

"No."

"All right. I will give you twenty kina a day. That's all."

Twenty kina was big money. They might not earn that much in months. But again the man did not hesitate. "No."

"What about your friend?" Powers said. "He hasn't said anything. You do all the talking. What does he have to say?"

The man addressed his friend in their tribal language and translated his reply. "He is not a man to talk much, you savvy. But he say he has wife and baby boy. He must go back and look out after them.

"The road to Engati is no-good true," he went on. "Big-fella mountains. Big too much. Not like these. No, these little mountains. And Menyamya men —" But here he hushed, recalling Yalu's presence behind him.

Resigned, Powers shook his head and reached into his pack for his money pouch. "All right," he said. "I'm sorry true you fellows won't help us. Here is your money. May God look out for you."

The men took their money and left. They had some hard walking to do to get to Maralinan before dark.

Peerson and Ramel sat staring at the ground. Yalu watched the treetops like a cat watching for a bird.

"Well, friends," Powers said. He shook his head and sighed.

"There's no way on earth we can carry all this gear. What do we do?"

Roy and Pam exchanged glances.

"We could dump some of the gear," Roy said. "We've got a lot more than we need. Just take enough food to get us to Engati, then buy what we need there."

"Ah, you have plenty faith, brother," Powers said. "Plenty faith."

"Roy's right," Pam said. "I think we can do it."

"Peerson? Ramel?"

They did not answer.

"Do you want to go back to Lae?" Powers asked. "We can go back. Ramel?"

Ramel, not looking up, nodded. "I want to go back."

"Peerson?"

Peerson considered for a long time. He looked searchingly at Pam, at Roy. Then he turned to Powers. "I want to go on."

"Yalu?"

But Yalu was not participating. He kept eyeing the trees, ignoring Powers's question and the discussion.

"All right, Ramel," Powers said. "I will give you ten kina and you can go back to Lae."

"No," said Ramel. "I will go on."

"All right, then," said Powers. "I guess we start dumping."

"Well, what about you?" Pam said. "What do you think we should do?"

"Majority rules," Powers said and stood up.

"But what would you do?" Roy insisted.

"It looks like we go on," he said with an air of great fatigue.

As they began sorting through the packs, they discovered that a can of insect repellent had burst in one of the bags, contaminating much of the food in it. This was hauled into the bush and dumped. The big sack of rice was also abandoned, and each person sorted through his or her gear to find the most expendable items.

At last the new heap, considerably smaller but still imposing, was assembled.

"We're still going to have a heavy load," Powers said.

No one spoke. A pall of depression hung over the group. Peerson and Ramel dug out the primus and rice, then took water containers down to the creek. Yalu slept, or pretended to. Powers spread out his foam pad and lay down, his hat over his face. Pam sorted through food and gear for a while, then stretched out on her sleeping pad and began to read. Roy pulled out his journal and began to write.

Much later, after they had rested and eaten and the air had begun to cool, life seemed to return to the little group. Peerson and Ramel started chattering again.

"I'm going to take a bath," said Powers. "Snakes won't be out for another fifteen minutes or so. That'll give us time to get our baths, Roy. Then Pam can have her turn." She flashed him a grin.

The two men followed the creek until they were out of sight of the clearing. The water here was murky, not nearly as inviting as the pebbly pools they had encountered earlier. They stripped and eased into the water, soaping themselves lazily in the gloom. The cold water and the sudsy rubdown eased their tired muscles.

"Do you think we made the right decision?" asked Roy.

"I sure hope so," Powers said. "It's going to be hard."

"I'm worried about that Yalu."

"I don't like him," Powers said. "I haven't liked him since he took that wrong turn."

"Seems like — I don't know — seems like he's up to something."

"I know. Like he can't be trusted."

95

"Well, we're stuck with him," Roy said.

Powers sighed deeply. "It's hard on the boys too. They're young. Scared. They're in strange country. That means something to a New Guinea native. Traditionally, over here, strange country means enemy country."

"You think they're afraid of the Menyamyas?"

"I know they are. They told me."

"Yeah, Peerson mentioned it to me, too."

"Did he? Ramel said he's afraid they'll eat him."

Roy could not deny a tinge of fear himself. "Do you think there's any danger?"

Powers looked at him and chuckled. "Here we are in the middle of the New Guinea bush, no carriers, a guide who gets lost on his first day, headed into mountains so big even the natives don't want to go into them — and you ask if there's any danger?"

Roy laughed too. He soaped his hair and ducked his head to rinse it. When he came up, Powers was doing the same.

"You'd better watch out," Roy said. "A snake could come out behind you. No joke."

Powers looked behind him at the dark, rooty, overhung bank. "I don't think we're in any danger, if that's what you mean," he said. It was a second before Roy realized he wasn't referring to snakes. "They won't bother whiteskins, and the boys are with us, so they're safe. Plus, we're coming in with one of their own people, even if he is a creep. And look, I know these people. At Aiwomba those were the friendliest people you'd ever want to meet."

"Yeah, but this isn't Aiwomba."

"Same people. Menyamyas. I told you they offered me a wife."

"Yeah."

"The old chief pulled me aside and said I could have a house, a piece of land, and a wife if I'd just stay there and live and start a church." He laughed. "I had trouble getting out of that one. But that's encouraging, you know? These people have a real hunger for the gospel. You don't see that back in the States."

"How do you think Pam's doing?"

Powers shrugged. "She's all right."

"I feel kind of sorry for her."

"Why?"

"Well, she doesn't have anybody to talk to. We should have brought another woman along."

"What about you? Why don't you talk to her?" Powers said.

"I do, but I mean — like this. We can come back here and cool off and hash everything out. Who can she do that with?"

"I tell you what," Powers said, standing up and picking his way to the muddy bank. "You stay here, and I'll send her over. I'll tell her you have some things you want to hash out with her."

"Very funny," Roy said, climbing out behind him. "You know what I mean."

"Yeah, I know what you mean. She's a good-looking woman."

"Knock it off."

Powers grinned. "And out here in the bush — who would know?"

Roy popped him with his towel and Powers hopped out of the way. When they were dressed and walking back, Powers said, "You know, we should have brought that Scrabble game. You still have a chance at the world championship."

"What do you mean? I won the other night."

"Yeah, but you have to win twice in a row to gain the title."

"What kind of rule is that?"

"Rule of the house. You're on my turf, remember? You're

the challenger; I'm the champ. One win, what's that? A freak accident. Got to be two in a row."

"It's a stupid rule, but all right. When we get back I'll do it. I hate to humiliate you in front of your wife and friends like that, though."

"Big words," Powers mocked as they walked into the clearing. "The bath is yours," he said to Pam.

"About time," she said. "I thought a crocodile had gotten you two."

"When you get back we'll have some hot chocolate ready," said Roy. "What say?"

"Sounds good," she said and headed down the path with her towel and bag of toiletries.

Late the next morning they left the kunai country for good and entered the jungle. At first it was a relief to get out of a sun that has been described as pitiless, brutal, cruel, tyrannical, and yet the effects of which still cannot be conveyed to one who has not labored in its tropical wrath. But while the jungle replaced the searing sunlight with moist shade, it also became cloying to the spirit. Gone were the views across endless expanses, mountains jumbled from here to heaven or hell or both. Instead of the open air, the sigh of the breeze, the rustle of the grass, there was a strange, dead silence — ironic in a place rampant with life.

They had been climbing steadily since leaving Watut Valley. Where, on what ethereal pinnacle, would Engati be perched? Roy wondered.

Up ahead there was a flash. Yalu had leaped aside, chopping at a snake with his machete. As Roy walked by, the slender, dappled, golden-black corpse was still writhing. What would happen if one of them were bitten by a poisonous snake?

The forest opened its heart and sucked them in. Set as it was on bitterly steep slopes, it offered no kindness. At its height, the air was clammy and cool, raising goosebumps on the flesh. Lower down, clusters of mosquitoes swarmed around them.

The trail was a nearly invisible dirt track used primarily by wild hogs who had left their fierce rootings everywhere. Brilliant blue butterflies fluttered in the sunlight. Now and then the silence surged with the whoop-whoop-whir of big-winged birds. And occasionally a strange whistle, a peculiar cry sounded through the forest, like the flute calls of a crazed and lonely spirit.

Yalu's face knotted with determination as he led the way. Little as they liked him, they were dependent on him now. Peerson and Ramel walked with somber frowns through this dark world, headed toward a destination even darker. Powers, Pamela, and Roy trudged along, too tired to speak. Their movements had slowed; they struggled up inclines so steep that at times they had to grab saplings to pull themselves up. Their feet went out from under them in the mud; their knees jarred on roots. Their bodies and clothes, hats and hair and packs, became begrimed with sweat and mud and flecks of bark.

When Powers called out "Malolo!" the group stopped to rest. Yalu and the two boys would stand impatiently, or sit waiting like dogs. They wanted to move on. But the other three would lie back, using their own packs as back rests. They would close their eyes and dream briefly, only to return and take up the bewitching brutal climb.

The top of the mountain offered no comfort. It was a narrow peak, distastefully chilly, with no view possible through the choked cluster of giant trees and clogging vegetation. Once at the top they could only head down again, and down was as mean as up but in a different way. Down worked on the knees. It endangered the ankles and sucked at the feet. Just as they had had to grab saplings to pull themselves up, they now grabbed limbs to ease themselves down without falling.

The path turned into a creek, and they slogged through shallow water and clambered over roots, praying that they would not slip on stones, that a snake would not strike out from one of a thousand dark nooks. Everything on their bodies — their clothes, their packs — worked against them, fought them, pulled them. The moisture was hothouse thick. It clogged the lungs like clusters of moths trapped in closets; it bathed them with steam, turned their hair to sticky clay. Inside their boots their feet shriveled and turned pale. The scratches on their legs began to fester, redden, and swell. In a few days these would suppurate, and tropical ulcers would be born.

At the bottom of the mountain there was no plain, not even a flat surface upon which to lie. Only a narrow rocky creek and a sharp uphill trail again — up this time toward a higher summit, a more exhausting climb.

When they passed through a mass of scarlet leaves, glittering in a rare belt of sunlight, they did not stop to admire or exclaim or exchange comments; they trudged on. When brilliant wedgewings fluttered before them, they glanced up through sweat, said nothing, thought nothing — just plodded.

Peerson and Ramel hurried along with frowns, quiet, glancing over their shoulders. They believed in the protection of Jesus, but fear of the jungle had settled deep in the unconscious of their people long before the first missionary set foot on their island.

Yalu alone was coming alive, like a shark who becomes lost in a freshwater river and, turning round at last, sluggish and sick, begins to scent the salt of its sea. His pace quickened; his eyes darted, noting and understanding his surroundings. He paused to listen to sounds the whiteskins were too tired to care about hearing; then he stepped on, saying nothing.

"How far to a house-wind?" Powers asked him.

"Close to," Yalu answered.

An hour later Powers asked him the question again, and Yalu replied, "Long way true."

And so they came to despise Yalu even more. Diminutive as he was, he led them like a shark leads its school of tiny scavenger fish, moving into waters — his waters — that the Maralinan men, for all their earlier contempt, feared to enter. What did they matter, those lowlanders? They were men whose fathers had died on the arrowpoints of Yalu's fathers.

"How far to Engati, Yalu?"

"Tomorrow morning."

That afternoon, at the foot of a mountain, they hit a stream and followed it, walking through water that was now ankle-deep, now knee-deep. At last they came to a sunny patch and found an old house-wind set there in the middle of the big bush, probably built by the old Menyamya warriors as a place to rest up on their raids to the Watut.

The roof had fallen in, weeds crowded round rampantly, but scattered in the torrent of green were banana and papaya trees — fruits set out for posterity by the men who had constructed this shelter. While the exhausted whiteskins rested, the other three fanned out in search of bounty; they returned with cooking bananas, a pumpkin, a tree pineapple, two coconuts, and a handful of giant limes. Soon they had a fire kindled and were roasting the pumpkin and bananas, passing the water-filled coconuts around. The sweet juice revived them all.

Roy in particular took to the limes, slicing them and dousing them with salt. He alone enjoyed this delicacy, so he consumed all three, charging his body with vitamins and salt.

After eating and drinking, Powers, Pam, and Roy waded into the stream almost hypnotically, their bodies seeking its coolness. The hole was deep, and they sat up to their necks in the water, not speaking, their eyes closed, faces pale with fatigue. Occasionally one would submerge, then come up blowing, face streaming.

Powers was the first to speak. "Feels good. Feels good."

Pam and Roy moaned agreement.

"How much farther today, you think?" Roy asked.

"I don't know," Powers said. "It's only early afternoon — maybe one or two. I guess we'll make it to the next house-wind."

"Praise God for house-winds," said Pam, her eyes shut. "Praise God for cold water."

"Amen," said Powers.

"Praise God for limes," Roy added.

"Praise God for tree pineapples," said Powers. Tree pineapples, or soursop, were white-fleshed, sweet, and juicy. They had shared one greedily.

"Praise God for malolos," said Roy.

Pam laughed loudly, a pleasant, refreshing laugh. "Amen!"

"Ah, please," said Powers, submerging. He blew bubbles underwater, stuck his head out of the water, took a deep breath, and went back under.

"Wonder how much farther to Engati," Roy mused.

"Yalu says tomorrow morning," Pam said.

"Yalu says a lot of things."

Powers emerged again. "What?"

"We're just wondering when we'll get to Engati."

"It can't be too much farther. Phil Sparks said it took him

two days from Maralinan. We've put in, what, a day and a half of hard walking?"

"We're bound to get there tomorrow, then," said Roy. "That's what I figure."

Peerson appeared at the creek side. "We're leaving," he said.

"What do you mean, we're leaving?" Powers said. "No, we're not."

"Yalu said time to go."

"Yalu's not the boss of this patrol. You tell him to come here."

Peerson disappeared. In moments he returned. "He's already gone."

The three hurried out and donned their packs. "Which way?" asked Powers. Peerson and Ramel led them up the creek. "Doggone his hide!" Powers said. "Wait till I catch up with him."

Before they caught up, however, the group found a big duffel bag — the one Yalu had been carrying — on a stone in the creek. "Ramel, you run ahead and catch Yalu and bring him back," said Powers, his voice seething but restrained. Ramel shrugged off his load and darted up the creek.

"We're not moving another foot until he gets back here," Powers said.

"What's got into him?" asked Pam.

Powers shook his head. "I tell you — he's no good."

Ten minutes later Ramel appeared with Yalu following slowly behind him.

"Yalu, why did you leave your load?" Powers asked in a voice that tried to be compromising, to show a willingness to understand. Yalu did not answer; he looked at the ground with an expression about to be angry, or ashamed, or something else. Powers repeated the question.

"Me no savvy," Yalu mumbled.

"I think you savvy." Power's face flushed with anger now. He paused. "Is the bag too heavy? Is that it?" Yalu nodded. "We can change the loads," Powers said. "Suppose yours is too heavy; we will scale things out. Suppose your load is heavy too-much; you must talk to me. No good you run away and leave it. All right?" Yalu nodded. "All right, let's scale out these loads."

With Yalu's load lightened, the group journeyed on. Further along Yalu turned at a tributary and led them up another mountain.

After awhile Powers said, "Yalu, house-wind how far?"

Yalu pointed ahead. "Close-to," he said.

"Close-to true, or close-to long way?"

"Close-to true," he said.

"Thank heavens," Pam muttered to Roy. "I'm exhausted."

Two hours later, almost sunset, they reached the top of the mountain. Powers and Yalu had been through the "how far" and "close-to" routines several times. Now night was near and there was still no house-wind.

The group was resting in a little grassy area that might be just big enough to camp on, but there was no water.

"Yalu," said Powers, barely controlling his temper, "soon it will be dark. What I want to know is, is the house-wind close-to true or no? If no, I want to sleep here."

"House-wind close-to true," Yalu piped and turned his back to adjust the strap on his duffel.

Powers looked as though he was about to kick the little rascal in the rear. Roy could see it coming, and both desired and dreaded such an action. But there was no kick.

"Come on," said Powers. "We can't waste time."

They set off down the mountain again. It was a long descent into gloom over rocks and roots and around trees immense enough to live in. There was not an inch of dry or level ground — a bad place to be caught at dark.

Yalu and Ramel were ahead, out of sight. As the other four neared the bottom of the mountain, they heard rushing water. Ramel came running back to them without his pack. "House-wind has fallen in," he said. "Yalu is working another one. The place to sleep is right ahead."

Down here there was no broad, grassy clearing. Instead, the forest opened out onto a river choked with neck-high grass right up to the current, which was studded with stones. They picked their way through the grass and found the damp, rotten remains of a tiny house-wind, completely overgrown. A little farther on Yalu had cleared a space with his machete, scarcely big enough for the group to lie down in. He was in the process of building a little shelter, but when Powers and Roy tossed their gear under it he left it unfinished and started on another one a few feet away.

The view was dismal. The sky was muffled with clouds and mist, and beyond the river were more mountains, choked and cloaked in jungle; there was no end to any of it. The path to the river was so muddy and the water itself so swift that washing was not worth the effort. Darkness folded in on them as they ate. Crammed together in the tiny clearing, among ants and weeds, Powers, Roy, and Pam lay side by side, with Ramel and Peerson on either side. Yalu lay at their head, wrapped in a sheet which was his only bedding; over his head was a tiny shelter of broad leaves he had constructed. A wall of dense wet grass surrounded them. Ants crawled everywhere. The river roared nearby. The thick mist was suffocating.

They lay for a while without talking in the clammy, damp darkness. Then, as fatigue eased out and their minds began to work, Powers stretched his hands behind his head and asked, "Pam, what do you think of Pentecostals?"

105

Roy was so drowsy he scarcely heard the question. It was an effort to listen.

"I believe what the Bible says: that speaking in tongues and other gifts of the Spirit ended with the death of the last disciples to know Jesus," said Pam in a dreamy voice, as though her thoughts had to reach out from a long distance.

"Then you think the Holy Spirit isn't active in our lives today."

"No, I . . ."

Roy drifted into sleep, then surfaced again. "What do you think, Roy?" Powers was asking. Evidently Powers and Pam had been discussing the question for a while, for the darkness around them was complete. A few stars showed among the clouds.

He mustered a sleepy reply. "I think God is out here. And I don't think there's any room out here for doctrines." He changed positions in his cramped quarters and fell asleep.

In the end he knew it was a sham, this Christianity. Power? These Christians had no power, except in the magic of their strange possessions. They could not even find their own path or food in the jungle. They gave no sign of noticing the birds hiding in the trees overhead, or the pigs that darted off without sound at their approach.

They were bunglers, big clumsy outsiders. They flaunted their authority, yet could not even carry themselves like men. They walked slowly and heavily, weighted down with useless clothing and boots. They did not even have guns! They let themselves be beguiled by the worthless

Watut villagers. They brought masses of food only to throw it away. A child could lead them astray in the forest.

He was disappointed and disillusioned. Hoping to return to his village with all the power of a new magic, he found himself instead encumbered with those who proclaimed great knowledge but in fact had none. What would become of him? He would return home a fool just as he had left. He had never been accepted among his own people, who were falling into the decadence of the whiteskins' ways. He had hoped to return and redeem himself, but now . . .

What recourse did he have except to recall the traditions of his forefathers, to summon the power he had once felt at the taste of the sacred foods — not biscuit and sugar-juice, but blood, skin, and flesh? He made his resolve and kept silent.

The torments of the day before increased when they left their river camp, but they were glad to get out of the place. Ants had invaded everything, and every item of clothing was damp from the dew and mist. They felt mildewed.

Roy noted by his compass that, for the first time, they were leaving their southwest course to turn north, following a trail parallel to the river. They were moving upstream, although the trail was perhaps a hundred feet above the torrent.

As trails go, it was ridiculous — no wider than a handspan and slick as grease. On one side was a steep drop-off through stone-strewn forest to the river; on the other was a rugged ascent. Along this tenuous track they threaded their wretched course. Sustained only by a breakfast of soggy, crumbly biscuits with limp processed cheese and cups of hot tea, they had little energy for the exertion.

"Will we get to Engati today?" Yalu had been asked various times throughout the morning.

His replies varied: "If we walk strong, we will get there this afternoon." . . . "No, Engati is a long-way true." . . . "We must climb only one mountain and we will be in Engati."

They almost ceased to care, like oxen plodding a circular track. When they stopped for rest breaks, as they did frequently, Roy dreamed of New Orleans coffee and pecan pie. These delights appeared before his eyes the instant he closed them; he could almost taste them. And he longed for the security of his car, driving through the familiar surroundings of an American city. He longed for a tall glass of milk — cold, the glass beaded with sweat. Then malolo was over and once more they walked.

They passed numerous mountain streams tumbling down through the rocks, but the air was too cool and the water too cold for them to bathe. They drank the clean water; they filled canteens and lengths of bamboo. But they did not go into the streams except to soak their feet.

In late morning they stopped for lunch. There was enough rice left for one meal, several cans of tinned fish, the canned ham Powers had been hoarding, a few packets of soup mix, and a supply of tea. Everything else was gone. They cooked the rice and mixed just two tins of fish in it, a meager amount. The meal and the clean gushing water they drank revived them. While the others rested in the sun, Ramel made himself a set of bamboo panpipes, as small as his hand, and played them. To Roy it sounded like some forest spirit.

Later in the day Powers began to weaken. "I don't know if it's malaria or a spider bite," he told Pam and Roy. There was a red, swollen knot on the side of his hand where he said a brown spider had bitten him. He took his malaria medicine and staggered on.

Weak, tired, hot, cold, wet, they struggled along behind Yalu, who padded warily ahead with his machete, at times backtracking in search of the negligible trail. Clearly this was not a heavily used pathway. To Roy, it was all but invisible.

Powers was in the rear now, shepherded closely by Peerson. His face was pale and he called for malolos often. They rested; they dreamed. They plodded through thickets of stinging nettle, through explosions of maroon flowers. They crawled over moss-slick logs, slipped down banks of mud. They grabbed roots and pulled themselves up over steep inclines. They were streaked and dirty and torn. They swatted mosquitoes in the shade, flies in the sunlight. They knocked leeches off their trouser legs.

When psychologists and mystics write of the five, or seven, levels of consciousness, they leave out the level of profound fatigue where all thoughts sink into a great gaping well of darkness; where purple spots dance before the eyes; where names and memories and opinions and emotions disappear; where the future is one painful step ahead and the past one muddy step behind. It's the level of consciousness where a human falls into and out of subhuman dreams, stumbling over snails and roots and stones. Just a dragging on, and then a stopping, and then a dragging on. There is no time or space but just a journey into the heart of something for which there are no words, the birthplace of fever and evil and pain and an all-encompassing nothingness.

"Time for malolo," Roy said. He sent Ramel on to stop Yalu, who was now far ahead. Powers's face had gone pale and he walked with a loping stagger. His eyes looked into the distance with an unfocused stare. Pamela put her hand to his forehead but he shook it off.

"He's got a slight fever," she said to Roy and Peerson.

"I'm all right," Powers said.

"Did you take aspirin?" she asked.

"I'm all right." He looked around him, then turned to Roy. "I feel sick, man," he said and sank onto a log. His voice had a pleading quality; it hurt them to hear it. Peerson stood by anxiously.

After a time Ramel returned with Yalu, who had a look on his face which might have been about to be irritated and might have been about to be questioning.

"Yalu, everyone, listen," Roy said. "Powers is sick. No good you-fella run away. We must go easy-easy. Savvy?" Yalu nodded, wide-eyed.

Roy said, "No good we walk strong and Powers come up with big-fella sick. All right?" Yalu nodded. "All right, malolo a little, then we go. Easy-easy." Yalu squatted.

Roy and Pam exchanged glances, then sat down a short distance away. "What do you think he's got?" he asked her.

"I think it's just a touch of malaria," she said in a low voice. "I'm hoping the chloroquine will fix him up. But if it's really a spider bite — I don't know."

He found himself marveling at the length of her hair, the braid falling to her hips. "When's the last time you cut your hair?" he asked.

She blushed slightly. "What's that got to do with anything?"

"I'm sorry. I just admire it, that's all."

She laughed. "If you can admire it in these circumstances, you've got some kind of imagination."

"We go now," piped Yalu. It was both a question and a demand, and it irked Roy.

He turned to Powers. "Pow? Can you make it?" Powers nodded and, gripping his staff, struggled to rise. Roy did not like the pallor of his face.

This time the trail led across a flat stretch of jungle full of stinging nettle. Roy walked fast, keeping an eye on Yalu. Ramel kept up with him, but the others dropped far behind.

111

Roy watched Yalu lose the trail, backtrack, and find it again. Suddenly Yalu stopped as though yanked by a cord and stared into the woods.

"Ramel, get knife!" he hissed.

Ramel, who was behind Roy, rushed ahead with a machete. Roy peered into the thicket where Yalu was staring. Forms became clear to him: an adult cassowary and two babies. Startled by the humans, they were on the verge of breaking into a run.

Evidently afraid to pursue them alone, Yalu waited until Ramel sprinted up, then plunged into the thicket. As lithe and small as he was, he became entangled by vines. He struggled to unfasten himself and leaped after the birds. Ramel followed him while Roy watched, his heart pounding. The adult bird was nearly six feet tall. It looked prehistoric, with huge muscular legs, tiny useless wings, and a strange long neck that glinted in a ray of sunlight.

The baby birds, as large as hen turkeys, were striped laterally. They stayed close to their mother. In seconds, birds and humans had disappeared, crashing into the jungle. Roy heard shouting as Yalu and Ramel pursued the birds.

For the moment all his troubles were gone; he was like a boy on a rabbit hunt. If he thought he could have run through that prison of vines and kept up with the birds, he would have done so. But he merely watched excitedly until the other three caught up with him.

"What's going on?" Powers asked.

"Cassowary," said Roy. "A mother and two babies. Yalu and Ramel have gone after them."

Powers managed a snort. "What do they think they'll do with them if they catch them?"

"Aren't cassowaries those giant birds, like ostrich or emu?" Pam asked.

"Yeah," said Powers. "In pidgin they're called muruks. And they've been known to kill adult humans. A stroke of their talons and" — he indicated his mid-section — "they open you up here. Happened last month to a woman up around Hagen."

"Gracious!" said Pam.

"If we'd only had a gun," Roy said, "I think I could have shot one."

"Be plenty of meat, that's for sure," Powers said. Some of his color had returned. Maybe the chloroquine was working. "How big was the mother?"

"Big as me."

"Oh, come on!" said Pam.

"True!" said Roy.

They heard Ramel and Yalu returning, and Peerson shouted to them, "You get muruk?"

"No got," they sang out. They were sweaty and grinning.

"He big-fella?" Peerson asked.

"Oh, big-fella true, big-fella too much!" Ramel said.

Yalu, still panting, held his hand high, indicating six feet or so. "Him big-fella," he affirmed.

"Yalu, why you no kill him?" Powers teased.

Yalu grinned back. "Me no can run that fast."

Powers shook his head. "Ah, me sorry true. Me like meat belong muruk plenty too much."

Yalu eyed him in wonder. "True? Ah, yes, meat belong muruk is plenty good-fella!" For the first time there was an air of friendliness among them all. Then Yalu turned to set off down the trail.

"Yalu," Powers called. "Engati — it close-to or long way?"

"Oh, close-to," he said.

Powers glanced skeptically at Roy and Pam, but they followed the others.

At five o'clock they came upon an overgrown garden spot

and a fallen-in banana-leaf lean-to. "We sleep here," said Yalu. "In morning we come to Engati."

"Morning true, or midday, or what?" Roy asked.

"Me no savvy," Yalu said and set about hunting food. The boys joined him, and Powers and Roy set off to find a bathing spot. They checked the river first, and in so doing came upon Yalu, who was returning with a marita — a large red fruit that grew wild in the Menyamya forests.

"Yalu, is river good for wash-wash?" Powers asked as the three walked through the brush to the riverbank, where it was a good thirty-foot drop to the roaring, rocky river.

"No good," Yalu said. "You no can wash-wash here."

Powers, clearly over his bout of fever, grabbed Yalu playfully and pretended he was going to throw him over the bank. The little native squirmed around in Powers's grip and fixed him in a bear hug. They wrestled, grinning and edging each other toward the river. Though Powers was considerably larger, Yalu was all fiber and sinew. Roy wondered what the outcome would be if the struggle were real.

"I think you like wash-wash, yes?" Powers said.

"No, me no like," Yalu panted.

"Ah, man, maski," said Powers when they had released each other, both panting. "I think you're dirty too-much. Maski you wash."

Yalu laughed excitedly and headed back toward the camp while Powers and Roy walked further along the trail. They found nothing but a muddy slough in which to wash. When they returned to the others, the boys had a fire crackling and food heaped around it: bananas, pumpkins, maritas, and an under-ripe pawpaw. They stuffed sections of bamboo with bananas, segments of pumpkin, and pumpkin leaves. They cut up the big red maritas and put them in a pot with a little water to boil.

114

Pam was stretched out in the lean-to, reading. Powers stayed at the fire with the boys while Roy spread out his sleeping bag under the lean-to beside her. "What are you reading?" he asked.

"It's a book of essays on prayer," she said, showing him the cover.

"I brought some books too, but I haven't had a chance to read yet," said Roy. He dug in his pack and brought out Byrd's *Alone*. "I could do with a little Antarctica about now," he laughed as he lay back on his bedding.

"I've heard of that," Pam said, looking at his book. "Is it good?"

"I don't know. I just started it."

They read side by side in silence, enjoying the coolness of the evening air and the background sounds of the crackling fire and the cheerful voices of the boys. Even Yalu chattered happily in a strange cadence that was almost musical. Powers kept them laughing with his sarcastic humor.

Unable to concentrate enough to follow the book's narrative, Roy browsed through it at random. Finding a section he particularly liked, he said to Pam, "Mind if I interrupt?"

"No."

"Listen to this. I like this." He read her a passage where Byrd was describing the beauty of the Antarctic while at the same time pointing out the lurking danger of which he was always aware — the peril that went with pure blue ice and flattened, brilliant sunset.

"That's good," she said. "You know, that's almost like a different way of putting a passage I just read. Here, let me find it . . . listen. 'Satan will come at any time. Most of the time he comes when we least expect him. He will come when we are weary and our defense system is tired. He will jump right in after we have seen great victories.'"

"Sounds almost like we're looking forward to bad times," he said.

"Oh, no. Listen to this. 'Since the Holy Spirit is much stronger than Satan, he is able to fortify us with the Word of God and to take over when Satan fights against us.'"

Roy nodded, not so much at what she had read as at his own thoughts. "You know, all these books about the jungle always . . . well, have you ever read *Heart of Darkness* by Joseph Conrad?"

"No."

"It's about a journey up the Congo, and it's a journey into evil, into the heart of darkness. It seems like every book about the jungle tries to turn it into a symbol of evil. I really get tired of that. They're all so melodramatic. We've been out here, what, four days? There's nothing necessarily evil about the jungle. I mean look at us. We're making a journey deep into the jungle, right? Listen. Does this sound like the heart of darkness?" They listened to the happy voices. "Tomorrow we should be at Engati, and according to Powers the people there — at least their kinsmen in Aiwomba — are the friendliest he's ever met. He said they showered him with food — pawpaws, sweet bananas, the works. What's dark about that?"

Pam thought for a moment before responding. "You're probably right, but to me the point is that whatever we find in Engati, good or bad, if we have the Holy Spirit with us we don't need to worry. Even if it really is the heart of darkness, with God we can conquer it."

The conversation had taken a dismal turn in Roy's estimation. "I guess I'm just not a zealot," he said.

"You don't have to be," she said. "I don't think of myself as a zealot either."

Roy heard her words but was not really listening. He turned over on his back and gazed out at the campsite.

"Anyway, I think you're right," Pam continued. "I mean, jungle hiking is horrible all right, but I don't see anything sinister about it. In a lot of ways it's very beautiful."

The sun was behind the mountains now. Butterflies twinkled in the waning blue light, and smoke filtered upward in the bowl of the clearing. In the center of the untended jumble of sweet potato and pumpkin vines, banana and pawpaw trees, walled in by tall dense forest, the group around the fire looked as wild as any pirates out of the last century: Powers with his beard and leather hat, the three natives digging their food out of bamboo stalks.

Just then a harsh, discordant note sounded somewhere out in the jungle, wholly out of harmony with the scene. "I wonder what that is?" Roy said. Somehow the sound disturbed him.

Pam grunted, absorbed in her book.

Again it sounded, disturbing in its shrillness, as though from another dimension. It told him there were other elements to this jungle world of which he knew nothing.

That night a sudden icy mountain shower burst through the darkness, penetrating the limp banana-leaf roof. Roy, fumbling in the darkness, spread his raincoat over his sleeping bag, but the rain ran along the ground, under and over him. Great damp patches soaked through his bag; water dripped on his face. There was nothing to do but endure the discomfort.

When the rain stopped, Peerson and Ramel rekindled the fire and curled up next to it. Powers stumbled out and joined them, tossing his sleeping bag onto the wet ground beside the fire. Roy stayed under the shelter for another hour, trying to fall asleep. Finally he gave up and climbed out into the sodden, pre-dawn stillness. Seeing Powers asleep by the fire, exposed to the chill air and so recently ill, Roy took his raincoat and placed it gently over his friend.

• • •

In the morning Yalu picked up his bag and left just as the others were sitting down to eat pawpaw and pumpkin. Since the trail disappeared into a thicket, no one else even knew how to find the way out of the garden clearing. Breakfast ended in confusion and anger. They searched for the trail and shouted for Yalu. At last Ramel found him. When Yalu reappeared, his expression was about to show anger.

"Yalu, why, why do you run away?" Powers demanded despairingly. "You must wait!" The atmosphere between them was hot with fury. All the pleasant feelings of the evening before had turned sour.

Once they started walking, they kept a clipping pace, afraid to lose sight of Yalu. Then they came to the highest, steepest mountain they had encountered yet. Since Yalu had sworn the day before that there were no more mountains to cross, Powers became almost unhinged with seething anger.

They dragged themselves up the mountain in the morning heat, using roots and saplings for handholds, pausing to brush away the leeches that attached themselves to boots, socks, and trousers, wriggling toward bare skin. Roy's compass showed that they had turned southwest again. There seemed to be no end as the mountain trail rose and rose, switchback after switchback.

Finally they reached the top where there was another tangled garden clearing. Here they found some sweet mulis, but the oranges were so acidic they blistered the lips.

The trail now followed the mountain range, and soon they

118

entered a vast open area where most of the trees had been felled over a network of gullies — battle fortifications? clearings for gardens? Yalu led them across these logs. Without the shelter of the forest, the sun was fierce. The air seemed heavy and putrid and smelled like raw sewage.

The blackskins, barefoot, scampered easily over the wooden maze. The heavy-booted whiteskins had to pick their way along gingerly, using staffs, for the gullies beneath them were sometimes eight and ten feet deep. Their attention was held fast to where they put their feet, for the logs crisscrossed everywhere.

Suddenly Pamela's screams made the others turn. She tumbled off her log, and Peerson sprang forward to grab her hand before she hit the ground. But she released his hand and fell to the ground where, coiled in a ball, she vomited into the deep grass.

Roy looked up and saw what had upset her.

Hanging from the limbs of standing trees around them were human bodies in various stages of decomposition. Wedged in the crotches of trees or lashed to makeshift platforms with vine, some had rotted to the point of bursting, with purple masses of entrails dangling out. The full force of the stench hit him now.

"I should have warned her," Powers said. He attempted to look calm, but his face was pale. Peerson and Ramel cowered on their logs in terror. Far ahead, Yalu stood, about to be impatient.

"It's all right, Pam," Powers said as he and Roy walked toward her across the logs. "It's just their custom. It's their graveyard."

She raised her face from the grass, a look of horror in her eyes. Then, seeing another body, she bent again into her fetal crouch, retching. The stench of the dead was overpowering,

119

and Roy fought his own nausea. There must have been nearly a dozen corpses strewn out across the area.

"All right, you fellas," Powers said, attempting to sound both authoritative and comforting. "It's nothing, really. I've seen it all the time in Aiwomba. Just don't look at them." He and Peerson helped Pam back onto the log, which was not easy since she had slipped into a deep trench with her heavy pack.

"We'll be past this section soon and then it'll be all right," Powers said soothingly. But Pamela was almost hysterical. As she shivered and sobbed and muttered, Peerson and Powers and Roy clustered around to comfort her. Roy felt like sobbing himself. The smell, the dangling corpses — some swollen, some withered, some skeletal — the whole thing seemed macabre, even evil.

"Hey," Powers joked. "This means times are good. When they're bad, they eat their relatives." Roy burst into a fit of laughter at the grotesque attempt at humor.

Pamela only shivered and sobbed harder. "I just want out of here," she kept repeating. "I just want to go home . . . I don't need to be here . . . just let me go home . . . just let me go home. . . ."

Roy pushed between Powers and Peerson, grabbed her by the shoulders, and shook her. "The Holy Spirit — remember, Pam?" he said. He struggled to recall what she'd read him the previous night. "He is much stronger than Satan. Remember?" She began to laugh and pressed herself against him. Then she was crying again, and he put his arm around her.

"Nothing to it, eh?" Powers said, patting her on the shoulder. "Nothing to it."

Even Peerson, who himself looked terrified, chimed in. "See, it's all right, Pam-mee. It's something-nothing. Maski this."

Somehow it was Peerson's attempts at consolation that

120

finally broke the spell. Pam laughed slightly and wiped her face with her hands. But she did not look up.

"Come on," said Powers. "Let's get on through this. We're almost to Engati."

They walked along the treacherous maze of logs with Ramel guiding them, since Yalu had once more gone ahead. Fortunately the boy had noted the direction Yalu had taken.

Roy lingered to take pictures of the grisly graveyard. At one moment it seemed nothing more than an interesting pagan custom; at the next the sight of the drooping entrails, the smell of corpse rot, and the sound of swarming flies conjured up a scene of demonic desolation.

They followed the log trail for nearly a mile. Then they were back on solid ground, in cool jungle, hiking through a deep gully, across a clear rushing brook, and up a steep hill. At the top, across a wide field of grass they saw a collection of huts and a group of tiny people racing toward them with beaming smiles and screams of delight.

Engati!

Outside in the darkness the mountain wind gusted cold rain. It blew under the springy floors of interlaced cane and sifted through the roof thatch. Occasionally enough seeped into the hut to billow the smoke from the fire that burned in the dirt-filled box in the center of the room.

The room was full of eyes. All dark, all aglow, all alive with fascination, joy, anxiety, wildness. The eyes watched the fire;

they glanced tentatively at the newcomers; they peered into fathoms of thought.

Roy sat with his back against the wall. Pam was next to him, on his right. His hand reached out and sought hers, squeezed it. She squeezed back. It was not a romantic overture, just a gesture of friendship and assurance. They had made it!

Whatever the rest of his life might bring, Roy knew he would never forget that moment when he had stepped onto the brow of the hill and seen the tiny people racing toward him. They wore aprons of thick grass, capes of beaten bark, ornaments of shell. The women, who stood just higher than his navel, had gripped him and his companions in tight hugs, babbling and crooning. Unaccountable though it seemed, their joy was undeniable. There were six or eight of them, mostly women and children, and they had led them, tugging at their hands, through the grass toward the cluster of huts. As they approached, three men came out. Pig tusks pierced their noses; great ropes of shell hung from their necks. They wore the same bushy grass aprons as the women. One had a ragtag, cast-off shirt. Mouths filled with buai grinned widely, teeth black, saliva red. Dirty hands reached out, seeking, touching. Bright eyes looked up, shining, wondering.

All of them — Pamela, Roy, Powers, Peerson, Ramel — had laughed involuntarily at this stunning reception. Yalu had disappeared, presumably to meet his friends.

They'd been led into the smoky hut and supplied with heaps of sweet bananas, ripe pawpaws, and cherry tomatoes. Weak with fatigue, delirious with relief, they spent the afternoon in lighthearted conversation, much of which had to be translated by one or two of the few villagers who spoke pidgin. Occasionally they stepped outside to observe the surroundings.

A chilly drizzle had set in late in the afternoon. By nightfall

122

everyone was clustered in the hut, including Yalu and a dozen or more villagers.

Peerson superintended a big pot of tea on the fire. The hot ambrosia would be scaled out to the crowd. Roy dug out a cigar, puffed it a few times, and then passed it around. From person to person it went, each one examining it, sniffing it, and sucking it savoringly. He retrieved another one for himself and smoked with the utter placidity that comes after profound exertion.

All afternoon Powers had regaled the villagers with talk — explanations, plans, proposals — speaking to them in pidgin. He spoke of his Aiwomba travels. Some of them had heard of the whiteskins who went there to preach. He spoke of wishing to talk with the villagers about the good news of Jesus. He and his companions did not make the trek, he said, to prove themselves against any mountains or to test their mettle against the jungle, but to speak the good news of salvation. He explained how happy the Aiwombans had been when they had heard the gospel, how they had clamored to start a church immediately, how they had begged that missionaries remain with them to tell them of this wonderful way to win eternal life.

The villagers of Engati nodded, inhaling it all with the smoke.

Powers told them that he wanted to leave these two boys with them for one moon — to visit with them and help them work their gardens and hold worship services and teach about Jesus. The visitors did not come with nothing, he said. Alas, thanks to the Watut River people, they had had to abandon great masses of rice which they had brought as a gift.

At this there were general nods of agreement, utterances of sympathy at the ill treatment, the abandoned supplies.

But that is over now, Powers continued. The visitors had arrived safely. The road was hard, but they were happy to be

123

here with the good people of Engati. They would leave the boys with money; they would pay for their food and lodging with money and with work. These are good boys, he told them. They understand the gospel; they are good workers. At the end of a moon they would walk to Menyamya Station and from there catch a plane to Lae.

More nods. Agreement. Understanding.

Now, as to Roy, Pam, and himself, he said that they wished to stay and visit with the good people of Engati. They would like to stay a long time, but could only stay for a day or two. Then they must go. Not tomorrow, but the day after, they would like to hire carriers to carry their gear and guide them to Aiwomba. In the meantime they would visit and hold worship, and this woman here, Pamela, would patch sores. She was a doctor woman, he assured them.

By bush standards, Pam was indeed a doctor woman.

Again there was understanding all the way around.

Now it was the natives' turn to speak. One man, a fellow who wore a tattered black shirt and a hat set awry on his head, and had a habit of sticking a finger in his ear and canting his head to one side, was the apparent spokesman.

Yes, we have heard about Jesus, he told the visitors, explaining that he himself was a Christian — a Lutheran.

Powers glanced frowningly at Roy. Roy wanted to question him but didn't dare whisper while the native was speaking.

The march to Aiwomba would be easy, the spokesman was saying. Plenty would carry for them. They would be happy to do so. As for the boys, they could stay if they liked. No one would turn them away. The people of Engati were their friends; they liked the white people.

Now it so happened, the man continued, that the people of Engati too had a problem — a problem perhaps the visitors could help them with.

124

Powers nodded his willingness to help if he could.

The man asked if they had seen the strip of grass outside the village.

Powers nodded. They had crossed the strip to enter the village. It was about a thousand yards long and a hundred wide, set on probably the least canted slope in the area, although it still angled rather sharply.

They had worked hard to make this airstrip, the villager said. They had flattened the earth and cut the grass with their machetes. Then one day a man came from Menyamya Station to inspect it. He gave them many white things to put alongside it. But he said it was not ready yet. He could not give them a permit yet for planes to land there. He said he would come back, but he had not done so. Why not? What was wrong with their airstrip? They had worked hard on it. They wanted it approved so that planes would land and bring them plenty of cargo. They wanted things such as knives, blankets, shirts, salt, pots and pans. They wanted a trade store. If the airstrip was opened, planes would come and land and open a trade store and the people of Engati would have all these things.

Powers translated all this for Roy and Pam, for they had had great difficulty in following the man's lingo which was stifled by a mouthful of buai. "They figure if the airstrip is approved they'll just get all these goods, bingo!" he said. "They have no comprehension of money. I guess they figure they'll trade food for knives and blankets. There's nothing we can do about it. Of course I'll tell him we'll mention it to the patrol officer at Menyamya Station, but it won't do any good. A place like this has nothing to offer. Even if the strip were open, planes would have no reason to land — except maybe to bring in poor fools like us and save us a lot of walking."

"What were those white things he mentioned?" Pam asked.

"Oh, those are fiberglass cones. When the airstrip is

125

approved, they line them up along either side so the pilots can sight it for landing. They're stacked against the hut out there."

Powers resumed his parley, and Roy turned to Pam and said softly, "This is getting pretty complicated."

"Yeah, I can't really follow it," she said.

Roy looked at Pam, her face shadowed by the firelight, and thought how good it felt to sit side by side in the smoky warmth of the hut, while outside the mountain wind whirled the cold rain across the miles of jungle.

"Powers can work it out," Roy whispered. "He understands these people and their ways."

Peerson leaned over and said, also in a low voice, "I think I will like it here." He popped a cherry tomato in his mouth from the heap. "The people are very friendly." He sat back and beamed.

"Sounds like we'll be lazing around the village tomorrow," Roy said.

"I'm ready for a laze," Pam replied. "I could sleep and eat for a week."

"Yeah, but after awhile it would probably get old. Especially out here."

"I don't know. Right now it sounds awfully appealing."

"You may be right. We could just leave you up here."

She bumped him playfully with her knee and directed her attention back to the discussion.

Roy, who had smoked three-quarters of his cigar, passed it to one of the native men, an old fellow with a sparse gray beard and a mouthful of buai who grinned at him and nodded his thanks. The man, the oldest villager they'd seen here, wore a brilliant but tattered purple shirt. He seemed to smile perpetually.

On Roy's left sat a native boy of perhaps thirteen. He wore the traditional Menyamya attire, including feathers in his hair, a reed through his nose — not being old enough yet for a pig tusk — and a large crescent-shaped kina shell around his neck. Roy had noticed him sitting there but, in his conversation with Pam, had forgotten him. His attention was recalled when he felt a gentle pressure on his left arm. Glancing over, he saw the lad touching the skin gingerly. Unaware that Roy was watching, the boy stroked the skin, felt its smooth hair, and finally leaned over and touched it ever so gingerly with his tongue, tasting it.

Roy chuckled quietly, then leaned back and closed his eyes.

That night the travelers — except for Yalu, who had not returned — slept in the back room of the two-roomed hut. When they were finally alone they clustered together and, by flashlight, celebrated their arrival in Engati with a feast of canned ham. Powers's previous illness, from malaria, spider bite, or whatever, had faded, at least for a time.

Morning grew lazily upon them. They slept as late as the village noises would allow them, then drifted sleepily into the front room. There, several villagers sat expectantly. After a breakfast of tea, pawpaws, and sweet bananas they went outside to check out their surroundings.

Engati seemed to consist of two clusters of huts strung out loosely across two ridges, separated by a deep ravine. Yalu, they learned, had spent the night with the villagers on the other side of the ravine. The huts where they were staying were immediately adjacent to the airstrip.

Beyond the ravine and the huts on the far side was a great

wall of mountains. It was staggering and depressing to think that, having climbed so high, they would have to hike even higher, for the natives told them that Aiwomba lay on the far side of that range. Roy was amazed that an area as relatively flat as the airstrip even existed out here in this tumbled, jumbled world. Except for the airstrip, village areas, and gardens, every inch of ground was covered in jungle. And the ridges upon which Engati sat, high as they were, were dwarfed by the mountains rising around them in every direction.

In this section of the village there were four huts, one of which was empty. This was a hut set aside for travelers. Roy and Powers, seeking greater privacy, moved their gear into it, while Peerson and Ramel stayed with the family in the hut in which they had spent the first night. Pamela was invited to stay with yet another family that was dominated by an ever-grinning, black-toothed woman. Yalu alternated his time between the house where Ramel and Peerson stayed and his cronies across the ravine who had not yet appeared to meet the newcomers.

After they had settled in, the travelers dragged out their dirty clothes, dropped some hints, and the obliging village women washed them in the creek. The travelers then hung their laundry from the roof edges to dry and spent some time bartering for fruit and vegetables, paying in coins.

About mid-morning Pamela opened the medicine kit. When news spread that she was ready to patch sores, about twenty villagers appeared. Men with gaping ulcers on their legs offered their dirty limbs to be washed and bandaged. A mother held out a screaming infant whose ear was full of pus. Eye infections were prevalent, and nearly everyone had malaria and its concomitant symptom, headache.

Roy observed Pam and took pictures as she competently, with an air of motherly authority, tended to the ailments of

128

these doctor-less people whose only palliative was buai. Buai, which helped the sleepless sleep, soothed aches, and relieved fatigue; which rotted teeth, eroded gums, and blurred judgment. In payment for her kindness Pam was given sweet potatoes, bundles of edible pitpit, and small bunches of bananas, both sweet and cooking. Now the travelers at least had some native food.

Powers and Roy walked around the area together, examining the airstrip, chatting with the natives, and climbing down the steep gully to the creek they had crossed coming in.

"Looks perfect," said Powers, with the air of a connoisseur of bathing spots.

"I'm about ready to try it, too," said Roy, who still felt stiff and sore.

They retrieved their washing gear — finding even that short walk laborious — and returned to the creek.

"I don't know how much privacy we'll have," Powers said.

"Let's just keep our shorts on." Both men were wearing denim cutoffs.

They walked upstream from the place where the path crossed, around a small bend, and found a spot perhaps three feet deep. Upstream from there the banks were choked in weeds.

"Looks like a good spot," Roy said.

Removing their boots and shirts, they eased out into the water. It was bitterly cold.

"I don't know about this," Powers shivered. The mountain air was not hot enough to make them crave the cold water.

"Well, I'm at least going to get clean," said Roy. He sat down, then stood up instantly. "Man, it's cold," he gasped.

Powers waded back out and sat on a rock, pulling his feet up out of the water. "I think I'll just watch."

Roy tried it again, forcing himself to stay under long enough

129

to soap himself thoroughly. He rinsed off quickly and clambered to join Powers on the rocks.

"I think our bathing days may be over," he said.

"They are for me anyway," Powers said.

Roy noticed a small sore on his left leg. It was merely a red swelling, slightly puffy and tender, the result of a kunai scratch. He splashed water onto it, soaped it, and rinsed it again.

"I've got one, too," said Powers, showing Roy his right shin. His sore had begun to turn white in the center.

"Better wash it," Roy cautioned. He leaned back against a rock and closed his eyes. The air by the creek was cool; the sky, which had been cloudy earlier, was clear and blue now. Behind them rose the almost sheer sides of the gully, choked with stones and grass. Across the stream trees and bushes encroached to the water's edge.

"That was a pretty grisly sight yesterday, wasn't it?" Powers said.

"Don't even talk about it," Roy groaned. "It's something I'd sooner forget."

"It'll be good for your article, though, huh? I remember the first time I saw one of those graveyards near Aiwomba. I puked my guts out."

"It was really hard on Pam."

"I guess nothing in Toronto prepared her for that."

"I don't think anything could prepare you for that."

"Didn't she work in a hospital?"

"There's a difference, Powers. Good grief."

"Well, I'm ready to go on to Aiwomba tomorrow. How about you? Or would you rather go back the way we came?"

"Not hardly."

"I was going to say, if you do, I'll give you my share of

130

kaukau and you can go. I don't ever want to see that trail again, brother."

"How did it compare with your other patrols?"

"It was as bad as — not worse than, but as bad as — the trail to Rakamunda," Powers said after a few moments. "And Rakamunda was the absolute worst. Rakamunda's a village in Enga Province. Have I told you about it? Anyway, the only difference between this and Rakamunda was that Rakamunda was higher up, so it was colder, and it rained all the time. I mean all the time. We were always cold. As far as the trail, it was pretty much the same."

"Hell on earth, huh?"

"If that's what hell is like, brother, I'm glad to be on the Lord's side."

Roy chuckled. "Do you think we'll have any problem getting carriers?"

"No. You see how friendly the people are. We only need three or four. In a pinch we could get by with two."

"Well, I'll still carry my pack if I have to."

"Bravo."

"But if we can get the extra carriers, let's do."

"That's what I thought."

"You think Pam will make a good missionary?" Roy asked.

"You're pretty obsessed with her, aren't you?"

Roy was surprised at the comment. "What do you mean?"

"You're always asking me about her."

"Hey, look. I just asked a simple question. I mean, I'm not interested. Especially in a missionary woman. No offense."

"That just shows your lack of taste. I'm married to one, and she's the best kind."

"She is." Roy already regretted his remark. "Jeri's great. You're a lucky man."

"As far as Pam goes, any woman — any man, for that

matter — who could make that trek and not be begging to go home has got what it takes."

"Not only that, she's been up there patching their sores."

"That's what I mean."

"So you think she'll stay in New Guinea, huh?"

"Well, she can't stay this time. If she decides to do it, she'll have to go back home, raise funds, get a work visa — all that. But if she wants to, I think she's got the stuff."

"But do you think she will?" Roy persisted.

"Hey, I don't know. The subject's getting old. Maybe it's because I'm a married man, but this endless talking about the pretty young single woman doesn't excite me. You're a single man; I can see your plight."

"Ah, lay off."

"What's your status, anyway?" Powers asked. "No kidding. Girlfriend? Engaged? Loved and lost, or what?"

"I'm a single, free, independent agent. Don't need nobody and nobody needs me. And I like it that way."

"Tough guy, huh?"

"That's right."

"Yeah, you looked tough whining your way up those mountains yesterday," Powers chuckled.

"Well, you know how it is."

"Don't I, though."

"Oops, hope I'm not interrupting." It was Pam's voice. She was coming upstream, rustling the brush loudly as though warning them of her approach.

"It's a community pool," said Powers as she came around the bend in the creek. "Besides, we were just leaving."

"You don't have to leave," she said, dropping her towel on the rocks beside them. She was wearing tennis shoes, shorts, and a jersey. "I just had to wash off after all that."

"It's cold," Roy warned her.

Slipping off her shoes, she eased out into the water. "Wow! You're not kidding!"

"Roy stood it for a few seconds," Powers said. "I wasn't man enough for it."

She splashed water onto her legs and, rolling up the sleeves of her jersey, began soaping her hands and arms. "Seems like the air is cooler here," she said. "But it sure is hot up on that airstrip."

"Yup," said Powers.

"So have you decided what we're going to do? Next, I mean?" she asked.

"We thought about staying here today and going on to Aiwomba tomorrow," Powers said. "They say it's a day's walk."

"And then?"

"I don't know. I'm kind of in favor of going on to Menyamya Station and catching a plane back to Lae," said Powers.

"What about that river?" Roy asked. "You said something about catching a river and floating to the sea."

"Yeah," said Pam. "That sounds exciting."

Powers shook his head. "We could try it. But I don't know where the river comes out, if we can float it, or how long it would take. Real chancy."

"Well, we can look at it when we come to it and decide then," said Pam. She had rinsed her arms and was unbraiding her hair. When she dipped it into the water, it became a heavy, dark mass.

"Well, I'm going back," Powers said, standing and stretching. "Coming, Roy?"

"In a minute."

Powers slipped on his boots without tying them and headed downstream and around the bend.

"How did you like doing the first aid?" Roy asked, watching

133

with some fascination as Pam began to rub shampoo into her hair. He was unable to resist the opportunity to look at her unobserved. Her legs were brown and smooth, except for the claw marks of kunai grass. The movement of her body under the wet jersey was appealing and sensual. He looked away, embarrassed.

"It's so pathetic," she said. "I don't see how those people live without doctors or medical help of some kind. I bet the infant mortality rate is something awful."

"'Something awful,'" he repeated jokingly. "Is that Canada or Arkansas?"

"I don't know. After four years at Searcy I get them mixed up." Now she was rinsing her hair, letting the current carry away the suds. "This shampoo is biodegradable, in case you're wondering," she said.

"That's good," he replied absently. "I don't think Powers is too excited about the river idea."

"I guess you can't blame him. This is probably all old hat to him. It's not an adventure like it is to you and me."

"I can leave if you want to wash off," he said as she twisted her hair into a thick rope, wringing out the water. His face felt hot, and he splashed it with the cold water.

"No, I don't want to right now," she said. "I just can't stand to have my hair dirty." She poured a white lotion from another bottle into the palm of her hand and began working it through the thick strands. "It's in a terrible state after all this. I'm hoping this conditioner will take out some of the snarls."

"Do you wish it were short?"

"No," she said, then added, "Would you want to try the river?"

"Yes," he said, "if it's feasible."

"Wouldn't that be an adventure! Floating a raft to the sea."

"I think it'll be a canoe."

134

"Whatever."

"Sure, as long as we get back on time."

"Oh, we would."

"How do you know?"

She shrugged and grinned, and Roy marveled at the way she had thrown off yesterday's horror so easily. More likely she was just hiding it.

"It sure sounds easier than walking," he said.

"Tell me about it." She rolled her eyes.

He laughed. "You wouldn't be afraid? We wouldn't know where we were going."

"It couldn't be any worse than what we've been through already. Could it?"

He shrugged. "Well, do you think you'll be a missionary?"

She looked slightly absurd, but cute, leaning over in the stream, her hair hanging above the water, as she waited the required time for the conditioner to work. "I don't know." She frowned, as though bothered by such a serious thought when she was feeling cheerful. She dipped her hair into the water again and massaged it gently with her fingers while the water rinsed the conditioner away.

"Biodegradable conditioner too, I suppose?" Roy teased.

"Yep."

"Would you hand me that brush?" she asked. Roy stepped into the water and slipped the smooth wooden handle into her hand. "This will take me forever," she groaned as she began to work the brush through the dark rope.

"Do you like it out here?" he asked as he took his place again on the rock.

"It's horrible. And it's beautiful. What more can I say?" She sounded a little irritated.

"Sorry. Don't mean to be personal."

"That's not personal," she said after a time. "I guess I just

135

feel like that's the question everybody's going to be asking when I get home. 'Did you like it? Are you going to go back?' I just don't want to think about it right now."

"I understand. I'm sorry."

"Don't be sorry. I can't stand it when people are sorry all the time."

"Sorry," he said automatically, and they both laughed.

"I'm going to leave so you can bathe."

"Is that a hint?"

"No," he said defensively, then saw her smile. "All right. See you later."

Later that day the three bartered for artifacts to take with them. Powers traded a good woolen blanket for a tribal costume — pig tusk, kina shell, apron, headdress, and bark cape. The young man he approached, enticed by the blanket, raced home to change into a pair of shorts, probably his only other garment, and brought all his native finery back to Powers.

Roy traded cigars, coins, and T-shirts for a set of bow and arrows, a shell necklace, a bark cape, bamboo juice harps, and a bamboo smoking pipe. Pamela bartered for jewelry — elaborate shells roped together with smoked vine, a huge half-moon kina shell, and bracelets of woven cane.

In the afternoon, at Powers's request, the spokesman who had said he was a Lutheran blew the gourd horn to summon people to worship. About a dozen villagers clustered around the cleared area in front of the huts. Yalu was there, too, trying to make himself inconspicuous under the eaves of a hut, although he had agreed to be Powers's interpreter when he was hired.

Powers made some opening remarks about traveling all the way from Lae to tell the good people of Engati about the good news of Jesus. He then nodded to Yalu and waited, but Yalu did not speak.

"Yalu," he said. "You must turn talk for me so all the people can savvy."

Yalu shook his head, like a schoolboy who has not done his homework. "Me no savvy," he said.

"You savvied pidgin in Lae," Powers said with a frown. "You savvied pidgin on the road. How come you don't savvy pidgin now?"

"Me no savvy."

Powers turned to the Lutheran, who was squatting on his heels, and asked if he would translate the sermon.

The man shook his head. "I am a Lutheran," he said. "I cannot turn talk for you. You come from another mission."

"All right," Powers said. "That's it. Peerson, lead us in prayer."

The boy stood up, cleared his throat, and prayed: "Papa God who stops on top, thank you true for all the things you've been giving me-fella. Thank you true for looking out for me-fella on the road. Thank you true for giving me-fella plenty food. . . ."

Roy looked around at the faces of the villagers. Their expressions were mild, benign. They had not understood a word of the exchange or the prayer. As they wandered off, Powers grabbed Roy's sleeve. "We're getting out of here first thing in the morning. I've had it with these people."

"What about the boys?"

"I don't know. I'm not sure about leaving them here. Maybe

we should take them on to Aiwomba. But the need is here. Maybe they could stay and just learn some of the language. If we could only speak the language . . . I think these people are interested. It's just people like Yalu and that Lutheran who are the bigheads."

"Do you think it's safe to leave them here? I mean, would they have somewhere to stay, something to eat?"

"Oh, sure, they could stay in the hut where we are. And I'd leave them enough money to buy food. I don't know — but one thing I do know. We're getting out of here tomorrow. I want to get to Aiwomba where I know the people are my friends."

Blocked from any further communication with the villagers on religious matters, the travelers whiled away the afternoon reading, writing, dozing, and eating. In the evening they gathered again in the hut where they had met the first night.

"We need four men to carry for us to Aiwomba," said Powers to the group. The Lutheran translated, since the subject was not religion. "We will pay three kina per day per man."

There was much discussion among the villagers, and Yalu participated energetically. At last the Lutheran addressed Powers. "The walk to Aiwomba is very hard. Two days."

"Two?" Powers muttered aside to Roy. "Yesterday they said one."

"And a very big river," added the Lutheran.

"Yes," Yalu said in fluent pidgin. "Very big river, strong too much. This river eats men. You cannot get across this river."

"A river lies between here and Aiwomba?" Powers asked.

Oh, yes, they said. A man-eater, a raging torrent. Impossible to cross.

"Maski river," Powers said. "I don't fear a river."

"You don't fear the river, hah?" Yalu exploded, his eyes like hot black gems.

138

"That's right," Powers said indifferently. "Maski river. I need men. Who will go?"

After more discussion, two volunteered, somewhat reluctantly: the kindly old man named Mausgras — pidgin for beard — whom Roy had admired previously, and who spoke not a word of pidgin, and a young man decked out in brilliant tribal attire, plumage and ropes of yellow beads, who had spoken little during the meeting.

"Morning morning true," Powers said. "You two-fella sleep here. Morning morning true we start."

"What about the boys?" Roy prompted. Peerson and Ramel eyed Powers uncertainly.

This started another lengthy discussion, the resolution of which was that the boys would stay on in Engati for three weeks, attempt to learn the rudiments of the language, then hike to Menyamya Station and be picked up by Hugh Larsen.

"Now let's turn in," Powers said with his laconic air of authority. "I'm tired of talking."

"What do you think?" Roy said when he and Powers were back in their own hut, burrowed down in their sleeping bags. The mountain night was chilly.

"I'm sick of this place," Powers said. "I'll be glad to get out of here, and I'll be glad to get rid of Yalu."

In the morning the two men who had volunteered to carry were not to be found; they had gone off somewhere. Yalu hung around though, watching like a buzzard as Powers stood amid the half-assembled cargo after shouting and searching for the promised men.

"We'll just signal an airplane," Powers said decisively. "I'm tired of dealing with these people."

They lugged logs and branches onto the airstrip, assembling it into three heaps. The plan was that, should a plane come over, the woodpiles would be doused with kerosene and lighted. These signal fires should be clearly visible from the air.

As Roy struggled to break a thick limb off an oversized log he had dragged onto the airstrip, he saw Mausgras and the other would-be carrier come up. They stood around watching benignly as though nothing had ever happened, as though they had not reneged on their agreement to carry. Yalu must have gotten to them, Roy figured. He gritted his teeth and broke the limbs with a loud crack.

By noon three planes had been heard and the fires had been lighted each time, wasting a quart of kerosene, for none had been sighted. In the brilliant sunlight on the airstrip the five travelers waited, fighting the aggressive flies, watching the sky, and listening for planes.

In the village, the natives went about their business. The women weeded gardens and cut grass for thatch; the men patched a roof. The children played around the airstrip. The novelty of the newcomers had worn off.

Peerson and Ramel moped around the log piles, ready at an instant's notice to slosh out kerosene and light matches. Powers leaned against a log, his hat over his face. Pamela sunbathed in shorts and T-shirt, her skin glistening with lotion and sweat. Her eyes were tightly shut; her hands fluttered, busy brushing away the flies.

Roy watched her for a few moments, a stem of grass between his teeth, then stared out across the wide view of mountains stretching beyond the lower end of the airstrip.

Covered in jungle so dark that at times they appeared a deep blue, the mountains rolled off forever. A huge dead tree protruded from one rocky promontory; perched in its limbs were big white birds.

His cap pulled low to shade his face, Roy felt a measure of the laconic attitude that Powers radiated — a sort of careless despair, a bored resignation. But he was also haunted by a sense of doom. What was this party of do-good voyagers doing here? Did any one of them, even the experienced Powers, have the slightest idea what they were about?

Signal an airplane? As in rescue? What was going on? Without their noticing it, something had fallen apart. What was it? Did it go back to Yalu's humiliation when he took the wrong turn toward Wau? Yalu was just no good; maybe that was it. At times the dark little gnome seemed the embodiment of evil to Roy. At other times he felt that they themselves had merely blundered everything, victims of cross-cultural breakdown.

But the ominous sense of evil persisted in the dark, malicious jungle and the ravenous mountains. Even the friendliest of villagers displayed a certain indifference, as though their expressions would not change if all the visitors lay down and died right there.

An image from the previous night in the hut rose inside him. After all the discussion, when Powers had left, Roy had lingered briefly just to listen and watch. Although disturbed by the talk of man-eating rivers and the reluctance of the men to carry, he was still mesmerized by his exotic surroundings: the smell of smoke, the low babble of strange tongues, the sigh of chill mountain rain outside in the night. Then Mausgras had taken out a bamboo juice harp and begun to pluck it, staring into the fire as he did so. Roy was hypnotized by the weird hollow music, the strange twangings that seemed to come from

141

another time, another world, another dimension. There was some strange dark current here. There were depths he had never imagined, ideas and behavior he could never understand. Even in the eyes of the old man, perhaps the friendliest villager they had met, there was something fearsome and unbreachable and alien. His eyes were dark and deep, or dark and shallow — there were no words for it. Maybe wild was the word.

The image locked itself into Roy's mind: the smoke, the night, the face, the primitive music. It strengthened his forebodings of evil in a way that no talk of man-eating rivers could. He had heard enough double-talk in his life to know the river was probably a bluff. And even if it were not, a river is a river, and rivers can be crossed. The words were not the thing. It was something else; it was a darkness of the spirit.

He remembered the passage from Pamela's book. He remembered the hanging bodies. And he felt terribly alone.

It was a good thing to draw the black palm bow, to fit finger and thumb around the thick string and pull back the cane arrow, feeling the hard pressure. It was good to release the arrow and send it flying with its brothers across the grass-choked field, raining down into the mass of the enemy.

The shouts were good, the yodeling, the acrid taste of buai, the whisper of the enemies' falling arrows and the sound they made going deep into the ground.

It was good at last, everyone together, to run across the field and find a man down, struggling, his eyes alight with fear, crippled with an arrow in the hip, trying to drag himself off after his friends who had fled. Good to gather round him and fling arrows into him, hearing them jerk into the flesh, hearing his moans and breathing and rattling, and the head man stepping out with his stone club for the finishing blows. Then everyone working together with sharp knives, cutting the legs loose from the hips, spilling out the guts, everyone getting a piece, everyone shouting and dancing and running back in single file, head feathers bobbing, to the village where the women would be full of song and the cooking fires ready.

It was also good, even better, to make friends with the enemy: engage in trading, hold a feast, invite them into the huts. Smiling, singing, and then at a signal pulling out the clubs and beating them down while the women scurried out of the way and watched with proud, happy eyes.

Those were the great deeds from days gone by when men did not skulk in fear and apathy.

The sight of the two warriors striding out of the jungle filled them with strange excitement — hope, fear. The men had walked halfway down the airstrip before Peerson saw them.

"Look," he said in a low voice.

A man and a teenage boy, carrying bows and arrows, walked down the grassy field with an air of strength and determination. As they neared, Roy's journalistic eye took in the details of their dress. Each wore a thick tuft of grass over the groin, as wide as a kilt. These were held up by belts of smoked bones the size of human thighbones. Hung from around their necks were capes of beaten bark which went down their backs, under the bone belts, and down the backs of their legs. Across their chests they wore great bandoliers of seashells, ropes of yellow beads, and necklaces of round shells. Downturned pig tusks pierced their noses. Around their heads were wide bands of scarlet cloth embroidered with tiny cowrie shells and a strip of bright yellow cloth. Above the headband stuck a wide tuft of plumage, presumably from a cassowary.

Roy had learned that to the New Guinea bushman, the cassowary and the wild pig represented the apex of dangerous game. There were no creatures more ferocious in the highlands. The man who wore trophies from these creatures was deserving of respect.

Their bows were made of black palmwood, the bowstrings of rattan, and the arrows of reed with charred wooden tips. The man carried a machete. Each had a string bag full of sweet potatoes slung around one shoulder.

Powers stood and advanced toward them with smiling face and outstretched hand. "Ah, afternoon, brothers! Afternoon true!"

They grinned; their mouths were full of buai. They offered their hands and seemed to size up the travelers, all of whom were standing now.

"You fellas do what?" the man asked after greetings had been exchanged.

"Ah, man," said Powers. He sat down, and the two sat beside him on a log. "We got one-fella heavy true. We need some men to carry cargo to Aiwomba, but we can find no one. So we wait for a plane."

The man clucked his tongue in sympathy.

"You two-fella look strong too-much. You think you're able to carry for us? We like to go to Aiwomba morning morning true. We have some bags. Not too much. We pay good — three kina each a day. You say what?"

The man's open countenance worked through a range of emotions; he crooned softly in his throat as he thought. Then he turned to the boy and they conversed in tribal lingo. Finally he stuck out his hand. "All right. We will carry for you."

Roy could scarcely believe his ears. Obviously the others felt the same. They hid their enthusiasm but exchanged radiant glances as the two men walked on into the village. Even the presence of Yalu, who watched from the edge of the airstrip, did not bother them.

145

"Can you believe it?" said Powers. "Praise Jesus! Our worries are over."

"Boy, they looked tough," said Pam. "Did you see those bones around their waists?"

"They looked like human bones to me," said Roy. "Do you think they were, Powers?"

"Nah," he said. "Cassowary. Say, they don't look like the kind of guys to be afraid of Yalu, do they?"

They all laughed in agreement, laughing at the thought of these two tough hunters and warriors being frightened of the impish Yalu. Peerson and Ramel chattered excitedly in Chimbu. Roy gazed at the mountain scenery and was amazed to think that the view that a short time before had looked so foreboding — positively evil — now appeared picturesque and lovely.

"Should we move this wood?" he asked.

"Leave it," said Powers. "Besides, if a plane comes over I'm still willing to hitch a ride. The walk to Aiwomba's not going to be any picnic."

After awhile, however, the heat and flies drove them back to the cool shade of the visitors' hut. Peerson and Ramel went off to cook some kaukau; Pam, Roy, and Powers decided to play a game.

"I still wish we'd brought the Scrabble," said Powers.

"What?" said Roy. "And be divested of your world championship out here?"

"Keep dreaming, hero."

"I think you two underestimate the power of womanhood," Pam said. "You both seem to forget that I came in second the other night — over you, Powers."

"Newcomer's luck. Besides, I like to make my guests feel comfortable. Next time . . . well. But what can we play? Did anyone bring a deck of cards?"

146

"The perfect game is Hangman," said Roy, producing a notebook and pen from his pack. "Paper and pen are all that's required." He explained the word game to them and they began in zest.

At dusk Yalu paid them an unexpected visit. Roy and Powers had just returned to their hut after another tiresome meal of kaukau when he appeared in the doorway, his head craned forward in a groveling attitude. He eased himself into the hut and crouched down against the wall. It was difficult to see his face in the darkness, but beyond him, through the doorway, was a scene of dusk-blue beauty: a sky abraded by sunset, punctured by stars, perishing over the mountains in the west.

"I have no mama," Yalu began in a whining, whimpering tone. "I have no papa. Suppose you leave me here, who will look out for me?"

Powers, who had not even looked at Yalu when he came in, now glanced up with a bored, indifferent expression. The waning light dimly illuminated the beard and handsome features of the face not unlike some portraits of Christ, but without the compassion just now.

"You will stay with the boys," he said after a long pause, his voice sighing as he spoke. He seemed to be dispensing mercy with extreme reluctance. "They will stay here one moon, then go to Menyamya Station. You will be looked after."

Yalu fidgeted. The sky was darkening quickly through the doorway; clouds moved in among the stars like ghouls.

"I have no mama, I have no papa," he repeated. The sing-song voice sent a chill of fear through Roy's stomach. Who was this cringing puppet? Was this doglike creature the same one Roy had imagined to be the embodiment of evil? "Who will give me something to eat? Who will look out for me?"

"Hear me," said Powers firmly, holding in his anger. "At Lae you agreed to guide for us and turn talk and stop in Engati one moon with the boys. Now we come to Engati and what? You don't turn talk. You don't want to stay here with the boys. You mess us up no good true. Hear me. You can stay with the boys, eat what they eat, stay where they stay. When they go to Menyamya Station in one moon, you can go with them. Hugh Larsen will pick you up and fly you back to Lae."

Yalu fidgeted again. "I have no mama, I have no papa. I have no place to stay, no one to give me food. Tomorrow, when you go to Aiwomba, I go with you, and when you go to Lae, I go on the plane with you." It was not a demand; it was a groveling, self-abasing plea.

"Maybe he just doesn't understand," Powers said to Roy. He launched again into his explanation. Step by step, speaking slowly in the most basic pidgin he could devise, he assured Yalu that he would be looked after — but that on no account could he go in the morning with the whiteskins.

Yalu crouched there for some time. At last he spoke. "I have no mama, I have no papa. I have no place to stay, no one to give me food. Suppose I stay here, who will look out for me? Who will give me food?"

With a disgusted snort, Powers reached over and grabbed his leather hat, settled back on his sleeping bag, and dropped the hat over his face. After awhile Yalu eased away as quietly as he had entered, disappearing into the dark.

• • •

The night air was crisp and clear. From the hut where Pamela stayed came the sound of talk, laughter, and singing. As Roy lay in his sleeping bag, relishing its warmth, he heard Pam's voice mingling with the others. They were teaching each other songs. Evidently the natives had learned some simple American tunes somewhere; there was a crazy pidgin version of "My Darling Clementine." The voices, led waveringly by Pam, suffused him with warmth.

Then they were teaching her a song, with much laughter and two or three false starts. The words were easily understood, the chorus anyway. Roy drifted off to sleep to the sound of Pam's tentative voice singing, "Pawpaw, pomegranate, sugar cane."

In the morning they were up at the first hint of light. A quick breakfast of cooked kaukau — it was all they had — and they had their gear stacked and ready. The two carriers showed up as promised. It was morning morning true — the sun was not even up — and the group was ready to go.

Roy, his boots tightly laced, his belt cinched, hoisted his pack and slung it onto his back. It felt good. He was ready; the prospect of mountain trails, so loathsome before, now filled him with happy anticipation. It would be good to leave this place.

Quick farewells were made to Peerson and Ramel, who stood by disconsolately. Powers had supplied them with money, medicine, and encouragement the night before. Still, they seemed depressed.

"All right," Powers sang out. "Let's go!" Roy grabbed his staff which had been leaning against the hut, felt its secure, smooth-barked grip.

The carriers hefted their loads and set off at a breakneck pace: behind the hut, along the edge of the ravine, down its steep, crumbling, rocky sides, and up the other side to the other half of Engati. So determined was Roy to keep up, so thrilled to be departing at last that he scarcely noticed Yalu darting ahead of the carriers as they went down the ravine. He spoke to them rapidly.

At the huts on the other side the carriers stopped and dropped their loads. When Roy, Pam, and Powers got there, Yalu was bouncing back and forth, his eyes aflame.

"What's up?" Powers said. "What's the delay?"

The lead carrier, the older man, turned nervously to Powers. "You have business with Yalu."

"No," said Powers with a stubborn edge in his voice. "I have no business with Yalu."

Yalu spoke up, his voice pitched high with excitement, his eyes fixed on Powers. His expression was no longer about-to-be. It was pure hatred, and it was directed at Powers. "You want to go to Aiwomba? All right, go!" His pidgin was amazingly fluent now.

Powers spoke sharply. "What do you want?"

"You take me with you. When you come to Menyamya Station, you put me on plane with you, back to Lae." It was not a plea; it was a demand.

Powers shook his head. "Yalu, if you mess me up now, I'll see to it that Hugh Larsen doesn't come and get you with the other boys! Now let's go." But the carriers stood uncomfortably, not wanting any part in this feud.

"Yes, go!" Yalu shouted hatefully. "You want to go to Aiwomba? Go!" He waved his arms wildly.

150

Roy, watching Yalu jerk and twitch, was filled with rage. Some part of him wondered calmly what would happen if he stepped forward and threw the little man to the ground. He took half a step.

But Powers turned around calmly, his face deadpan, his voice bored. "What do you want to do?" he asked Roy and Pam.

Pam had gone white, as though struggling to suppress some inner horror that threatened to strangle her. Roy knew his own face was red with fury, and his rage terrified him. If he gave in to violence here, what would the outcome be?

"I say we stay here and try to signal an airplane," Powers said. "I'm not giving in to him."

"All right," Roy agreed. "I don't think we should give in to him either."

"Pam?"

For a moment she had seemed almost throttled, as though invisible hands were clenching her throat. Now a calm expression — or nearly calm — came to her face. "Why not do what he says?" she asked. "Save a lot of trouble."

At this Powers showed some emotion. He turned his back to the others and hissed, "We can't give in to him! If we give in to him now, what about later? What else will he want? What if he gets us out in the middle of the bush and makes some other crazy demands? Then what? At least here we've got a chance of getting out. And what about the ones who come after us? If we show them we give in, it will be that much worse for the next ones."

Pam shrugged. "Are you sure this isn't a matter of pride?"

His impassive expression returned. "If you want to go on, we'll go. You can have full responsibility for the rest of this patrol."

She shook her head, refusing to play that game.

151

"All right!" Powers said, turning around. "Let's go back."

The carriers picked up their loads. By the time they got back to the hut across the ravine, the sun had risen, yellow and hot. Peerson and Ramel watched them return with looks of doubt, fear, and perplexity.

The three of them took turns at the airstrip, dividing the time into one-hour watches. The flies made it unbearable to remain any longer than that. If the person on duty heard a distant drone, a shout was given, and Peerson and Ramel raced out, ready to light the fires. But they spared their fuel now, having agreed to light the fires only if a plane came into sight.

Sometimes they shared watches to relieve the boredom. "Why don't we just go back the way we came?" Roy asked Powers at one point when they were together. "I'll bet the boys could find the trail. And I have an idea of the general direction. I think we could do it."

Powers lifted his hat and held it out, pointing toward the mountains. "Do you realize what would happen if we got lost out there? We could wander forever. Besides, we don't have any food."

"Kaukau."

"Kaukau! That doesn't give you strength." He clamped his hat back over his face. "I don't think I could survive it, man. Our best hope is to wait here and signal a plane."

But the absurdity of their signal was beginning to disturb Roy. Three fires on a mountainside? What did that signify?

What pilot would go to the trouble and expense to investigate what might be natives burning garden spots?

Later in the day, when the three of them were sitting on the airstrip, the two would-be carriers wandered up sheepishly and sat beside them.

"Hello, brothers," Powers said resignedly.

"Afternoon," they chimed.

Roy was amazed that Powers would even speak to them after their treachery. "How can you talk to them?" he asked.

"Aw, man, it's not their fault. This guy told me Yalu threatened to kill them if they carried for us. These people are so screwed up. If they'd have carried for us — who knows — it could have started a tribal war. The Menyamyas are like that. They don't get mad; they just get even. They let it build up, and then they kill each other. That's one of the reasons they have so many problems."

Roy looked at the two villagers they now knew to be father and son. Their attitudes and expressions did seem to show genuine sympathy for the whiteskins' plight. "I tell you what," Roy said. "I don't understand these people."

"They're unpredictable," Powers agreed. "Like sharks."

During the afternoon a layer of cloud moved in low, obscuring the mountain peaks and bringing with it a malaise — depression, fatigue, maybe a touch of fever. The sores on their legs were festering. Pamela had one just above her ankle, and the sore Roy had told Powers to wash was oozing pus, even though he kept it bandaged and salved with antibiotic ointment. Roy had a bad one forming on his calf.

The heavy cloud cover made it futile to man the signal fires; yet they were afraid to stray too far from the airstrip. Finally Pam went to her hut and stayed there for several hours. Roy wondered what she was doing. Reading, praying, crying? He had finished *Alone* as well as Bligh's brief account of his

153

adventures. In desperation he had borrowed a New Testament from Powers, but even reading became tiresome. A game of Hangman held their interest for an hour or two, but that also palled, like the bland and starchy kaukau.

All their food, even their tea, was gone, but so were their appetites. They were able to buy kaukau, cooking bananas, and pitpit from the villagers; and occasionally friendly ones, like Mausgras and the family Pam stayed with, gave them food and refused payment. Still, they had lost weight and strength.

Their greatest problem, however, was depression: the bleak sense of being imprisoned by walls of mountain and jungle, by natives either unable or unwilling to help, and by Yalu, who stayed across the ravine now, but who would show up periodically, slinking around and watching them. Powers had instructed Ramel and Peerson to give him none of their food.

The boys suffered, too, but not as badly, for they were young and easily amused. At times though they were visibly swamped with despair, and spent hours lying motionless, in some limbo between sleeping and waking.

The bleak tedium was interrupted the following day when Roy hit upon the idea of arranging the white fiberglass cones into an SOS. Immediately everyone came alive, even Powers, who was pale and weak with intermittent fever. They raced out to the airstrip where Roy paced out the design, a huge SOS stretched lengthwise down the grass. The others set out the cones. Villagers stood in their gardens or by their huts, watching with idle curiosity.

The white-on-green pattern should be clearly visible from high above, and any trained pilot should know the meaning of the signal. As the day passed, however, the surge of hope subsided. No planes passed over this area, nor ever seemed to. Occasionally they would hear a drone far, far away over the mountains, but no aircraft came into sight. Their ears and eyes strained when they heard a distant sound. Sometimes it was only the rushing of the stream or some off-key moan from the jungle. It grew maddening, listening for a plane.

That evening twin rainbows arched out over the mountains, clearly visible through the doorway of the men's hut. Roy tried to absorb their beauty, but could not free himself from misery. He sat in the hut with Pam and Powers, mulling over their woes.

Pam and Roy gravitated toward each other now when they were together; tonight they sat side by side, their arms lightly touching. Powers was leaning back listlessly on his sleeping bag; he had suffered all day with fever. Along with this, he seemed afflicted with a peculiar apathy.

"There's got to be something we can do besides wait," Pam said. "I mean, I have a lot of hope that our signal will eventually be seen, but isn't there anything we can do in the meantime?"

Roy said, "Sometimes, out there, I get the feeling I'm just lying there waiting for a big hand to scoop me up."

"Me too, brother," said Powers weakly.

"We've decided we can't go back the way we came in," said Pam. "And none of us knows the way to Aiwomba."

"It's that Yalu," Powers said plaintively. "He won't let anybody help us. I swear, I think he hates me."

Pam and Roy looked at each other; they were obviously thinking the same thing. How much it hurt to hear Powers sound so weak and querulous. Roy wondered how many other thoughts and feelings they shared. He reached for Pam's hand, and she did not resist. Her touch was warm, a salve to the bitter aloneness that was oppressing him.

"You know," said Pam, leaning forward suddenly, "Yalu won't let them help us, but what about the boys? Do you think he would stop them?"

155

"You mean just them and not us?" Powers asked.

"Sure," she said. "We could send the boys out, to Menyamya Station maybe, with a message. Isn't there a radio there?"

Powers sat up. His sudden burst of laughter was sweet music, and Roy's eyes welled with tears of hope and with admiration for both of his companions. "Yeah," said Powers. "Send a message. They can radio Lae and have them send a helicopter. But who will guide the boys?"

"I know who," said Pam. "There's a boy in my hut. He'd do it. I know I could get him to do it."

"Wait just a minute, wait just a minute now," Powers said, mentally calculating. "Let's say they leave in the morning, really early."

"Morning morning true," put in Roy, and he and Pam laughed.

"Before Yalu can even learn about it," Powers went on. "We can arrange it all tonight, and they can be gone before daylight. By the time Yalu finds out, it'll be too late to do anything even if he wants to. Pam, can you get that kid in here tonight?"

"Sure."

"You get him. Roy, you go get Peerson and Ramel. I'll get my notebook, and we'll write out a message."

Soon they were clustered like spies in the darkness of the hut. The boy agreed to do it. They would pay him two kina to guide Peerson and Ramel to Aiwomba. From there they could get a guide to Menyamya Station.

Peerson and Ramel were eager to go; the plan energized them. At last some action, some hope, some excitement. They would leave morning morning true, carrying only their meager gear and a bag of food. They would walk strong. Maybe they really could get to Aiwomba in a day. They would tell the Aiwombans of Powers's plight. Those people knew him; they

156

would be outraged at the shabby treatment of their young friend. Then the boys would hustle on to Menyamya Station with the message. As Roy held the flashlight, Powers wrote out the message: "Stuck in Engati. No food, no carriers. Send helicopter. Powers Stivell."

"In three days we can be out of here," Powers said.

"Now don't get too hopeful," cautioned Pam. "It may take four."

"I don't care, sister. If I know that chopper is coming, I don't mind at all. Once those boys hit the trail in the morning, our worries are over."

Peerson, Ramel, and the Engati boy were on the trail as soon as it was light enough to see where to put one foot in front of the other. Roy, Pam, and Powers whispered their farewells, and the three boys jogged off silently on bare feet. The three left behind watched the sunrise together in quiet exultation. Today it rose in full glory, with banners and battle-dress, like their spirits. They had not even a cup of hot tea to share, only baked kaukau, but it seemed like a feast.

When Yalu appeared, skulking, shortly after sunrise, they almost laughed, but he did not seem worth even that. They watched as he entered the hut where Ramel and Peerson had slept, no doubt intending to visit them. If he suspected anything was amiss, his countenance did not reveal it when he stepped out of the hut.

With the SOS in place, it was unnecessary to stay out on the airstrip. If a pilot saw the signal, he would know there was

157

trouble. Besides, they had learned that they could hear an aircraft before they could see one. With this assurance, they settled down to a serious game of Hangman.

Even with their high hopes, however, the hours dragged. They concluded their game of Hangman at mid-morning, and it was difficult to resist the temptation to count the hours. To pass the time, Powers immersed himself in one of Roy's books while Pam and Roy went out to walk around the airstrip.

It was a good walking place. The children followed, running wide figure eights around them, screaming and laughing and falling to the ground in temporary exhaustion before getting up to race some more.

"No wonder they never get tired," Pam said. "They get this kind of exercise as children."

Roy leaned on his staff as he walked, for the painful infected sore had weakened his entire leg. Pam's leg had healed without festering. In fact, the ordeal somehow seemed to be making her healthier, while leaving the two men weak and limping. She was lithe, lean, and wonderfully tanned; her hair, bleached from the sun, was growing tawny as a lion's mane. Today she had left it unbraided, and it trailed down her back in golden brown waves. Limping slightly beside her, Roy felt the contrast. Unshaven, his beard had grown out scraggly and goatlike; his hair flowed shaggily over his ears and down to his collar. He had become thin to the point of gauntness — not so much lean as frail.

At least he had kept his color. Powers, besieged by fever, was sickly pale. He stayed inside the hut, resting or reading, emerging only when absolutely necessary. When he walked he staggered, and the outdoor light seemed to dazzle him. The only times he came alive and showed any energy were during games of Hangman or when talking of Jeri and the coming baby and a planned feast at the restaurant in Lae.

They had agreed they would all go to the restaurant once they got back; they craved an orgy of food. In Engati they were eating the sickeningly bland kaukau morning, noon, and night. Sweet bananas were no longer to be found, so only the occasional pitpit or cooking banana gave any variety to their diet. Even meat was a rarity in these parts. The only meat they had seen was a piglet that inhabited the village and a wild piglet a boy had brought in from the jungle. But that was meat on the hoof, not on the plate.

Roy and Pam held hands as they walked. Roy's affection for Pam was growing, but it was a cautious, tentative growth. He was uncertain whether his feelings were genuine or just a product of circumstances. Would he feel the same in Lae, or back home?

They did not discuss any of this, but Roy knew these concerns were mutual. And yet he was willing to give the magnetic warmth between them a chance. There was electricity when they held hands. Their conversations sparkled; their words seemed imbued with fascinating qualities.

As they strolled, they told their histories. Pam talked of Toronto and college in Arkansas, he of New Orleans and journalism. They discussed parents and pets and siblings, opinions and flavors and preferences and dislikes. Books, movies, and songs. Things that were funny and things that were sad. Dangers they had encountered. Woes they had experienced.

She told him of Mike, who had been killed in a motorcycle accident when she was seventeen. He told her of Linda, who had jilted him in his senior year of high school and kept his ring.

They had reached the upper end of the airstrip and were sitting in the grass, constantly brushing away flies. The long green carpet spread out below them with its curious hieroglyph of white cones. It seemed almost ridiculous that they were trying to be rescued. The mountains around them formed an idyllic scene. The children playing among the cones sounded cheerful. Occasionally one would race up, throw himself onto his belly and peer at them awhile, then get up and run off to join the others.

Ignoring the alien world spread before them, they discussed the limitless future beyond their immediate horizons. She didn't know yet if she wanted to be a missionary; he wasn't sure he wanted to be a journalist forever.

They did not dance too closely to the flames of religion, but they touched on the subject lightly — just enough for her to elicit from him that he believed in God. Both feared a clash of opinions, an unwanted rupture.

Later they walked to the creek and dangled their bare feet in the cold water. Roy thought he heard the drone of a plane and looked up idly, forgetting that a plane was a momentous event. But the sound stayed far away. Some of the children followed them to the water; a woman passed them with clothes and cooking pots. She smiled at them.

The ravine was cool, the sound of the water peaceful. As they sat together on the rock, he slipped his arm around her back. She leaned her head against his shoulder. They sat like that, without speaking, for a long time. Then they heard a pop, like gunfire, and they raced up the hill to investigate.

From the clearing by the huts came a scream and more pops. Hurrying across the airstrip, Roy and Pam saw Powers standing outside, supporting himself on his staff, grinning wildly; in his hand was a lighted firecracker — one of the assortment he had brought with him as possible trade items. He tossed it at one of the boys, who screamed with laughter and jumped out of the way.

Several adults had clustered around to watch the fun,

including the Lutheran spokesman. Powers hobbled up to him with a mischievous grin and reached up and slid the pig tusks out of his nose. The Lutheran just grinned in a slightly bewildered fashion. Powers replaced the tusks with a firecracker. The children stood by, hands clamped to their mouths to hold in their laughter. But when Powers struck a match, the old man jumped away with a grin.

"Powers!" Pam exclaimed. Roy just laughed at Powers's reckless streak.

The children were begging for firecrackers, and Powers doled them out with matches. They raced around, lighting them and tossing them behind adults to make them jump. In the midst of the raucous fun, two strangers — teenage boys — appeared in the village. At first frowning with confusion, they soon joined the fun, asking for a share of the firecrackers. Powers obliged until he had handed out all his supply.

Only after things had quieted down a bit did the two visitors deliver their message: Ramel and Peerson were stuck at a wayside hut just over half a day's march away. Tribal fighting had broken out; two men had been ambushed and cut into little pieces; the road to Aiwomba was closed. Ramel and Peerson had sent word that they would wait at the hut until things grew calm, whenever that might be.

Once again gloom and despair descended upon the trio.

Roy wept that night in his bed, silently, so Powers would not hear him. It was a woeful weeping. Even the thought of Pam could not soothe him, for if things were to go badly for him they would go badly for her as well.

It was hopeless. Just when they saw an open door it was slammed shut. Each plan came crashing down like a jail door slamming shut, like a cat torturing a mouse — allowing it to make a quick dart for freedom, then bringing down the paw.

There was no escape. Forces beyond his ken and power were keeping them here. Was it God or fate or Satan or Yalu? Was this to be his death spot? This wretched mountain, this fly-swept ridge? Would these villagers be the last people to see him alive? These people who did not know enough to wipe the snot from their faces; who allowed the same flies that swarmed over the corpses of their dead, over their gelatinous mounds of feces, to walk across their own faces, over their eyes, into their ears? And what about Powers, whose pregnant wife waited for him at Lae? And Pam. Was any possibility of a future with her to be strangled away at the hands of a wretch like Yalu, or gradually killed by indifference, disease, emaciation?

He shook with weeping, stifling his sobs in the shirt which served as a pillow. He was sick of it all — all of it! The flies, the people, the food, the heat, the mountains, the endless days and tedious hours. Surely he would not die here?

He did not remember falling asleep, but late in the night he was awakened by something — a heartbeat? — drums? He came alert instantly. The slow, ominous pulse sounded from across the ravine, where Yalu stayed. Accompanying the beat was a man's minor-key chant, followed by a refrain of deep voices.

Still close enough to sleep to have the instinctual awareness that springs from the unconscious, Roy knew that the drums and the chant had one meaning and only one: death. He lay listening, his bowels burning with fear. He thought of any weapons that might be handy. There were only the bow and arrows he had gotten in barter — the bow not even strung — and Powers's hunting knife. What good were these against a group of armed men?

A shadow appeared in the doorway and he sprang up. It was Pam. "Are they coming to kill us?" she said, her voice surprisingly calm.

Powers spoke out of the darkness. "I don't think so."

"What is it then?" Roy asked. His teeth were chattering; he hoped the other two could not tell. "You don't think Yalu's working them up to come get us, do you?"

Powers waited, listening. "I think it's a funeral ceremony. Somebody probably died."

Roy sat back down. Yes, that made sense. Death, but not murder. He had known — known without doubt — that those sounds meant death. They were the sounds of mourning — the living grieving for the dead.

"Are you sure?" asked Pam. Now that he had given her hope, her voice quavered.

"Yeah," Powers said. "I've heard them before." His voice was quiet and reassuring, like a big brother's. "You can sleep in here if you want."

"No," she said and turned to leave.

"Are you sure?" Roy said.

"Yes, it's okay," she said softly.

They lay there awhile after she left, listening to the drums. The hollow thud and the chant burned into Roy's brain.

"Do you think we should bar the door?" Powers said.

The suggestion propelled Roy upward as he realized Powers's reassurances had been for Pam's sake. Fumbling for toilet tissue, his teeth chattering audibly, Roy raced outside. When he returned a while later, Powers merely said, "I know the feeling."

163

• • •

Each morning the earth smoked with cloud. Dragons rose from the deep ravines around the village, snorting and turning in upon themselves to devour their tails and emerge anew. Thus fattened, they spread out and became clouds high in the air. Sometimes they slithered along the mountainsides and swallowed them completely so there were no mountains to be seen anywhere. Other times they lowered from above, impaling their bellies on the ragged crests, slowly engulfing the mountains and forests like some gigantic sky-borne amoebae.

In this bleak and desolate dawn, Roy accepted a baked sweet potato from one of the village women who had treated them kindly. She came into the hut and gave them the food with a smile, then left. Powers took a bite of the hot, pale potato, then spat it violently onto the ground.

"I'm sick of kaukau," he said, lying back and throwing his arm over his face.

Roy said nothing, but ate less than half of the tasteless mass — and that almost gagged him. He stretched out on his sleeping bag with his journal and pen. He had written pages since he had been here, but they were mostly descriptions of his thoughts, emotions, and impressions. What had happened to the image he once had of himself, strolling around villages, mingling with natives, exploring the countryside with camera and notebook? From a certain point of view he was missing a wonderful opportunity. He should be out there inquiring into native customs, examining species of flora and fauna, sketching mushrooms, identifying birds, photographing sunsets. But the image meant nothing to him any more. He scarcely felt like standing. When he did, his head swam and the sore on his leg throbbed. Sunlight was painful. Activity was distasteful.

He could not have cared less about native customs, or flora and fauna, or landscapes. Landscapes! He glanced out the door of the hut at the same view he had seen for the past few days. The hell with those mountains. The hell with scenery.

It was not just that he was uninterested in exploring his surroundings; he felt contempt for the very idea. He despised this place; he would not grace it with his curiosity. Let the people keep their customs; let the species of birds remain unknown to him. If he could just get out alive it would be enough.

He put his journal aside and opened the New Testament he had borrowed from Powers. He was over halfway through it, at the book of Galatians. He hoped he would not have time to finish the work before he got out of this place. Nonetheless it inspired him: the lean tales of Jesus and his wisdom; the wild adventures of the apostle Paul and his stern courage. The New Testament was a work with meat on its bones. He vowed he would complete it — but please, God, not at Engati.

He saw little of Pam that day, although she did bring them the news that a child from the other side of the village had died from malaria during the night, accounting for the death chant. He and Powers lay in the hut for hours, reading and dozing but seldom talking. Only when Powers, staggering in after a trip to the bush, said, "My urine's turned brown," did Roy come alert.

"What's that mean?"

Powers flopped onto his sleeping bag with a sigh. "Black-water fever."

"Is that bad?"

"Could be."

165

Later Roy sought out Pam and asked her about it. She knew a little about the condition and confirmed its seriousness. "It's the worst form of malaria. Fifty percent fatal."

"What can we do?"

"That's just it," she said, lines of exhaustion and worry showing under her brown-sugar eyes. "I don't think there's anything to be done. Just keep him still. I think regular malaria medicine doesn't help it."

"Rest and liquids, huh?"

She nodded grimly.

Powers lay motionless and silent for the rest of the day, like a monk in profound meditation. Occasionally he would lift his head to drink when Roy or Pam offered him water. And water was about all they could offer him — water, kaukau, and aspirin.

By evening when the air cooled, he showed some improvement. It was about that time that yet another newcomer arrived, a native man who strode into the village with a silent tread, walked into the visitors' hut, dropped his bag of sweet potatoes, fixed Roy and Powers with a pair of steady eyes, and said, "Afternoon, friends" through a wad of buai nearly the size of a baseball.

"Afternoon true," Powers said.

"Afternoon," said Roy.

The man wore the usual grass loincloth and an old U.S. Army shirt. He seemed seasoned and tough.

"You fellas got some kind of heavy?" he asked, squatting on his haunches.

"Where do you come from?" Powers said.

"This is my place. I come from the bush."

"This your house?"

"No." He motioned somewhere with his arm, then spat a great wallop of red buai juice in the corner.

166

"Ah, yes, brother, we got one big-fella heavy true," Powers said.

"Yalu, huh?"

"You hear, eh?"

"Yes, me hear."

"Yalu is one no-good man," Powers said.

The native laughed heartily, every vocal sound muffled by buai. He nodded appreciatively. "Yes, he's a rubbish-man."

Powers managed a smile. "Well, Yalu, he messed us up no good true."

The man grunted.

"We want to go to Aiwomba," Powers said, beginning to recite the old story. "We want to hire carriers. No one will carry. All fear Yalu."

The man laughed again. He put his finger to one nostril and blew his nose violently onto the ground; he repeated this with his other nostril, topping it off by spitting great gobs of buai juice into the corner again.

"What about you?" Powers said. "Do you fear Yalu?"

The man just laughed.

"Would you carry for us? We pay plenty kina."

"Me alone?" said the man. "I'm not enough. Not just me."

"Well, can you get some-fella man to help you?"

The man stood up and walked outside. Roy and Powers heard him shout to the huts across the ravine. He shouted loud and long. After a time a voice answered in reply. The man came back in and squatted down.

"What do they say?" Powers asked.

The man shook his head. "They say, 'Let them find their own road.'"

• • •

Outside on the airstrip more than a dozen men were gathered, cutting the grass with their machetes. Expert with the sharp blades, they kept the cleared area trim as a suburban lawn. Roy glanced out of the hut. In the bright morning light he saw Pamela walking across the field, carrying her washing gear. The men did not look at her or speak. She disappeared over the lip of the ravine, headed for the creek.

"They're cutting the grass," Roy told Powers.

"Tell them not to move the cones," said Powers.

Roy went out and stood where the men could see him. "Hey, no good you-fella move those white things!" he shouted. They looked up, and he heard a laugh. Then he went back inside.

They had lain in silence for about fifteen minutes when Powers sat up suddenly. "Listen!" he said. "A chopper!" They ran outside and stared up into the bright sky. Roy heard it now, too. He glanced toward the airstrip.

"There it is!" Powers said. "Praise God, there's our chopper!"

"Powers," Roy said in a low voice, tugging at his arm. "Look."

When Powers looked over at the airstrip, the sight struck him like a physical blow; he seemed to stagger back a step. The SOS had been removed; all the cones were stacked neatly on one side of the cleared area.

The helicopter passed directly overhead, never pausing.

Grabbing his staff, Powers hobbled out to the field as quickly as he could, with Roy close behind.

"What have you done, you rubbish-men?" Powers bellowed. "We told you not to move those cones!"

Yalu stepped up to him. The muscles in his arms were taut; his fingers and knuckles worked tightly around the handle of his machete. "You don't want us to move them, eh? Why not?"

Roy knelt down and picked a blade of grass. He chewed the stem and watched.

"That was a sign to call a helicopter," Powers said, shaking his staff threateningly. "Now you have messed us up no good true! You don't savvy. A helicopter man will look at our sign and stop to get us."

"Oh, you savvy and I don't, eh?" Yalu replied arrogantly. The others watched solemnly. Some, like Mausgras, looked away.

"That's right, I savvy. You don't," Powers said angrily. "You don't savvy this. This sign is something of ours."

Yalu laughed derisively. "A plane is not going to land here. A helicopter is not going to land here. Your boys did not get through to Aiwomba. Your message didn't get through." His voice was shrill, and little tremors seemed to surge under his taut skin. "You will not get out of here."

Roy felt his heart drop into his belly and throb there like a panic-stricken bird beating against the inside of a cage. He glanced instinctively behind him. When he looked back, Yalu's motion had already begun. The little man swung the machete blade upward and then across, slicing smoothly and with great force through Powers's neck.

Some part of Roy knew he would see that scene for the rest of his life, however long or short that might be. The other part of him was already up and running. His sore leg forgotten, he bounded over the edge of the ravine. Pam was walking up the steep slope toward him, her towel draped over her arm.

169

"Run!" he shouted in a voice too hoarse, too low. He forced the volume out. "Run!"

A bewildered look crossed her face, but she turned ahead of him, dropping towel and bag, and began to run, across the creek and up the far side of the ravine. At first she was not running fast enough; Roy was about to tread on her heels. But when next he shouted "Run!" she sprinted suddenly, like an athlete, like a deer, leaving him slipping and sliding behind her in his heavy jungle boots as they raced down the path toward the field of hanging corpses.

She sprang onto the logs where the trail ended and the maze-work of felled trees began and scampered unerringly across the tortuous course. Some animal instinct or divine guidance allowed her the balance to bound across those bare logs. She could not consciously have picked her way through that maze on her own. Instead, it was as if the course had been imprinted in the circuits of her nervous system that day when they first crossed this ground. She now knew exactly which way to go.

Roy followed closely, spurred not just by panic but by the indelible image of the cutting blade, the severed head. The picture in mind blotted out the stench of the rotting dead in the trees around them and the sight of the skeletons hung with shreds of skin like ancient parchment. They whisked by, unseen, insignificant.

Pam bounded off the last log and back onto the trail which led into deep grass and, beyond that, forest. Roy glanced behind him before they entered the trees. He saw shadows — men running, or dots before his eyes, or the shadows of hanging corpses — but he could not dwell and discern.

When they reached the garden where they had eaten sweet mulis, they were weaving with exhaustion. Pam stumbled in the deep grass, and he leaned over to catch her. Their breath came in great moaning draughts; foam trailed down the corners of their mouths; their hearts were beating like lunatics against cell walls.

"Wait," she gasped. "Wait. Listen."

They stood still in the bright sunlit clearing, but their hearts were galloping too fast, their lungs roaring too loudly, for them to hear anything else.

"Maybe they're not coming," she said. "What is it? What's happened? Where's Powers?"

"Wait," he said. He stumbled back to the edge of the forest, seeking a view down the trail. The shadows made his skin crawl. Every sound — every bird call, twig snap, insect drone — startled him. He could see nothing, and was afraid to go any farther lest he be caught or ambushed. When he returned to the clearing, Pam was holding a gourd-shaped green-and-orange pumpkin.

"We've got to go," he said, his voice hoarse and cracking. "They got Powers."

A sound behind them in the forest sent them leaping forward again, resuming their race. In the overgrown garden there was no sign of a trail. Pam, leading the way, burst blindly into a thicket of greenery, fighting and tearing through the entangling mesh of vegetation. The ground went out from under them, and they were falling — brutally, harshly — raking their shins and slamming their knees, sliding on their butts and reeling over on their sides down the mountainside. Their body weight carried them through vines which held for a moment and then burst, across saplings, between tree trunks, over stones. They came to a tumbling halt on a broad ledge of moss-covered rock sticking out from the steep mountainside like a pouting lip.

They lay there, exhausted, confused, in pain, having done their limit. They had run they knew not how far at top speed; had tumbled a hundred feet or more down a steep mountain slope. Now they waited, half-conscious, hidden in the green and golden patterns of the jungle.

Roy heard a moan. He looked up and saw Pam sprawled beside him. It was like awakening from a long sleep. He had trouble connecting his thoughts. A part of him thought he was in his New Orleans apartment; he felt a strong desire to get up and make a pot of coffee. It would be good to sit and drink fresh coffee, the bright sunlight falling warm across the breakfast table. He looked at Pam again, wondering for a moment who she was. Her eyes were shut, her face dirty and scratched. Her long hair, unbraided, was a tangled mass around her. He reached out and touched her. She shook her head and moaned again softly, not opening her eyes.

Roy looked up the steep slope above them, through the forest. Sunlight filtered sparsely through the leaves. There seemed to be a crest up there ... something ... bright sunlight — a clearing? Fear clutched his heart in a tight fist. Were there faces up there in that indecipherable network of light and shadow, eyes peering down at them, predatory eyes?

"Pam," he whispered, shaking her. She licked her lips and her eyes fluttered open. "Shhh," he said. She looked around in panic, consciousness returning to her more swiftly than it had to him. She looked upward to the thicket through which they had blundered.

"We've got to get away from here," he whispered. He looked around. "We've got to go down. Come on." He grabbed her arm. Supporting one another, lending each other strength, they

172

began to pick their way down the side of the mountain. The descent seemed to go on forever as they worked down and down, sliding, gripping roots and saplings. Tiring, they paused to rest, then continued down.

As they went lower the air grew warmer and thicker. They wended over stones, among plants that seemed remote and alien. They passed between trees fighting mutely for their lives among the vegetative clamor in this forgotten wedge of the earth; through gooey patches of moss, through nettles, across hog-rootings; through belts of fragrance both sweet and putrid. They were slick with perspiration, sprinkled with bark, smeared with dirt. Leaves tangled in their hair, dirt clogged their nails. Knots of pain surfaced here and there — forehead, shin, back — throbbing and subsiding and turning to bruises.

At last they came to a glen through which a tiny stream, perhaps an inch deep, sluiced over black pebbles a damp steaming shelter, a hole in which to hide from the sword-slashing world.

They drank the water and huddled together in this streambed, a place both hot and cold — the air warm, the mist chillingly penetrating — overhung with eternally dripping leaves and dangling roots growing out of the banks. In the black wet gravel they crouched, leaning back against stones and moss wet as sponges, smelling the damp fungoid earth.

Somewhere far above, leagues and fathoms above, there was a sun at work in endless fields of blue sky. Down here they shivered in silence, torn and abused by a thoughtless, thankless earth, each scarcely aware of the other except as a body from which some warmth, some comfort radiated.

It seemed like hours before Roy spoke. "What happened to the pumpkin?"

Pam looked around her, slightly bewildered. She did not

173

remember losing it. "Should we go back and look for it?" she asked in a weak voice.

They both made a sound which could not have been called a laugh, though it sprang from the same internal sources as laughter. Only a touch of hysteria would make her suggest climbing the mountain for a lost pumpkin.

"We're going to need it," she persisted weakly.

He shook his head. "We can't. We'd never find it anyway."

Roy's thoughts circled on themselves, avoiding the truth — dreading the question she finally had strength to ask. "What did they do to Powers?" she said quietly.

He shook his head, bit his lip, began to speak. But instead of words there came a tearing sound, and he wept. She moved closer to him while he cried, trying to flood the memory away with his tears. Wash it away, sluice it, drown it. But it would not leave.

"Yalu," he began.

"Is Powers dead?" she asked.

He nodded. "Yalu killed him, Pam."

A fierce shudder passed through Pamela's body. "What happened?" she said.

"They moved our signal. Powers got into an argument with Yalu and —" His words choked. "His machete, and —"

For a long time they hunched up together in the most hideous, hopeless state of misery either had ever known, incapable of speech or thought or action. Water dripped and sighed its thousand sorrows. Mist probed them hungrily and swelled on.

"We've got to do something," Roy said as dusk gathered in, his voice edged with panic.

"Not now," she said. "Tomorrow."

Night moved in around them, and they twisted and turned to make themselves a bed. When they stretched out, their feet were in the stream, but they did not care; their heads were pillowed on the damp spongy moss under the overhanging earth bank. They removed the stones under them and curled up in their nest. The darkness was absolute. There might have been starlight or moonlight above them, but it could never penetrate the depths where they huddled.

"I don't know what we're going to do," he said after a time.

"We'll figure it out tomorrow."

"I'm afraid they'll come after us."

"They won't find us," she said. "They can't find us down here. Falling off the mountain was probably the luckiest thing that could have happened to us."

"And what about food? How will we get out of here?"

"We'll get out," she said.

He laughed bitterly. "How? It's like Powers said. We could wander out here forever and never get out."

"We'll figure out a way. Tomorrow."

"If they catch us, do you know what will happen?"

"Yes."

"We've got no food and no —" He stopped abruptly and reached into his pocket. "I've got it!" he said, sitting up. "I do have it. I'd forgotten."

"What?" she asked, sitting up beside him. They could not even see one another's silhouettes in the darkness.

"My whistle!"

"Whistle?"

"It's a combination whistle, compass, and match-holder. I've got matches and a compass. And —" He felt in his pocket again. "My penknife." It was not much of a knife, barely two inches long.

"Do you know which way to go?"

"Sure. I kept checking our direction before we got to Engati. We left Maralinan and traveled almost due southwest for, let's

175

see, two days. All right. Then we hit the river and turned due north for almost one day. Then we angled back to the southwest and went straight into Engati."

"Then all we have to do is reverse that?"

"Well, let's see. Travel northeast till we hit the river, go south a day, then turn northeast again. If we can keep a northeast course we're bound to hit the Watut."

"Yeah," she said bitterly. "There's just the problem of five or six mountain ranges in our way."

"So?" he said excitedly, their roles reversed now. "All we've got to do is follow the compass."

"Follow a compass straight up a cliff maybe? With no food?" Her voice had risen a few notes. "And Yalu following us?"

He put his arms around her. "We don't know he's following us, Pam. Like you said, how can he follow us the way we've come? We'll stay away from any trails. And food . . . we'll find food."

"How?"

"Well . . . maybe we'll find another garden."

They sank back together into their damp bed.

"You know we may never get out of here alive," she said, her voice low now.

"I know," he said. "But maybe we will," he added, his tone free of unrealistic hopes. "We can try."

Later that night Roy experienced his first genuine attack of malaria. So far on the trip he had felt only the malaise that sometimes occurs when medicine suppresses the brunt of the disease's force. But he had no medicine now, and the hardship of the day coupled with the night's chill began to make him surge with chills. His violent shaking woke Pam. She tried to wrap herself around his back like a blanket while he lay in a fetal position, hoarding all the warmth he could. The shivering gaze following hers to the treetops where a large black bird with a big beak was cleaning its feathers.

"It does sound pretty scary, doesn't it?" she said. "Have you ever done anything like this before?"

He was tempted to say yes and compare it to some campout he'd been on or maybe to some of his experiences south of the Rio Grande. Somehow though, he knew Pam would detect any dishonesty. "No," he said. "Sounds interesting, though. I'm excited about it. I can't wait." Adrenalin coursed through him at the mere memory of last night's plans over the map.

"Isn't that a hornbill?" she said after awhile, still watching the bird.

He glanced up again. "I don't know." He was not interested in birds, although this one was beautiful in a harsh, abstract way. Huge, jutting beak. Brilliant orange head, black body. Sort of like a crow decked out for a tribal dance.

"So how do you like it here?" she said.

"Here as in the mission, or New Guinea in general?"

"Take your pick."

"New Guinea I like, so far anyway. Like when I first landed at the airport in Port Moresby. I was standing waiting for my luggage and I looked across the crowd and saw this black man staring at me. Fierce, like a real warrior. He was frowning like he was ready to start chucking spears.

"I wasn't sure how to react. Ignore him? Try to look fierce myself? Well, I decided to smile and wave. And the funny thing is, he broke into the biggest grin I ever saw. Just like a kid."

She nodded. "Yes, I like the people, too. What about the mission?"

A sudden feeling of bitterness unaccountably swept over him. "Oh, I don't know," he said. "I like to drink; I like to smoke cigars. All this praying — "

33

"My father smoked cigars," she said, interrupting him in a quiet, musing voice.

He waited, slightly surprised. He had been prepared to alienate her.

"The doctor told him to quit, and he did. He was afraid of lip cancer." She looked at Roy's mouth.

"Pam!" Jeri's voice called from the mission center.

Pam walked across the patch of open sunlight to where Jeri was standing on the porch, then turned and called, "She wants you too, Roy."

In the mission center Powers was slapping a tennis racket against his leg. "Do you play?" he asked when Roy came in.

"No." He went to the sink and washed out his tea mug.

"Powers wants to play some tennis," Jeri said. "How about if he and Pam go play, and I'll take you around town, Roy? Anything you'd like to see?"

Roy shrugged.

"You want to swim? There's a pool by the tennis courts, and there's a pretty good public beach."

"Better take advantage of the offer," Powers said. "This may be our last day of fun. Tomorrow it's all work. We're supposed to meet a guide at dawn to plan out the details. Then find us somebody with a boat and buy supplies." He shook his head. "Thursday morning we leave, you know."

"The beach sounds good," Roy said.

The four of them crammed into the Stivells' small car and Jeri drove out onto the road into town. Hunched up in the back seat, his elbow jostling against Pam's arm, Roy watched the natives along the roadside: all ages, all postures, all manners of dress. An old woman, bare-breasted, sat in the shade of a palm tree. A group of men wearing ragged T-shirts and shorts talked and spat great gobs of red betel-nut juice onto the pavement — like bloodstains. A slender young man

34

with the light skin of a coastal tribesman, wearing a brilliant blue sarong, stood in the center of traffic for no apparent reason. An old man carrying a bow and arrows, fresh out of the bush by the looks of him, wore a grass loincloth in front and an astanket — a large, single leaf — in back; the leaf bounced up and down as he walked. He was bedecked with shells, and a tusk pierced his nose.

"Tonight we'll eat out," Powers said, turning his head to address Roy and Pam. "It may be our last feast in quite a while. There's a real good restaurant up the coast."

"They have native singers and everything," Jeri said.

She dropped Pam and Powers off at the tennis courts and, after stops at the post office and the bank, drove a short distance up the coast to a public beach.

"You swim all you want," she said. "I'm going to sit in the shade and read. Be careful though. Sometimes sharks come in." She cut off the ignition and got out. Large palm trees leaned toward the sea, shading the car and a long edge of coconut-strewn sand.

Jeri sat down, leaned against the trunk of a palm, and opened her book while Roy stripped down to his swimming trunks and walked across the hot sand. A few other swimmers and sunbathers played along the beach.

He waded out into the water, dazzled by the expanse of sea and sky, sun and heat. In the distance, the palm trees formed an arboreal chorus line along the coast. He waved at Jeri, hunched over in the shade.

He waded out, chest-deep, and stood bracing himself as each foamy mound moved into him, lifting him and pushing him backward a little. He tasted the brine, felt the coolness of the water washing over his sun-warmed skin.

He floated on his back, letting the waves carry him under. Then he backstroked farther out, watching the perfect blue sky

35

puffed with small white clouds. A trio of seagulls wheeled by, squealing. He flipped himself upright and treaded water, over his head now. He thought of sharks, of the saltwater crocodiles he'd been told about, and turned to face the open sea, an instinctual thrill of fear kissing his spine. The crocodiles grew to twenty or thirty feet long, they said, and were extremely aggressive, ranging the coastal waters of New Guinea and southeast Asia, traveling up freshwater rivers as well. They made freshwater crocs seem like Boy Scouts.

Thirty feet long! How many tons would they weigh? What would happen if a thirty-foot croc met a thirty-foot shark?

Driven back to the shallows by his imagination, Roy felt the pure pleasure of the warm wind on his salty, wet body. He walked up the beach to Jeri and spread a towel out in the sun a few yards from her. Rubbing down with suntan lotion, he lay on his back to sunbathe.

"I wouldn't do that long," she said. She was knitting now.

"What are you making?" he asked, one arm thrown up over his eyes.

"Booties."

"You want a boy or girl?"

"We'd like a boy."

"Have you picked a name?"

"Hundreds of them. We can't decide. I like Aaron. Powers likes Mark."

"Mark Aaron sounds good."

"If it's a girl, we've agreed it will be Rebecca Ann."

Roy thought about Jeri having her first baby in this strange land. Did she worry about that? He didn't think so. Somehow, as young as she was, Jeri was at home, even knitting booties among the coconuts.

"You'll stay here then, after the baby?" he asked.

"Oh, yes. Powers and I plan to make our home here."

36

"For good?"

"Let's say indefinitely."

"You like it that much?"

"We like it, and there's so much work to be done. Oh, Roy, if you could see some of these people. The need here is so great."

"And you really feel like you're helping them?"

"Yes."

"What about the money? Things are pretty high here."

She sighed. "It's tough. Our church at home won't send us our money on time."

"You're kidding."

"Well, it goes deeper than that. But we're already behind in our notes on the car. Powers is going to call the elders today and try to find out what the hold-up is."

"It's not cheap calling overseas."

"No, but . . . I don't know. There are just problems."

"Like what?" he asked, sensing that his curiosity would not offend her.

"Doctrinal beliefs. We don't always see eye to eye with the church. They expect you to toe the line all the way. And through our studies and prayer, Powers and I have come to believe differently on some things than what they teach."

"Like what?"

"Like the Holy Spirit. He's alive. Today, now. But they seem to think the Holy Spirit quit working when Christ was crucified."

Roy was out of his depth now. Religious discussions were beyond him. But he did care about the Stivells' plight. He sensed the gap that lay between them, but not an awkward gap.

"I was raised in the Methodist church," Roy said. "But religion was never very important to me."

"When you're out here," Jeri said, "dealing with people in real, genuine, sometimes life-and-death situations — well, the people back home just don't understand what it's like."

"So what will you do?"

"I don't know. They're wanting us to come home, to tell you the truth. I'm afraid we may have to go back and find another supporting congregation."

"Sounds like fun."

"It's a headache. It really is. You can't imagine."

"And you with a baby coming."

"And then there's this patrol."

"Are you worried?"

"Oh, Powers can take care of himself. I mean, he's been on plenty of patrols. He knows the bush and the people."

"It's just a bad time for him to be gone, right?"

"Right."

"Want me to talk to him?"

"What do you mean?"

"Try to get him to cancel it."

She laughed. "You don't know Powers. No, he's going. He's got faith. I wish I had his faith."

Roy turned over on his belly, adjusting himself on the towel and applying more lotion. Then he closed his eyes again. "I haven't known you long, but I'd say you have at least that much faith."

He felt her smile.

At the restaurant that night there were the four of them, along with Tim Harkins, and Hugh and Janice Larsen and their two children. The restaurant, at one of the country's few hotels, was a house-wind, a large open-sided building with a thatched roof. It allowed a view of the sea, and the breeze kept insects away.

The buffet was outrageously sumptuous, with roast pig, tenderloin, shrimp of all sizes, crabs, fish fried and broiled, vegetables both native and European, every sort of tropical fruit, rich highland coffee, and homemade rolls.

"You won't find a feast like this for many a mile," said Powers as they sat down, their plates loaded, at a large table.

"You can count on that," said Hugh, a pudgy, jolly fellow with a full, black beard.

"Madang's got a good restaurant," said Janice, who spent most of her time attending to the two squirming youngsters. Though in her twenties, she looked older. Perhaps dealing with the endless hardships, petty and otherwise, involved in raising a family in a place like Lae caused the dark circles under her eyes. And Roy sensed that jolly Hugh might be something of a bully.

Tim, a bachelor in his late twenties, was a strange sort, too. Roy had seen him consume thirteen pancakes, a piece of chocolate cake, and two bananas for breakfast the previous morning. Though intense and friendly, he seemed a bit slow mentally — or perhaps not so much slow as on a different track altogether. Despite his legendary appetite — a source of pride to him — Tim was gaunt with a scraggly goat's beard and thick, rimless glasses. He made rather an odd figure, and his speech seemed slightly impeded, his words like pieces of a jigsaw puzzle cut not quite to form. But Roy warmed to the rare sincerity radiating from the man — the sincerity of Dostoevsky's Mishkin, whom society called an idiot but whom other, wiser persons might have called a saint.

"Yep," said Hugh knowingly, "eat up, Pam and Roy. Starting Thursday it'll be kaukau and pitpit."

"Sweet potatoes and edible grass," Jeri translated. "Actually, I like pitpit."

"Well, when we went to Aiwomba — remember, Powers? — I got enough kaukau and pitpit to last me a lifetime," Hugh said.

"Pitpit's a little like asparagus tips," Jeri explained.

"You can have your pitpit and your kaukau," Powers said. "I've decided to hire an extra carrier just to carry canned hams."

"Rice and tinned fish is more likely what you'll be eating," Janice said. "That's the usual patrol diet."

"Hey, they can take whatever they want," Powers said. "We'll go to Burns-Philp, the grocery store, tomorrow and stock up. You don't know, Pam might be a caviar eater."

"I'm pretty much an omnivore," she said.

"A who?" said Hugh.

Tim, his thick spectacles glinting, broke in with a voice that was always a shade too loud. "There's plenty to eat in the bush. Pawpaws, sweet bananas, cooking bananas, maritas, tree pineapple, sweet muli — "

"Look," Janice interrupted. "They're setting up."

"What do you call that?" said Pam. A group of native performers dressed in colorful sarongs had brought in a huge bundle of hollow bamboo tubes lashed together. Some of them had guitars, and with no ado, the music began.

"I don't know, but it's nice," whispered Jeri. Janice agreed.

The bamboos were played by a man who sat astraddle them and slapped the open ends with rubber flip-flop sandals. Each tube produced a different note, and all were deep, hollow, calming, like the heartbeat of a big friendly beast. The air was rich and warm with the sound and feel of the South Pacific.

40

The sea stretched out in the blue dusk, framed by thatch. The breeze carried a suggestion of bougainvillea and raintree, brine and brown skin.

Roy excused himself and took his coffee cup into the bar to have it laced with amaretto. Then he returned, wandering easily past the performers, among the ranks of food, through the humming conversation, the candlelight and dim yellow incandescence. The sea breeze and the music flirted with him.

At a small table in a corner sat an extraordinarily attractive couple: a young man and woman, both deeply tanned and dressed in cool tennis whites. Her hair was honey rich in the warm light, and Roy could see her tanned skin under her thin white blouse. At another table sat a white man with a black woman. She was dressed in a dark blue floral print wraparound dress, and the rich tones of her skin glinted warmly. A group of men sat around another table, drinking beer with their meal and talking too loudly, ignoring the music. A solitary gentleman sat at a small table watching the musicians, his head moving back and forth with the music. The scene filled Roy with a strange sensation, and he half expected to have that ceiling view again. He took a gulp of coffee to steady himself and returned to the table. The coffee, rich but not dark like Colombian — in fact, almost as pale as tea, but quite strong — warmed him and added to his light-headed sensuality. The gentle music sang of easy living in paradise.

"Get some more food," Hugh urged him.

"Eat up, man!" Powers agreed. "You'll be dreaming of all this soon enough."

Roy got another roll and a slice of pork and ate that, then slid his chair back from the table, disengaging himself from the conversation. Occasionally he heard Hugh's loud laugh, the Larsen kids whining for ice cream, an earnest conversation between Jeri and Pam, Powers's energetic description of a

41

tennis match, Tim's awkward attempts to join in, but for the most part he tuned them out.

Soon — much too soon — the musicians quit and another group, utterly different in appearance, brought in a huge hollowed-out log. The men were much darker skinned and wilder looking. They wore loincloths, shell necklaces, and head plumage.

"What's this?" Roy asked Jeri.

"Looks like a Sepik River group," she said. "That's a garamut — a big drum. On the Sepik each village has at least one."

Roy excused himself again and slipped into the bar for another drink. When he came out, he leaned against the wall to watch instead of joining his group at the table.

Some of the Sepik group carried small wooden drums with tops of reptile skin, and they began the same pulse-beat — bumBUM bumBUM — Roy had heard last night. Women had joined the group, and they stood in place, swaying with the music. The loud, deep garamut sounded and the group danced out into the circle.

Roy's eyes were drawn to the women, their bare skin glistening with oil and sweat. All of them were young and shapely, but one in particular caught his eye. Her face was fierce-looking but arrestingly attractive. Haughty. Around her neck and ankles she wore circles of fur, and there were feathers in her hair. Her only clothing was a dark loin cloth. The dance was not especially erotic — it was mostly a jog-trot movement, each dancer holding the waist of the one in front — but Roy felt a stirring of desire. He glanced at the table of missionaries across the room. No outrage, no curiosity. To them this was just another group of native performers.

Half-ashamed, Roy devoured the dancer with his eyes, now and then looking away idly so that no one would notice his fascination. He sipped the strong mixture of coffee and alcohol. The drums added another dimension to his passion: it was a pulse-beat, all right, the pulse of dark jungle passion that lived in his heart and brain and blood and muscle like a caged, drugged tiger.

And yet, how foolish he felt — like a kid sneaking his first copy of *National Geographic*. Foaming at the mouth like a teenaged boy. His own desire bewildered him. Yet the drum-pulse had settled in his throat, in his chest, spreading down like raw heat.

He gulped the last bit of coffee and returned to the table.

"Those are some dancers!" Powers was saying.

Everyone had finished eating, and they got ready to leave. On the way out Powers stopped beside a black man in a suit who stood watching the dancers proprietorially. "Who are they?" Powers asked, nodding toward the entertainers.

"The Sepik Group," the man said, and the pure unimaginativeness of the name almost made Roy laugh.

"What do they charge?" Powers said. "I might like to hire them sometime." He turned to Roy. "Don't you think some visiting church members would get a kick out of being met at the airport by a group like that? It'd be great, man!"

Roy turned and followed the others to the cashier's desk.

Roy was being dragged deeper and deeper into fatigue. He was not sleeping well at night. Each morning he woke with raw, burning eyes, cotton mouth, and skin slick with perspiration. He braced himself with a cold shower and strong tea, but his brain was clogged with aching tiredness.

Wednesday morning at dawn found him sitting in the church minibus on a deserted jungle road. He blinked at his surroundings, half-awake. Powers was outside somewhere. In the seat behind him sat Peerson and Ramel, who would be their native companions on the patrol. This morning was the first time Roy had met them. They were about sixteen years old and were training to be preachers. Now they sprawled in the back of the bus, half-asleep, as tired and uncommunicative as he was.

All around was jungle — towering trees slung with vines — except off to the right, where there was a clearing of sorts. It was not a natural clearing. Someone had made it by cutting down trees, burning them until they were reduced to gigantic black carcasses, and planting sweet potatoes, pumpkins, bananas, and pawpaws among the rubble. The potato and pumpkin vines had spread out rapidly to form a jungle of another sort. Two or three huts stood in the middle of this jumble.

A heavy mist lay in the clearing and among the trees. The sun was not up yet. *It lurked behind the huge jungle of trees, waiting to spring on the world and seize it by the throat.* Roy tried to think of other metaphors. After all, he would eventually have to produce an article. He really needed to get one off today before they left, so he toyed with ideas.

The mist lay coiled among the trees like a huge serpent. Trite, overused. Everything was serpentine, especially rivers.

The mist lay entwined with the jungle like a lover. Leave out the entwined. *The mist lay with the jungle like a lover.* That was good. It reminded him of last night's dance. He looked at the mist and the jungle and the clearing and the huts. In fact, the mist did not lie with the jungle like a lover. They were just words.

44

The scene itself was just jungle and fog. But everything has to be like something else — the writer's trade. You don't have white hills; you have hills like white elephants. Only by thinking of something else could you imagine the actual thing. Just tell the actual thing like it is and what do you have?

The article should begin: *There was jungle and fog.* Nothing especially exotic about that. *The mist lay with the jungle like a lover.* Exotic? Maybe. But it didn't describe the scene before him now. He'd probably use the line in his article anyway. They'd like it back at the office.

Powers emerged from the thicket of the clearing followed by a small brown man. Roy clambered down from the bus into the clammy dawn heat.

"This is Yalu," said Powers. "He's a Menyamya, and he'll be our guide."

Yalu was the shortest native Roy had seen; he could almost be classed as a pygmy. His skin was the color of dirty copper, his hair slightly darker. His eyes glittered like the flat black ivory pieces of a Chinese Go game. Wild, blank, animal eyes.

He appeared to be young, perhaps twenty or so, and had evidently never known soap. He wore ragged khaki shorts and a T-shirt so faded and filthy that whatever logo it had once sported was now an indiscernible smudge. His legs were scaly, his feet broad and tough.

"Yalu, this is Roy." The small man grinned and nodded.

"Yalu is a new Christian," Powers said. "He's been coming to our church about a month now. Engati is his place. True, Yalu?" Again Yalu grinned and nodded. "Engati place belong you?" Powers said.

"Ah, yes, Engati place belong me — true!" Yalu said in a high, emphatic voice.

"And you savvy the road to Engati?"

"You think what?" Yalu said disparagingly.

Powers turned to Roy and smiled. "I explained to him that we'd leave with the boys and Hugh would pick him up in a month at Menyamya Station."

He turned back to Yalu. "True, Yalu? You stop in Engati one moon something with two-fellow boys. All right? Then you fellows walk-about to Menyamya Station and whiteskin missionary Hugh get you then, and you fellows come back to Lae. Savvy?" Yalu grinned and nodded.

"You sure you know the road to Engati?"

"You think what?" Yalu repeated with mock contempt.

"All right. Morning morning true we will come and get you here. You be ready. Have all something you like carry to Engati for one moon. All right? Morning morning true, same as now." He motioned to the sun just clearing the treetops. "You be here; we get you." Yalu grinned and nodded.

"All right," said Powers, offering his hand. Yalu took it heartily and they shook. "See you."

Roy shook Yalu's hand. It felt crusty. "See you," he said.

"Now we've got to make arrangements for a boat," said Powers as they got into the bus.

When Roy looked back, he saw that Yalu stood by the road watching them.

As a boy, Yalu remembered, he had been so frightened he wanted to vomit. He had to fight down the sensation. He and the other boys his age — they were still young, just about to enter young manhood — sat for interminable periods in the hut listening to the old men hammering at them with their words.

46

Then, weary from listening, they were led down a path through the thick jungle. The path led to a low tunnel of brush, and one by one they were forced to squat down and crawl into the tunnel. Once inside they heard monstrous noises, the sounds of masalai, spirits of the dead, spirits of the mountain and jungle. At the end of the tunnel — hurrying, hurrying — hard hands clamped over their eyes and they heard horrible bird shrieks from the other world, the world of the dead that lives in the jungle. The air roared like thunder.

They were halted in a line before a log and the hands were removed. Angry men surrounded them, men who looked like their elders but were full of rage and madness. He remembered the feel of cold water rubbed against the septum of his nose. He wanted to flinch, but strong arms held him. Fingers pinched his nose and held it out and a sharp bone pierced the septum. Blood ran in a trickle over his upper lip; he felt the slide of a tiny bone into his nose. For the first time he knew a sensation of strength amid the howl of his fear.

The boys were led to an altar and shown the three sacred foods — foods they could not touch until they passed the rites of manhood many years later: red maritas for blood; black sugar cane for skin; a dead tree opossum for flesh. His bowels had trembled with fear and power as they were warned not to eat the sacred foods until the right time.

Then they were forced to run, run, while the men shouted and whipped them with barbed canes. But the running was happy now, and free. Even as the blood ran down their backs and shouts filled the air, they glimpsed the road to manhood before them, a destination they would someday reach with power, treachery, and fearlessness.

By mid-afternoon they were back at the mission center where the floor was a mountain of gear and food. Powers sorted through it while Jeri checked off a list of items.

Powers looked exhausted from the day's scrambling. After several wrong turns that morning they had found Noa, a little clearing on the Markham River, where they made arrangements with a man who owned a motorized dugout canoe to meet them in the morning and carry them upriver to Maralinan. At Burns-Philp they had purchased a twenty-kilo sack of rice plus a dozen one-kilo sacks, a carton of tinned mackerel, a carton of hard biscuit — plain unleavened crackers — a canned ham, and odds and ends such as canned grape juice (for communion services in Engati), chocolate powder, tea bags, peanut butter, honey, cheese, salt and pepper, dried soups, and drink mix.

Back at the center, Jeri had already dragged out Powers's patrol gear: duffel bags, backpacks, socks, boots, tennis shoes, cutlery, cookware, primus stove, fuel, sleeping bags — all the thousand and one things required to make life bearable for the civilized person in the jungle.

Roy had his own camping gear, and Jeri was loaning her gear to Pam. Miss Nellie had assembled a well-stocked first-aid kit inside a small, water-tight metal chest. She had included aspirin, chloroquine, bandages, gentian violet ("blue paint"), sulfa powder, sunburn cream, swabs, disinfectant, and ointments for ear, eye, and skin infections. Pam would be expected to administer medical treatment to the natives at Engati. With her limited knowledge and experience, this would essentially amount to first aid.

As the four of them sat around organizing the various items, Roy sensed a dual air of excitement and fatigue. Why did they need so much gear for a mere two weeks? he wondered. The bush natives could go anywhere with a string bag full of sweet potatoes and a machete or bow and arrows.

"What about a tent?" he asked Powers. "Do you have one?"

"I usually just stay in the huts. The villagers always provide you with a house."

"What about on the trail?"

Powers shrugged, preoccupied. His lack of attention irked Roy, who prided himself on his camping skills. "I've got a little two-man tent," Roy said.

"Take it if you want," Powers said, not looking up.

It was after dark by the time they had assembled the mass of bulging packs and duffel bags into a stack against the wall. Jeri had gone out for fish and chips, and they ate hurriedly. The other missionaries had already left for the Wednesday night church service.

"Are we going to try to go to services?" Jeri asked when they had finished eating and sat slumped around the table. They could hear the group singing the first hymn.

"I'd like to," said Pam.

"Might as well," Powers agreed. "Coming, Roy?"

He nodded and looked at the others as they stood up. What a ragtag crew, he thought. They would not have been ready for church services in the United States. Powers in his ragged jean shorts and a sweat-soaked T-shirt, Jeri in a sleeveless maternity dress, and Pam in jeans and a "Lae" T-shirt. Roy wore a pair of old khaki trousers and a rugby shirt.

But this was not the United States, where Sunday-best clothed church-goers and a clean, temperature-controlled building housed the family of God. It was Papua New Guinea, where no amount of grooming could survive the withering heat, where church doors stayed open to admit the slightest breeze, and where dogs or pigs sometimes took advantage of those open doors and wandered in to check out the commotion.

The four left the mission center and headed across the grounds to the church, which glowed cozily in the early tropical night.

Nine o'clock. Roy sat in his room with his portable typewriter and stared at the blank sheet he'd just inserted. The hymn-singing of the native congregation hung resonant in his memory. They'd sung in pidgin English with full-hearted feeling, and the service had been entirely in pidgin, so he was able to follow only some of it. But it was one of the nicest services he'd ever attended. The broad, beaming smiles of the people made him feel welcome, and many of the hymn tunes were familiar. He had hummed along, sometimes even singing the English equivalent.

Now, staring at the white sheet, he had no idea what the topic of his article should be. He did not feel like writing at all. He should turn in; the next day promised to be long and hard, the beginning of the Menyamya patrol. Yet he felt obligated to send something to his editor before taking off for two weeks. If he could get something on paper, Jeri could mail it for him in the morning. He had a couple rolls of film he had shot, just general photos. They would do.

He rehearsed the experiences he'd had since leaving New Orleans. The flight over? Tiresome, uneventful. The Honolulu layover? Ditto. Guam? He had only been there a few hours, and that at night. Port Moresby? Just one night there, and on to Lae.

And Lae? Visits to the market, around town, the beach, the mission, the restaurant, the dancers. Nothing that would make an article. He'd have to write a general, local-color, feel-for-the-tropics piece. He sighed with boredom and typed, "The mist lay with the jungle like a lover."

Then he stopped, reviewing his impressions of Lae. Certainly he'd been struck by the colorful clothes, the anything-goes attire. He liked his own new shirt, purchased in Lae the day before. T-shirts with logos abounded in New Guinea, and his was the most cryptic and arresting he'd seen. On the front, in blue letters, it said "The One to Eat" with no punctuation. Just under that was the word "Man" in red letters followed by an exclamation point. He had seen a native wearing one of the shirts in town and had thought the slogan was a tongue-in-cheek reference to the nation's history of cannibalism: "The One to Eat Man!" When he saw the back of the shirt, which read "Morobean Biscuits," he realized it was merely an advertisement for a biscuit company. He preferred his original, more macabre interpretation.

Scratching the line about the mist — he'd save that for another time — he started an article entitled "Tropical Attire: Anything Goes" and did not emerge until eleven o'clock, when he slid into the inviting embrace of the sheeted mattress.

51

• • •

By the time they had loaded the church bus with gear, picked up Yalu, and soared up the straight, flat Markham highway, then turned off onto the twin dirt ruts that carried them, jouncing and bouncing, through head-high kunai grass to the edge of the wide muddy Markham River and a view of the green grassy mountains beyond, it was no longer "morning morning true." No, nor anywhere near it. It was after nine o'clock on a hot and brassy tropical morning. Blackskins sat around the smoking embers of cooking fires in sparse shade; they turned and looked at the minibus and the people and gear pouring out of it.

While Ramel, Peerson, Roy, Pamela, and Jeri unloaded the bus, Powers found his boatman and began the usual harangue over details. When the gear was at last heaped beneath a solitary tree on the short bluff overlooking the mud flats leading to the river two hundred yards out, Powers returned with the news that all was ready except that the boatman had no fuel for his motor.

To Pam and Roy with their American view of schedules, of making plans and following through on them, this was a disappointing setback. To Jeri and Powers, well acquainted with the way things worked in the tropics — the way gears don't mesh, cogs don't fit, and plans are made to go awry and be reformulated — it was "something-nothing," as the pidgin expression so appropriately put it.

"We'll have to go back to town for fuel," Powers told Jeri. The boatman, a lank black ostrich of a man wearing a

52

weathered and crumpled black golf hat, stood behind him sheepishly. "Why don't you and Ramel go and we'll stay here with the gear?"

Jeri frowned, a hand over her brow to block the sun. It was a frown that could easily become a habit to her pretty, young face. Observing it, Roy remembered Janice Larsen's young-old face and wondered if this was what happened to white women in the tropics.

"Take him with you," Powers said, pointing to the boatman. "Have you got plenty of money?"

Roy turned away from the discussion to the broad river vista. The water was not particularly wide, but the riverbed was. Obviously there were floodtimes when this river became angry. Right now it would be a long, hot, muddy trek to haul their bags of gear out to the beached canoes. Across the slow-swirling brown water the mountains rose abruptly like emeralds. The kunai grass that covered them looked close-cropped from this distance, showing their soft, numerous spines. Farther back were dark jungles, slung like capes over the shoulders of the mountains.

Around him, soft voices mingled with gentle acrid smoke. An old woman poked sweet potatoes in the embers. Naked fat-bellied babies with caterpillars of snot molded under their noses stared with the frowning curiosity of infants.

"All right," Jeri was saying. "We should be back in an hour."

As she backed out and drove off with Ramel, Yalu, and the boatman, Powers turned to Pamela and Roy and said, "It looks like we wait."

"How long do you think it will take us to get to Maralinan?" Roy asked.

Powers shrugged. "We ought to get there today." He stood with his hands on his hips, surveying the surrounding natives with a friendly gaze. Their returned glances were equally mild. "Might as well get comfortable," he said and went to the foot of the single big tree. After checking its base for ants and clearing away the twigs, he sat down, leaned back, and tilted the wide brim of his leather hat down over his eyes.

"Well," Roy said to Pam, feeling awkward, uncertain what to do next. Pam shrugged slightly, and together they walked over and joined Peerson who was sitting with his back against a duffel bag. Peerson smiled broadly at them as they leaned comfortably against the gear.

"All right, man," Roy said, feeling the strange discomfiture of eagerness deferred. He'd been ready to embark into the wilderness and here they sat on a riverbank. "Are you ready?"

"Oh, yes, I'm ready," Peerson said.

"Are you excited? Scared?"

"Yes."

Roy laughed. For breakfast he'd eaten only a few bananas, but he'd stowed away a sack of cold fish and chips from the night before. He rummaged through his pack and pulled out the paper sack.

"Pam, you want some?" he asked.

She shook her head. He suspected she felt more out of place than he did. A straw mesh safari hat threw a tight grid of shade across her face. Beneath it her hair was braided into a thick rope, pulled tightly behind her head. The tip of the braid peeked around her waistline like the head of a python. She wore what Roy assumed was her safari outfit: the khaki shirt and hiking shorts and huge, red-laced mountaineer boots with thick white socks pulled halfway up her smooth brown calves. A yellow bandana was tied scout-fashion around her neck. The entire outfit looked crisp and new and, although ostensibly designed for a tropical safari, seemed incongruous here. As his article last night had indicated, natives wore catch-as-catch-can outfits. Peerson's oversized hand-me-down trousers were rolled up around his calves. He was barefoot, of course, and wore a T-shirt of indiscernible parentage. The natives around the clearing wore similar motley outfits.

Missionaries dressed only slightly better. Powers's blue jeans were stuffed into laced green canvas jungle boots. He wore a long-sleeved red plaid shirt with the sleeves rolled up, a big hunting knife on his belt, and his crowning glory, a wide-brimmed leather hat that appeared to be the veteran of numerous bush patrols.

Roy wore lightweight canvas pants and Vietnam jungle boots he'd picked up at an army surplus store back home, along with his new light blue "One to Eat Man" T-shirt. For headgear he had a baseball cap with an extra-long bill and the emblem of a leaping bass on the front.

After a while, Roy fished out his Olympus and snapped pictures. The others dozed.

It was nearly one in the afternoon when the minibus bumped back down the road to the clearing. The clutch had malfunctioned and they'd spent two hours in a repair shop. In the interim Peerson and Roy had devoured the fish and chips, exchanging details of their lives with growing friendliness. Pam had joined in occasionally but mostly dozed. Powers had slept, waking only once to tell some of the natives a fabulous story about the time a crocodile had bitten his leg off and he'd had to replace it with a steel one. For a moment they had believed him, then broke into laughter.

Now, in the blazing heat of the day, assisted by the boatman and his partner, they toted the gear across the mud flats, arranging it in the long dugout canoe. Roy and Pam found seats in the boat while Powers and Jeri said good-bye. Powers held her by the waist and kissed her lightly. Roy heard their low voices and soft laughter.

"Rebecca Ann will be waiting for you," Jeri said, apparently referring to their unborn child. Powers gave her a final kiss and stepped into the canoe.

The motor caught after several false starts, and suddenly they were in motion, motoring up the Markham River.

Roy sat near the front directly behind the boatman's assistant, who used a pole when necessary to push away from shallows. The boat was narrow and cramped, and there was half an inch of water in the bottom in which he sat. The duffel bag immediately behind Roy was uneven and poked him uncomfortably in the back. He was too hot to be hungry, and the water in the canteens was warm. His bare arms were cooked in no time, and the area of his chin not shielded by his cap brim began to burn among the stubble of his new beard.

He glanced around behind him. Peerson's open face was a blend of boyish excitement and anxiety, while Ramel's Chimbu features were set into a sullen mask; Powers flashed an adventurer's grin; Pamela surveyed the scenery impassively from behind the shade of her cool straw hat; and Yalu watched his surroundings with the glitter-eyed gaze of a forest animal. At the rear the boatman, his hand on the tiller of the outboard, smiled placidly, constantly watching the river.

Roy turned back to the view of his own boots and the assistant boatman's bare black back. The man was smoking tobacco rolled in newspaper; it smelled like wild perfume.

This is great! Roy thought, looking up into the blinding tropical blue with its islands of white cloud. The brilliance was

56

unbearable. He watched the land — the mountains on his left, thick grass on the right. Here and there he spotted a native with bow and arrows. Despite the sun's searing heat, the movement of the boat created a pleasant breeze. It felt good to be moving at last, upriver where the roads ended and there were no newspapers or phones or electricity — just wild country and mystery and things that were going to happen to him which he could not imagine no matter how hard he tried. The pit of his stomach tingled.

They stopped once, a few hours later, to stretch their legs, beaching at a spot where a small clear stream ran into the Watut; they had left the Markham behind at a big fork and turned up into the Watut, which, like the Markham, was the color of gravy. If Pamela had not been there, Roy would have stripped and plunged into the cool water. As it was, he and the rest waded out into the shallow stream. The water soaked his trousers and cooled his legs.

There was a clear line of demarcation where the stream joined the muddy Watut, from jewel dark to opaque gray. Roy waded out thigh-deep and stood in the muddy part. He turned back to Peerson and Ramel, who crouched in the shallow, pebbly water of the stream.

"Come on out here and swim!" he called to them.

They just shook their heads and grinned. The assistant boatman muttered something in his tribal language; it went the rounds of translation, and Powers said to Roy, "They won't swim out there. They're afraid a crocodile might come up and they won't see it."

Roy felt foolish but not fearful. Pamela was grinning at him.

Soon they were under way again. When the sun went down, the air cooled noticeably. Roy's exposed skin had gone through several shades of redness, and the cool dusk air felt good against his blistered, burning arms and face.

They were far up the Watut now, which had become shallow and rocky, making navigation difficult. The assistant boatman used his pole frequently and signaled the boatman with his hands. Towering jungle lined the banks, and mountains ranged away in all directions.

As darkness fell the man in front took out a weak, battery-operated flashlight; its yellow beam limped ahead into the blackness. He shouted directions back to the boatman. It seemed to Roy that they were zigzagging back and forth across the river.

At last up ahead there was a dim light. The assistant boatman shouted; voices answered. The canoe puttered over to the light, and the voyagers clambered out stiff-jointed into mud. A little boy held a kerosene lantern to guide them up the slick bank. Villagers grabbed gear and trotted with them along a damp grassy path overhung with the shadows of great trees and into an open village where fires twinkled like amber.

"This Maralinan?" Roy asked Powers, who walked beside him.

"I think it's the boatman's place." Powers called to the boatman, who answered back in pidgin that Roy could not follow. "We'll come up to Maralinan tomorrow," Powers said.

Roy's main sensation was thirst. They had long ago finished the tepid water in their canteens and hadn't dared drink the water of the Watut. The gear was heaped around a small house-wind, and Pam and Roy stood beside it in exhaustion and confusion while villagers babbled, Powers conversed with the boatman, dogs barked, and hogs snorted.

"Hey," Roy said, interrupting Powers. "Tell him we're dying of thirst."

"Yes, please," Pam said weakly. Roy looked over at her sympathetically. She'd hardly spoken all day. How was she feeling, this Canadian girl ten thousand miles from home?

Powers and the boatman talked some more. "The only water is the river," he said after awhile.

"We can't drink that," Roy said, figuring he'd opt for perishing thirst over a case of dysentery.

Pamela slumped down against one of the corner posts of the house-wind. Ramel, Peerson, and Yalu had hauled out the primus and were firing it up to cook a pot of rice with river water. Suddenly a little child padded up to Pam and held out a fat green coconut with the top lopped off. Pam looked at it wonderingly.

"Drink," said the boatman.

She tilted it to her mouth and, once drinking, could scarcely bring herself to stop. Then she passed it to Roy, who guzzled his share of the sweet, cool coconut water, then passed it on to Powers.

"More, please," Roy begged. The boatman spoke to the child, who soon returned with two more coconuts.

Soon the scene was orderly again. The three boys sat around a big pot of simmering rice. Pam, Roy, and Powers shared biscuits and cheese, none of them being especially hungry. The villagers, not far enough from civilization to be fascinated by whiteskins, had retired to their own huts, leaving the travelers in peace under the house-wind, which was just a thatched roof set on poles with neither walls nor floor.

"I don't know about you people," Powers said, wiping his knife on his jeans, "but I'm about ready to turn in. I'm beat, and we've got a long day tomorrow."

"Me too," Roy said.

"Do you know how much more river we've got ahead of us?" Pam asked.

"I'd guess not much," Powers said. "Probably a couple hours. We want to get started early, before the sun comes up."

"Morning morning true, huh?" said Roy.

59

"Yeah."

"I'm so tired," Pam said.

"Probably never got over your jet lag," Roy said sympathetically.

"Well, kiddies," said Powers, standing up, "you ain't seen nothing yet."

They spread their sleeping bags on the ground and burrowed in. Sleep did not come easily in the tropical night, however. One of the villagers had a battery-powered cassette player. The fact that the batteries were nearly dead did not keep this household from playing a recording of a Lae radio show late into the night. The program was a motley blend of island music, drum-throbbing singsings, and American country and rock.

Tired and overheated from the long day in the sun, Roy's brain swirled around like taffy — pulled in outlandish and sickening shapes, stretched thin as thread, then massed into fat, sticky lumps. Woven throughout was the ridiculous cacophony of music, voices, laughter, hogs grunting around the crumbs they had left, the fitful breathing of his companions, and the hungry refrain of mosquitoes defying the acrid scent of the repellent they had so ardently applied before retiring.

On the first day of their final initiation into manhood their foreheads were pricked with sharp quills while they were told of their inadequacy as boys and their mandate to become men and warriors.

On the second day they were painted with maritas juice, which dried sticky and crisp along their flanks and chests. They were then given sips of the blood-red juice, and in the night they heard their elders dance and beat the drums and sing the deeds of old battles, prowess, treachery, and victory. The old men, becoming excited, grabbed some of the boys by their cane-pierced noses and dragged them to the ground, shouting, stomping, until the boys thought they were about to be killed and their red nose-blood spilled into the dirt.

On the third day they arose as men.

Groggy and stupefied, they at last were allowed to partake of the sacred feast at the altar in the clearing which they had witnessed years before in their first ordeal. This time the three sacred foods were imbued with the richness of their imminent manhood. He would always remember their flavors: the maritas juice, thick and pasty like hardening blood; the sugar cane, sweet as a man's toasted skin; and the opossum, rich and meaty as a man's thigh.

The ceremonial supper over, it was time for celebration.

Wakefulness arrived as spitefully as sleep had been kept at bay. Roy heard what he fancied to be a dysenteric splatter, followed by the raw gurgling bugle of a rooster. He realized the screeching roosters had been chasing him in and out of slumber for some time now. A newly wakened baby screamed with displeasure at its surroundings. The hogs, returning from their dark grovels, mulled around the house-wind, and Roy felt one nuzzling the mound that his feet made in the sleeping bag.

He sat up angrily. "Get back!" The hog trotted off.

His eyes were grainy and sore, but his heart throbbed with novelty and anticipation. Pam and Powers were still lumps in their respective sleeping bags, but Roy's exclamation must have sifted through to Powers. He sat up groggily, rubbing the back of his head with one hand.

"Morning," said Peerson. Roy looked around and saw the boys hunkered around the stove again, heating water. Hot tea!

"No time for rice," Powers said, clambering out of his sleeping bag.

"But let's have tea," Roy hurried to say.

The sun was not up. The air was gray and thick with cool mist.

Pamela rolled over. "Already?" she said with a sour face.

"Rise and shine," Powers said cheerfully. "You two aren't big breakfast eaters, are you?"

They had biscuits and honey and hot tea, eating and drinking with little talk. Roy was wide awake with adrenalin. The tea was ambrosia. A coffee-drinker back home, he felt a novel pleasure in drinking hot tea here. No sugar — just rosy, clear, and strong. Bitter and biting to the stomach.

The village, which last night had been hidden in the darkness, was alive with sounds and smells. The houses were simple huts surrounded by bare dirt; smoke sifted through their thatched roofs. Coconut palms rose here and there.

Pamela stood looking around her, apparently lost in thought. "Just anywhere you can find," Powers told her with the wisdom of one who had been on many patrols.

Within an hour they were headed upriver in the canoe. The air felt cool as they motored through it; its briskness was invigorating. The hot tea had charged Roy, and the coolness renewed that energy. Life was clean and new and exciting. Pure mystery lay before him like a deep-sea dive or a space voyage. The waiting was over; he was moving into a story that had not yet been written.

"Surely this is not why they put the dot on the map," Pam said, standing with her hands on her hips in a clear, sandy spot in the shade of some big trees on the river bank. The boatmen were pushing off, drifting downstream without a word of good-bye.

"This is it," said Powers. "Actually, there's probably a village back off the river. It's nearly one. What say we have some lunch?"

"I'm famished," Pam agreed, and she and Peerson began to rummage through the packs. Two young native boys had appeared and stood watching.

"Hey, you two-fella," Powers said in his friendly, laconic way — the result of years of dealing with natives and knowing how to put them at ease. "Drinking water close-to?" The boys looked at each other; then one nodded.

"What about sweet muli? You got sweet muli?"

They shook their heads.

"There's got to be some oranges around here somewhere," Powers said. "I saw some floating in the river."

"I would love an orange right now," said Pam, who was setting up the stove.

"Yalu, you and Ramel go fill up the water bottles," Powers said. "When you get back we'll make rice." Yalu and Ramel gathered up canteens and cooking pots, and the two young boys led them down a path into the woods.

"There's only one thing to do at a time like this," said Powers. "Sleep." He arranged himself a resting place among the duffel.

"Well, I'm not sleepy," said Pam.

"I hope you two aren't gung-ho hikers," said Powers, tilting his hat brim over his face in his tough cowboy manner. Roy and Pam looked at each other. "I'm not out to break any records," Powers went on, talking to his unseen audience. "Tony Hill tried that. You haven't met him; he lives in Goroka. He was a Marine, figured he was tough. He was going to out-hike his carriers. Carried his own pack." He laughed. "Had to fly him out on a stretcher."

"Why?" asked Pam.

than this stretch of stream and forest. It had been made for them, given to them by God himself. There was no awareness of time or an outside world. There was only this intimate universe of life and loving.

When the afternoon sun had moved beyond the treetops, leaving them in deep shade, they once again sensed the encroaching shadow of exhaustion. For a brief time the sunshine and their love had renewed them. But the fatigue that struck now was unlike any they had experienced before; it was quite unlike the weariness of fighting mountains and rivers.

"Maybe we should go," Pam said, breaking a long silence.

Roy sighed deeply.

"We can't stay here forever. We can only go so long without food," she reasoned.

When they sat up, they were both alarmed at the weakness that swept over them. No longer energized by passion, they felt utterly drained, frail and weak and rubbery.

"I don't know if I can go anywhere today," Roy said, lying back.

"We've got to," she urged. "The longer we wait, the weaker we get. If we don't keep moving, we'll just weaken until we can't move any more."

"I may be at that point already."

She prodded him, almost angrily. "No you're not. Roy! Get up."

He sat up. He was dizzy, and great purple blotches blobbed before his eyes. "We need food," he said weakly.

"Maybe we'll find some on the trail. Come on. Get up. Get dressed." She began slipping on her clothes. He watched her idly, regretfully. "Come on," she insisted, nudging him with her toe.

In relatively clean clothes, her hair braided neatly, Pam looked amazingly fit. She had lost weight, to be sure, but seemed lithe and alert. He shook his head in groggy amazement.

"How long do you think we can last without food?" he asked as he laced his boots.

"I've read that people can go a month or more," she said.

"Yeah, but that's without a lot of activity."

"I know," she acknowledged. "The ones I've read about who fast for long periods don't do anything."

"And here we are, exerting ourselves to the limit. I don't know where all our energy came from today."

"I do," she said, and they looked at each other and smiled.

"Here." He handed her the compass. "You lead the way."

"We just follow this stream to the top, right?" she said. "Then swing back north, northeast."

"You got it."

"All right. Let's go."

With Pam taking the lead, they started up once more, stepping among the rocks of the stream, leaving behind the site where they had become husband and wife — a site identifiable on no map, and which they could probably never find again.

They entered the high moss forest where the ground trembled under their footsteps and Roy's spear-staff often plunged two to three feet into the spongy earth. Their stream had dwindled to a trickle, a narrow runnel along which they picked their way. Huge fallen trees, saturated and rotten, were covered with pelts of moss; even the living trees were furred. The stones, the ground itself, all had succumbed to the moss; it steeped the world in a dim, luminescent green. The moss seemed to absorb sound, so that their footsteps were silenced, their occasional words muffled.

Now and then strange bird calls echoed around them, and streaks of color fluttered above as the crazily colored creatures pursued their alien occupations. This was a zone uninhabited by man, a strange world of fungus and cold rot. But the air at this altitude was crisp and cool, and its freshness gave them a measure of energy.

By late evening they were at the top of the mountain, and to their pleased surprise they found it to be broad and flat with ample room for a good camp. Surveying the weird greenish scene, his lungs expanding with the thin pure atmosphere, Roy said, "Why don't I make us a good camp and you go look for food? You've been a better food-finder than I have."

Pam returned nearly an hour later to find a snug lean-to — albeit clumsily made and not necessarily rainproof — in front of a heavily smoking fire. "We're lucky to have a fire at all," he said in apology, rubbing his hands in the smoky warmth. "Everything around here is wet."

"It looks good to me," she said. "You've done better than I have."

She had found only ferns, but of ferns there was an endless supply in this area. She had great bunches, far more than they could eat. "It didn't take me any time to pick these," she said. "I spent the rest of the time looking for maritas or fruit or something, but I couldn't find a thing."

211

"That's all right," he said. "At least we can cook them. Boiled greens."

As darkness closed in, they sat before the fire and cooked the greens with water in the bamboo container. There were springs close by; water, too, was no problem in this saturated place.

"I wish I weren't such a city boy," Roy said as he sat on a log with his back to the lean-to, facing the smoldering fire. "I wish I knew how to snare animals and track game and hunt."

"My brother is a hunter," said Pam. "He hunts deer in Canada. Sometimes he'll go a whole season without getting a shot. Once he went five years without killing a deer. And there are deer everywhere, where he hunts."

"Is he just a poor hunter?"

She shook her head. "No, he's a good hunter, actually. He's got some trophy antlers, and he's killed plenty of deer. I think hunting is just an unpredictable thing. That's what he says, anyway."

"So you're saying that even if I were a great hunter and had a rifle, we still might be eating ferns for supper."

"I guess." She grinned.

"It's going to be cold up here tonight. I wish we had a blanket."

"We'll keep warm." She moved over beside him, and he slid off the log onto the ground. They sat there together, their backs against the log.

"It's not so bad, really," he said. "We've made good progress. I haven't had any more fever. We are getting something to eat. Not much, but something. And we have a general idea of where we are. I think we may make it out of here yet."

"A general idea of where we are, huh?" She laughed. "Where are we, then?"

He laughed too. "East of the sun and west of the moon, I guess. South of heaven and north of hell."

"It's heaven enough here," she said, snuggling close to him.

He wrapped his arm around her, and they watched the fire drowsily as their supper stewed in the canted bamboo tube.

"Even if we die, we've had enough happiness for a lifetime," he said.

"Yes," she said, "but I don't want to die. I want a real lifetime of what we have."

His mind felt strangely detached; maybe it was the thin air. "But if we do die, we've still been blessed," he said. "Just today. Just today was probably better than most people's whole lives."

"Yes, Roy, but please don't talk like that. I don't want to die out here." She trembled slightly, maybe with the cold. The fire, which put forth as much steam as it did smoke, did not offer much heat.

"We won't die," he said gently. "We'll get out. We've got a compass. We've got your faith. We've got that guidance you were talking about. We'll get out."

"I don't know," she said, shivering heavily now. He held her closer. "I'm afraid, Roy. It's not just the land. It's not just being lost." He waited, knowing instinctively what she was going to say. "I'm afraid he's out there," she said. "Following us." She voiced the fear that haunted him, try as he might to rid himself of it.

"No, no," he said softly, hoping to reassure himself as well. "Not even an Apache could have tracked us through all this. Besides, what would he want with us? His grudge was against Powers, not us." A tremor swept through him as the suppressed memory surfaced: the swinging blade, the spurting blood, the toppling head. He felt a momentary surge of panic. "No," he said, trying to talk himself down into calmness.

213

"Besides, it's like you said, God is with us. He'll take care of us."

"But what if he wants us to die?"

"You mean God?"

She nodded, snuffling a little.

Tremors were beginning deep in his belly now — suppressed fear surfacing. He hoped she didn't feel them but knew she probably did.

"If God wants us to die, then we'll die," he said, his voice resigned. "Maybe that would be best. Maybe if we lived, there would be worse things to come after. Maybe we would get old and stodgy and fall out of love and live rotten lives."

"No!"

"Who knows? If that were true though — just if — don't you think it would be better if we died now?"

"No!" she said. "I don't know. I just don't want to die." Logic was one thing, fear another.

He knew exactly what she meant. He didn't want to die — not for any reason, not even if God wanted him dead. He wanted to live. He was trembling with fear. He felt they were being watched by Yalu's wild, glittering eyes out there in the darkness — gloating, watching, waiting. That image, that image — God, remove that image from his brain. The swinging blade . . .

"Come on," he said, jostling her. "I think the greens are ready. We're just tired and hungry, that's all. Some hot food will do us good."

She sat forward. Her eyes were wild and listless, like a dying animal. Roy was a city boy, but he had hunted a time or two in his life. He had seen that look in a rabbit's eyes as it lay crippled with shotgun pellets. Panic, shock, resignation. He had to shake her out of it.

"Mmm!" he said, rolling the cane out of the fire and sniffing the aroma. "Mama's good home cookin'. Just you try a bite o' these greens, dahlin', and you won't never go back to yo' English peas."

"I'm not hungry," she said. But she ate.

Giving up on the fire, which seemed to be self-extinguishing, they retreated to their lean-to and nestled in together, warming one another on the winding road to sleep. Pam fell asleep first. Roy heard her regular breathing while he lay awake imagining tigers and cobras — creatures not even found on the island of New Guinea.

The prospect before them in the morning was encouraging. The mountain ridge sloped off away to the north, a gentle, easy walk. The woods were broad and open. For a while, at least, there would be no brutal descents.

Breakfasting quickly on raw ferns and cold water, they left early, walking with loose, easy strides through the highland forest, clambering over logs, wading through thickets of fern. The air was brisk and refreshing, like a spring morning back home. They walked rapidly, hoping to make good time along this relatively easy stretch.

At mid-morning they paused for a break and heard the gurgle of falling water. Leaving Roy to rest on a log, Pam went to explore the sound.

"Roy!" she called. "Come look at this." She had found a spring running out of the side of a mud bank, dropping perhaps five feet to the surface of a deep pool.

"Nice," he said.

The sound of the water was soothing. They sat with their feet dangling over the side of the bank, looking at the water several feet below them. The pool was murky, so they could not tell just how deep it was.

"Roy," she said, "have you ever been baptized?"

"Yeah," he said. "When I was a baby."

"Would you like to do it for real now?"

Her question startled him, but he understood the seriousness and complexity behind it. If they died out here, she wanted to be sure his ticket to heaven was punched. She wanted no partings at death's door.

"Sure," he said.

"Come on then," she urged, as lightly as though she had suggested a swim.

She dropped down into the pool cautiously; it was only knee-deep. But as she waded out to the center, it crept up to her thighs. "It's cold," she said.

He dropped in after her, landing with a heavy splash. Wading out to her, he asked, "Now what do we do?"

"First I ask you a question."

"Shoot."

She looked tentatively into his eyes, as though both afraid and hopeful of what she might discover. "Do you believe that Jesus is the Christ, the son of God?"

He heard the water bubbling noisily around them. It was chilly in the pool; muddy, mossy banks rose around them. "I do," he said.

"Now I hold you like this." She put one hand behind his back, the other over his face. "I'll say the words and then dunk you under backward."

"All right."

"By the authority vested in me, I now baptize you in the name of the Father, the Son, and the Holy Ghost."

He took a deep breath and shut his eyes tightly, and she lowered him into the water. She held onto his weight and brought him up again quickly.

"That's it," she said.

He wiped the water out of his face, then looked around as though expecting to have emerged into a new dimension. Everything looked the same. Then he turned to Pamela. Her face was radiant with love, joy, gratitude, and faith. Exuberance swelled within him and he hugged her tightly, standing in the deep bowl of the forest.

"I love you so much," he said.

"I love you too," she said.

He did not know about religion. Maybe it crept up on you, a habit acquired. Maybe the spirit of God had alighted on him like a dove, but his worldly eyes had been incapable of seeing it. He didn't know. It didn't matter.

"I'm freezing!" he said.

"Let's get out. We'll have to walk fast to warm up."

The little man frowned, glaring around him with irritation. He wasn't even sure this was the right stream, the right mountain. He had wasted needless hours finding their river crossing. The rain had almost obliterated their deep footprints in the riverside mud. He had almost lost them!

And now they were headed into the high moss forest, if this indeed was the way they had come. It was country alien to him, not his type of place. He peeled some wild buai and stuffed the bitter nuts into his mouth. Then he stepped quickly along the rocks up the stream. His chest heaved in and out with the thin, high air. Moss forest was not good for tracking. The foot left a print, but then the sodden sponge swelled back into place, filling the depression.

His supply of meat was getting low. He should have brought more with him. The wild hogs had probably raided his cache by now. He had not thought it would take this long to find them. He jumped along angrily.

Up here there would be no maritas, no tawns, that sweet-fleshed fruit found in low areas. His people had no gardens this far out. And if they kept on, these two doomed, wretched, worthless wanderers — his prey — they would come to a country inhabited with well-used trails and villages and people happy to help the whiteskins. He could not waste time. He had to close in fast, like a hawk swooping on a snake, a pair of snakes.

Reaching the top of the mountain, panting in the chill damp air, he looked around unhappily. No sign, no sign. Where had they gone? Along the ridge to the north or downhill toward the east?

He took a few more steps. Night was coming fast. But it was in that last dim light that he found what he was looking for: a little cavern of limbs and leaves heaped clumsily against a tree — a shelter. He danced over to the spot and found the charred wood, the cracked bamboo, and the smooth place where they had lain. He hunkered down.

He would use their shelter, their fire spot. He would sleep lightly and rise in the earliest dawn. He was gaining on them.

They strode through the forest, conscious only of advance, prodded by the thought of the distance they were covering. They felt light-headed, light-bodied, as though they were suffused with air — thin as spider webs, fluttery as butterflies, unfettered by gravity. Thin air, lack of food, and flat ground combined to make them giddy and swift. In minutes, miles seemed to pass under their long strides. The earth was conforming to their wishes, for this flat forest, a broad saddleback in the mountains, continued steadily north by northeast.

Roy's thoughts scurried in silly directions. Maybe this was it, a shortcut to the Watut Valley. Maybe they had found a new passage. Maybe it would be like this all day, and then they would go downhill and there would be the Watut, muddy and fast, down in a hot climate of coconuts and lethargy.

The air affected them like helium. They bounced along just above the surface of the ground. Food? What was that? Only something heavy, something to weigh them down. Their hunger had passed, replaced by a giddiness that only at rare intervals bordered on dizzy nausea. They glided along like eagles. Roy's staff sank into the ground satisfactorily and propelled him forward. Pam's lithe legs kept her close to him with the easy gait of a huntress.

Their lungs had to swell to unknown proportions to take in the elusive oxygen. Sometimes they had to stop and gasp, drinking in the air, inhaling it as though from great carafes. They guzzled water from springs, streams, and rainpools, wetting their knees in the mossy mud.

There came a time in the afternoon when the broad, flat forest narrowed and they realized they were walking on a ridgetop. The ground became rocky, slippery, harder to travel. And then the ridge turned, angling away to the east. They continued to follow it for a ways, but when Roy's compass needle dropped below the east mark and nudged slightly toward the south, he stopped.

"This is it," he said. "We've got to go that way." He nodded toward the northeast, all downhill.

"Oh," she said, panting. "If it could only all be this way. I like this. It's like Canada."

They sat down to rest. "I wouldn't be surprised if we've covered eight or ten miles," he said.

"Maybe eight."

"That's a long way, in the right direction."

"Oh, Watut, where are you?"

"Who knows? Maybe it's right down there." He nodded to the downhill slope before them.

"Don't get my hopes up, Roy!"

"Okay. I know it's not that close. But still, I feel like we're getting somewhere now. Not all this snail-crawling over the mountains."

She grabbed his arm and squeezed it. "Maybe we should stay here for the night."

"Are you kidding? Look at the sun." Then he understood her meaning, and he gave her a light kiss on the forehead, then on the lips. "Under any other circumstances," he said. Then added, "Don't tempt me."

"All right," she said with a laugh, standing up. "We've got to conserve our strength. It wouldn't do to love ourselves to death out here."

They began to pick their way down the slope, which soon became alarmingly steep. Soon they were almost crawling, letting themselves down by saplings, helping one another on mud-slick banks, losing their footing at times and sliding several yards through stones and mud. It was the tortures of the road to Engati all over again.

The air became warmer and more humid as they reached the lower altitudes. They sweated heavily and felt again the old anointing of mud, grime, bark, and leaves. The descent was steeper and longer than logic or geology had reason to dictate. Occasionally where a tree had fallen and the forest gaped, they had views of staggering proportions, mountain blades razing the sky with thick clouds bleeding into their hollows. As they dropped lower and lower, they passed through entirely different zones of flora, fauna, and climate, from Canada to Louisiana in a single, rock-jutted swoop.

It took the whole afternoon to get down the mountain, but when they got to the bottom there was nothing to make them happy — just a narrow, rocky stream and another mountain rising nearly straight up beyond it. In the profoundly deep chasm where they now stood there was not a breath of sunlight. Vegetation crowded everything, and the air was dusky, humid, and warm. It was a lousy place to have to camp.

"Do you want to keep going?" Roy asked.

Pam shook her head despondently, examining the new scratches on her legs. Some of the older cuts had begun to turn into small sores, young versions of the sores on Roy's legs which he washed at every opportunity but which continued to fester and hurt.

They made a makeshift shelter on a sloping, rock-strewn patch of ground, not bothering with a fire.

"Roy, I've never been so exhausted in my life," she said as they huddled in their lean-to. They had no strength for lovemaking or levity. What dim light there was quickly faded. The stream was loud nearby, and other sounds were coming alive in the jungle — hums and throbs and crooning, moaning whines. "I just don't know if I can make it," she said.

Strange how our moods go to such extremes, he thought, like our minds are all unhinged. There was nothing to keep them rooted. No food, no decent lodging. It hit him suddenly: they could die out here, and soon. The fear of Yalu paled before the prospect of starvation, of succumbing to fever and crippling ulcers. If they did not get food or find help soon, they could not go on much longer through this horrid country.

Yalu was like an old memory now. Roy was certain they were not being followed. He had read about Indians and frontiersmen tracking their enemies through the woods relentlessly, but that was the kindly landscape of America, not brutal New Guinea. Besides, if Yalu were following them, they would have heard from him by now.

No, Yalu did not concern him any more. The mountains did. They offered nothing. They just took — took strength, health, and hope. After today's horrible descent, he could see that Pamela was visibly weakening. The thought of a major climb tomorrow scared him, more for her sake than for his, though he did not see how he could endure it. And what if — God, let there not be — what if there were more mountains after this one? What if his calculations were wrong? He knew that a slight error in orienteering could throw hikers miles off course. And they weren't calculating carefully with maps and checkpoints; they were trekking along on hope and faith and a plastic whistle-compass.

What if Powers's words had been prophetic when he said that an attempt to return to Maralinan could mean wandering forever in the mountains? Powers — God rest his soul. And poor Jeri. How could he ever tell her what had happened? She was waiting for them to come back to Lae, dirty and tired and safe. And the boys, Ramel and Peerson. He hadn't even thought about them. Had they ever gotten through? Were they still languishing in that hut midway between Engati and Aiwomba? Or had the Menyamyas gotten them too, killing them, eating them . . .?

The swinging blade . . . God, no. God, remove that image from my mind. God, I believe in you. I was baptized. I'll believe anything, do anything. In return, just remove that image from my mind. And get us out of here safely.

Roy woke in the early dawn when the jungle was coming alive with dim light. Raucous bird calls sounded up on the mountain. Pam was still asleep. Roy looked at her and felt a shiver of alarm. She was so pale, so thin, so weak! Her face was slack, like an invalid's.

He eased himself away from her and walked down to the stream with his spear-stick. He knelt and drank, then splashed the cold water on his face. He was weak and tired, groggy and old. He could not tackle any more mountains; he wasn't sure he could take even another step. He wanted to lie back in the shelter with Pam and never get up.

223

But he had to go on; he had to find her something to eat. Holding his spear lightly in his right hand, he turned and began to walk down the stream. Would wild animals be more likely to be down here near the water or up on the mountain? He did not know, but maybe he could surprise some creature at its morning drink.

The stream was wide and not easily followed. Head-high vegetation crowded against one bank, and a sheer bluff rose from the other. He stepped from rock to rock, but eventually they were too far apart. He tried wading, but the footing was slippery in the fast water, which in places was thigh deep. He looked for mussels or little fish or crabs. Nothing. Fruit or seedpods or tree pineapples. Nothing.

After awhile he came to a place where a tiny tributary plummeted into the stream from the left bank. Clambering up among the rocks, grabbing clumps of vegetation for a handhold, he lifted himself over the steep drop-off and was able to walk warily up the little stream. Its bed was a narrow corridor through rampant vegetation, scarcely wide enough to admit his body.

An explosion to his left set his heart thudding. He crouched and tried to peer through the screen of undergrowth, gripped by the adrenal thrill of both potential predator and potential prey. There was movement in there, something dark and man-sized. Gripping his spear, he stepped into the bushes and knelt to elude the net of vines and limbs. A dark shadow darted away from him. He moved at a crouch, trying to see what he was pursuing.

Suddenly the looming darkness of a cliff confronted him through the greenery. Between him and that wall of stone was the shadow. He took another step and saw it: a cassowary, dark-bodied, blue-necked, with a great hump of gray-black bone on top of its head. Its legs were great shafts of savage muscle ending in sharp, hard talons. He had surprised it off its nest. Panicked, the big bird ran this way and that, cornered in the cove of cliff wall. Suddenly the bird, which had been crouching in its attempts to run, turned and faced him and raised its neck to full length. Roy found himself staring at a creature as tall as himself. It was only then that he noticed the baby at its side, a striped little bird the size of a chicken.

The man and the cassowary sprang at each other in the same instant, the bird armed with talons, the man with a pointed stick. The cassowary kicked — better than kenpo, oh, better than karate! — and Roy felt a talon puncture the skin under his breastbone. He knew the next thrust could be a killing stroke. He twisted to the side and fell to the ground. With a great screeching and flapping of its fierce, tiny wings the cassowary jumped on him. Roy thrust blindly upward with his spear. It met air.

His eyes were shut against the raking, stabbing talons. He jabbed again and again and was surprised to find the point of his spear meeting resistance. There was a soft puffing sound and the slight odor of intestines. Roy pushed harder, rising onto his feet and driving the impaled bird back against the cliff. Filled with rage now at the beast that had tried to take his life, Roy shoved the spear completely through the cassowary's body until the spear point pressed against the rock wall behind it. The bird's head flailed wildly from side to side on its long, rubber-muscled neck. The legs kicked out, slashing the air.

Roy understood that his work was not over; he had not hit a vital spot. The cassowary, impaled through the guts, was mortally injured but a long way from being dead or defenseless. Afraid to release his grip on the spear, Roy wondered what to do. Ridiculous amounts of time, gobs and volumes of time, seemed to pass as he stood there facing the screeching bird as it tried to peck his face.

With one movement, Roy let go of the spear and moved in close to the bird, between its legs, and seized its neck with his hands. For a moment it seemed an embrace of love, torso to torso, face to face. But he took the head and slammed it against the rock wall, repeatedly, with all his strength.

Realizing at last that the bird was dead and he was safe, Roy sank onto the ground in a sitting position. Looking at his vanquished quarry sprawled out beside him, Roy grinned, his body flushed with exultation. He stared admiringly at the rich, dark textures of the bird's plumage with its subtle rainbow colors; the brilliant hues of the neck; the formidable thighs and hard, yellow, sharp-pointed talons; the strange tissue of the legskin; the enormity of the bony head crest. What a beautiful primeval creature. And what meat! He reached out and touched the leg. It was still warm. The skin was thin and tough. All that meat!

What would it weigh? He jumped up, oblivious to the blood that ran down his belly and the myriad scratches on his face and forearms. Grabbing the bird by its neck, he attempted to hoist it. How had God ever invented such a creature? He lugged it upward. It must have stood about six feet, his own height. Must go eighty, maybe a hundred pounds. He dropped the toilsome weight.

Oh, Pamela, what a breakfast I have for you! he thought, almost laughing aloud in his excitement. If only he could get it back to camp. But first he needed to wash; he was dirty and sweaty. He walked back out to the stream and knelt in the water, splashing his face and torso. Only then did he see his wounds. He tested the belly puncture: a jagged cut, but not serious. With his fingertips he probed the lacerations on his face. He'd look rough for a while. His arms were scratched too, but thankfully his wounds seemed superficial. If only they didn't get infected. Still on his knees, drinking out of his cupped hands, he looked up into the choking tangle of greenery, the sky scarcely visible — he couldn't even tell if it was blue or cloudy. "Oh, thank you, God! Thank you, thank you, thank you." He gave a whoop of laughter, then sank into the cold water and howled with exuberance. A crazy cry — wolf, loon, wild man.

When he finally stood up, a great wave of fatigue rolled over him. No matter. He would get the meat back to camp. They could stay put all day, cooking and eating and regaining their strength. Oh, they could do it now! They were going to get out of here!

With his penknife he released the bird's heavy load of guts, then dragged the carcass to the creek to wash out its intestinal cavity. As it lay in the shallow water its colors glowed in places like mother-of-pearl while its blood trailed rainbows downstream.

After rinsing the bird out and cleaning his own hands and arms, Roy lifted it by its neck and heaved it over his back like a sack of feed. He dreaded the long walk back. Body heavy, heart light, pausing now and then to adjust his load, Roy staggered down the creek.

As he approached the place where the little stream dropped off into the bigger creek below, he heard darting footsteps on his left. The baby cassowary? He bent down to drop the big bird, thinking a baby cassowary might be easy to catch, and in doing so he avoided the brunt of the downward swing of the blade.

The cassowary's neck absorbed most of the blow, but the razor edge of Yalu's machete traveled on across and bit into Roy's right shoulder. The action threw both men off-balance, and when they faced each other they were both sitting in the stream.

They leaped to their feet simultaneously. Yalu stepped in

with an overhead swing, headed down toward Roy's collar-bone. Roy intercepted the strike by grabbing Yalu's wrist. Their other hands locked, and they stood face to face, struggling and groaning. Then, a shred of his old training resurfacing, Roy aimed a kenpo kick at Yalu's groin. The kick went high and hit his belly instead, landing against muscle as hard as wood. Yalu dropped his left hand to protect himself from the next kick and Roy, his right hand suddenly freed, remembered the words of his old kenpo instructor.

"If you must use the eye-strike — and you should only use this technique in a life-and-death situation — you'd better be prepared to go all the way. You have to stiffen your fingers and sink them to the hilt — that's right, to the hilt — in the eyesockets. It sounds gross, its sounds grisly, and if you don't think you can do it, then use a different technique."

Roy stiffened his fingers and thrust them forward. The fingers parted at the bridge of Yalu's nose and kept on going, soaring into a dimension of horror. A high-pitched squeal came from Yalu's throat. Remembering the cassowary's fight, Roy did not stop with the single strike. Sliding his fingers out, he grasped the top of Yalu's head and brought it down directly onto his rising knee. The collision made the splitting sound an overripe watermelon makes when it is first cut with a knife and bursts open of its own accord. Yalu dropped straight to the ground and began the twitching tango of death, jerking, frothing, bleeding. Roy turned away, fell to his knees, and vomited a thin green gruel.

It was a long time before he could force himself to turn around and look. Yalu was still now. His eyes were red globs. Blood trickled from his ears, nose, and mouth. Sitting back in the water, Roy looked at him much as he had looked at the cassowary, noting the fine network of muscle, the chest like a nail-keg, the stomach distended from a diet of kaukau, the legs

228

pure sinew and muscle, the feet broad and tough for mountain walking. A creature of beauty, a creature of God.

When Roy prayed this time, he did not turn his gaze up to heaven but bent over and laid his forehead against a stone. His supplication came in wordless weeping, tearing moans. His tears ran out into the creek until it seemed he was part of the running water, the mud, the hard stone. The clamoring crowd of vegetation, the possessive clutch of the earth seemed to entwine and cover him. If only he could be free of it, free of it all — his grief, his hunger, his grisly sin.

He heard a sound behind him and wheeled wildly, his face a contorted mixture of savagery and vulnerability. Pamela stood above him, staring at the scene of death with an expression of absolute shock.

Looking up at her, Roy was equally surprised at what he witnessed, for he saw something more than a frail woman in a state of shock. He saw the answer to his prayer.

Halfway up the mountain they found a trail, broad and well-used. Accustomed now to observing and understanding the lay of the land, they had little trouble following the path. A half-day's walk away they came to a garden, where they dallied to eat sweet bananas and pawpaw. Just beyond it was a village. There, the people seemed unaccountably but undeniably happy to see them. Many were eager to guide them to the town of Bulolo, two days away to the east, in exchange for the abundance of cassowary plumage the couple possessed.

In the village they had an entire cavernous hut to them-

229

selves. On the night before they were to leave on the long walk to Bulolo they lay in the darkness on the springy cane floor of the hut. They curled close together in the cool night, accustomed now to sleeping without covers, to finding warmth in one another. The village was silent; each family had retreated to its hut, and only a low murmur could be heard now an

They were rested and clean. One of the villagers had had a cake of soap — real soap — and they had used it liberally, on clothes and skin and hair, in a nearby stream. The villagers had cooked a great mumu in their honor, and they had found themselves confronted with mounds of food. But to their own surprise, despite their hunger, they had been unable to eat much; their stomachs had shrunk. So they had fed sparingly on good, bland, nourishing food: bananas, pawpaws, kaukau, pitpit, all the village had to offer. What they had eaten nourished them subtly and surely, restoring a glow to their skin, an inner warmth, a growing strength, and most of all a sense of security.

"Well, how do you feel?" Roy asked at last, and his question was like a sudden opening in the clouds after days of gray, a blue sail ready to be inflated by the wind and carry them onward swiftly to where they wanted to go. It was as if for the first time — after the blurred, delirious entry into the village, the turbulent explanations, the long fireside talks with villagers — they realized their ordeal was over. The trail ahead posed no threat now. Some part of them knew with certainty that the road home lay before them, clear and uncluttered.

Pam seemed to grope in the darkness for an answer. "Do you remember those cartoons where the character — Mickey Mouse or the Road Runner or somebody — would walk across a rocky precipice and the precipice would cave in behind them at each step and they would go on and never even know it?"

230

she asked. "Danger behind every step, but they just waltzed over it as if by magic? That's how I feel. We've been like that. Everything fell apart right behind us, but we stayed one step ahead."

"Magic?"

"No. Like being carried in the hand of God," she said.

"Through the fires of hell," he added. He could feel the movement as she nodded. He delighted in the clean scent of her hair. The smoke of the village was friendly in the night air. It was not as chilly as it had been in Engati; they must be at a lower elevation.

"When we get back," she said, encircling his neck with her arms, "I want to sleep for a week."

"All right," he said. "And we'll have to get married — officially."

She laughed, her voice sleepy. "Let's not have a lengthy engagement." Her arms drifted loose from him, and he lay on his back, wide awake, staring at the darkness of the ceiling.

"It wouldn't be so bad to stay here, would it?" he asked. "I mean, to come back. I don't know. To find a village where the people will listen. Know what I mean?"

She murmured something, a drowsy, drugged sound. Perhaps she was already dreaming.

"If only they'll listen," he said. Then he laughed, thinking of himself, and his laughter turned into a melt of tears from some deep core of warmth living inside him now that had never been there before. "If only we'll listen," he whispered.

His whisper jarred Pam slightly from her sleep. "What?" she mumbled.

He kissed her forehead lightly. "Nothing," he said. "Just sleep."

His own road to sleep was paved with prayers. Drifting, he thought of Yalu, to whom death had given a certain innocence

231

and beauty. Such a sorrow for the beauty to have come too late. God, don't let it be too late for him, or for me. Restore that beauty and innocence to me. To all of us. Please.

Roy woke before Pam and clambered quietly out of the hut. It was morning morning true: cool, gray, and smoky, the sun still hidden below the mountains. He stretched and walked over to an ashpit where the mumu had been held the night before. The man who was to be their guide to Bulolo squatted there on his heels, staring idly at the smoldering heap, a sleepy smile on his face.

"Morning," said Roy.

"Ah, morning."

Roy squatted across from him, and the man reached into the ashes and pulled out a sweet potato. He brushed the ashes off meticulously, then offered it to Roy.

"No good you give me your food," Roy said.

The man just shook his head and smiled, so Roy took the potato. The man pulled another from the ashes for himself.

As Roy peeled back the skin and bit into the soft hot potato, he thought about the cassowary meat, so lean and tough. When he and Pam had returned to their camp with the huge bird, they cleaned it hurriedly and toasted strips of the meat over a fire. It was nearly inedible, but they chewed and chewed until they could swallow it. After appeasing their immediate hunger, they had cooked other meat from the bird more slowly, but it was still tough.

They never went back for Yalu. He was probably lying there

now on his back in the stream, staring at heaven with an eyeless gaze. Wild hogs may have gotten to him by now, and ants. . . . Roy shook off the grisly thoughts.

"This road to Bulolo, it hard too-much, or just a little?" he asked the man. He had been over these details with the villagers a dozen times, but he never tired of discussing the trip back.

"It no hard too-much," the man replied lightheartedly, munching his potato.

Roy had the trip all planned out in his mind. They had been in this village three days, resting and eating, gathering their strength for the journey out. It had been both honeymoon and convalescence. Though they were eager to get back to Lae, it would have been dangerous to attempt a trek through the mountains too soon in their weakened condition.

Soon he would rouse Pam, and with this man they would set out for the town of Bulolo. There Roy would find a telephone and call the missionary in Wau, which wasn't far up the road. When he explained their situation, the missionary would drive down and pick them up and take them to Lae. The mere thought of Lae filled Roy with contentment.

The guide had finished his potato and had lighted a thin hand-rolled cigar in the coals. He took a drag and offered it to Roy, who reached for it and slipped it between his lips. As he sucked the pungent smoke into his mouth, he wondered: Do missionaries smoke? The thought made him chuckle. If not, maybe this would be his last cigar. He passed it back to the man, savoring the cloud of smoke that hung around him.

The morning was brightening considerably; the sky above the mountains was acquiring a golden glare which presaged a hot day. He would have to waken Pam soon.

Just then he heard footsteps and, looking over his shoulder, saw a naked child scarcely old enough to walk. The child

233

stopped beside him and stared with wide-open nugget eyes. His hair was coppery, his skin the color of buttered toast. A thread of drool spun its way down a corner of his mouth as he watched this strange visitor in fascination.

Roy smiled broadly and reached out toward the child. The boy started to cry but stopped after the first croak. His attention wandered from Roy to the guide, and he tottered over to the squatting villager who beamed through his short beard, revealing a mouth short on teeth. He picked the baby up and murmured words in a language Roy did not understand.

Sunlight was spreading over the mountains like a wing now, reaching down into the clearing where Roy crouched. He stood up.

"Pam," he called, then decided to wake her more gently. He stepped to the hut and crawled in beside her. "Hey baby, time to get up."

Eyes still closed, she smiled and put her arms around his neck. "I dreamed we were on the beach," she said sleepily.

He bent down and kissed her lightly on the lips. "It's time to go," he said softly.

"Let's just stay here," she said.

He chuckled. "Come on. It's time to go to Bulolo. It's morning morning true."

She released him and opened her eyes, staring at the smoke-blackened roof thatch above her. "We were on the beach, swimming and playing. The water was so nice. Can we go to the beach when we get back to Lae, Roy?"

"Sure."

"Good," she said, sitting up and rubbing her eyes, then favoring him with a smile. "In that case, I guess I'll go with you to Bulolo."

He smiled back at her, and together they went out of the hut into the bright morning light.

By the time the Land Rover entered the outskirts of Lae, Roy and Pam had told their missionary driver everything there was to tell about Powers's death, and much about their own odyssey. They also learned that Peerson and Ramel had made it to Menyamya Station and radioed the missionaries, who had them flown to Lae. By now the missionaries had learned of Powers's death, but they had remained mystified over Roy's and Pam's whereabouts.

When they pulled into the mission compound, a mass of schoolboys spilled out to greet them, Peerson and Ramel in the lead. But when Roy and Pam climbed out, the two boys stopped and stared as though they could not believe their rescued companions were not some ghostly deception. Then the spell was broken, and the two joined the crowd that was clustering around them.

In the midst of the chatter and excited welcome, the screen door to the mission center creaked open and Jeri stepped out onto the porch. Roy pushed through the crowd, his eyes fixed on hers, and walked across the grounds and up the wooden steps onto the porch. The noise faded out behind him.

He reached out his arms and Jeri buried her face against him. She made a noise that sounded like the beginning of a long time of weeping.